KLEPTO

KLEPTO

a novel

Jenny Pollack

viking

VIKING
Published by Penguin Group
Penguin Young Readers Group, 345 Hudson Street, New York, New York 10014, U.S.A.
Penguin Group (Canada), 90 Eglinton Avenue East, Suite 700, Toronto, Ontario,
Canada M4P 2Y3 (a division of Pearson Penguin Canada Inc.)
Penguin Books Ltd, 80 Strand, London WC2R 0RL, England
Penguin Ireland, 25 St Stephen's Green, Dublin 2, Ireland (a division of Penguin Books Ltd)
Penguin Group (Australia), 250 Camberwell Road, Camberwell, Victoria 3124, Australia
(a division of Pearson Australia Group Pty Ltd)
Penguin Books India Pvt Ltd, 11 Community Centre, Panchsheel Park,
New Delhi – 110 017, India
Penguin Group (NZ), Cnr Airborne and Rosedale Roads, Albany, Auckland 1310, New Zealand
(a division of Pearson New Zealand Ltd)
Penguin Books (South Africa) (Pty) Ltd, 24 Sturdee Avenue, Rosebank,
Johannesburg 2196, South Africa

Penguin Books Ltd, Registered Offices: 80 Strand, London WC2R 0RL, England

First published in 2006 by Viking, a division of Penguin Young Readers Group

1 3 5 7 9 10 8 6 4 2

Copyright © Jenny Pollack, 2006
All rights reserved

LIBRARY OF CONGRESS CATALOGING-IN-PUBLICATION DATA
Pollack, Jenny.
Klepto / by Jenny Pollack.
p.   cm.
Summary: In 1981, fourteen-year-old Julie, a drama major at the High School of
Performing Arts in New York City, becomes best friends with an attractive new girl
who introduces Julie to the exciting but dangerous world of shoplifting.
ISBN 0-670-06061-5 (hardcover)
[1. Shoplifting—Fiction. 2. Stealing—Fiction. 3. Best friends—Fiction.
4. Friendship—Fiction. 5. New York (N.Y.)—History—20th century—Fiction.] I. Title.
PZ7.P7566Kl 2006
[Fic]—dc22
2005015809

Printed in U.S.A.
Set in Granjon
Book design by Kelley McIntyre

For J.K.,
with all my love

KLEPTO

It Wasn't Like I Hadn't Done It Before

I wore my baggy red overalls 'cause Julie Braverman said to, and she wore her big army pants. Wearing baggy pants to Fiorucci, this totally cool clothing store, was really important, Julie said. She was acting like what we were gonna do was no biggie. She said it was so easy at Fiorucci. Especially on a Saturday if it was pretty crowded. We headed straight downstairs to the jeans department. There were floor-to-ceiling wooden shelves that held all the different kinds of Fiorucci jeans and pants by size and color and style. Leaning on the counter in front of the shelves was a guy with spiky green hair, ready to get down the pair you wanted.

Julie went up to the spiky green hair guy and said, "Hi. Could I please try on one pair of regular jeans, size twenty-eight, one pair of turquoise corduroys, size twenty-seven, and ummm . . ." She paused to act like she was mulling it over even though she knew exactly what she was going to

1

say. "One pair of the rust-colored jeans? Twenty-eights?" Then I asked him for my three pairs.

As we walked toward the dressing rooms with our armloads of pants, Julie said under her breath, "Try on all three and decide which are the ones you want, okay?"

I was pretty sure it was going to be the regular blue Fiorucci jeans. *Oh my God,* I suddenly thought, getting excited, *I'm gonna have a brand-new pair of Fiorucci jeans for free!* I tried to my hide my nervousness. I mean, it wasn't like I hadn't done it before. I'd done it once or twice. Only, it was just little stuff, like candy or lipstick from Woolworth's. I'd never walked out of a store wearing a pair of expensive jeans under my pants!

I tried on the pink corduroys, but they made me look fat. I've always wished I was one of those skinny girls like my sister who could eat anything all the time. When we were little, Ellie was really skinny, so Dr. Beaumont said she should drink one milk shake a day to gain weight. Mom didn't want me to feel left out so she let me have a milk shake, too, even though I certainly didn't need it.

I tried on the regular jeans and thank God they fit. Then I put my red overalls on over them and looked in the mirror. Pretty good. You couldn't really tell. A little bulky, but not much more than usual. I felt my heart kind of beating fast then, and for some reason I couldn't stop smiling, even though I was alone with myself in the dressing room.

1

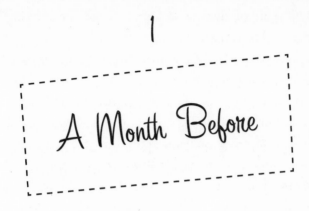

A Month Before

I got off the subway at 50th Street and Broadway and walked down to 46th Street feeling excited and thinking, *I can't believe I'm finally in high school*. It was the Tuesday after Labor Day in 1981, the first day of freshman year. I was actually going to the High School of Performing Arts (or P.A. for short, as everyone called it), where I got accepted as a drama major. There were only three departments: drama, dance, and music. P.A. had academics, too, but just the basics like English, math, history, science, and foreign language. You spent half the day in your major and half in academics—what a change from my old school.

As I walked up to the old brown stone building, I saw this girl on the top of the steps, and I knew I recognized her from somewhere. I thought, *My God, she's so pretty!* She looked kind of like Brooke Shields. She was wearing these dark-blue-and-purple-striped painters pants from Reminiscence, and I thought, *What a coincidence,* 'cause I was wearing my new striped cotton boat-neck shirt from Reminiscence. I had bought it as my first-day-of-school shirt. Reminiscence was my all-time favorite clothing store. It was on Macdougal Street in the Village. They mostly sold 1950s-type stuff, which I totally loved, and these really cool pants in a zillion different colors. It was a store that made me wish I was rich, 'cause I wanted almost everything. The rest of my outfit included my Levi's and white Keds—I had carefully laid out this combination of clothes on my orange pillow chair the night before. *Maybe we'll be friends,* I thought, looking at this girl, since we had the Reminiscence connection.

As I stood that morning outside P.A., the sun made me squint my eyes and scrunch up my forehead. It was just before the first bell, and it seemed like there were zillions of kids hanging out outside, not going in. Some were in covered-with-pins jean jackets and tight Jordache jeans. I could hear a few different boom boxes playing WPLJ or The Police or Human League or whatever. All I could think was, *How do I know that girl in the painters pants?*

I noticed this cool-looking group of friends: two girls and a guy smoking clove cigarettes. The girls were wearing black suede boots with their jeans tucked in. They also had identical hairstyles—long one-length perms and frizzy bangs with lots of mousse—only one was a dark brunette and the other was kind of an orangy-blonde. They must have been upperclassmen, 'cause they seemed to be a little clique already. I started to get that annoying hollow feeling in my chest, like no amount of deep breaths would make it go away. My parents always said I had no trouble making friends, but I was still nervous. I knew I'd see my old friends Kristin and Olivia sometimes, but it wouldn't be the same since we were going to different high schools.

"*Eye-ee-sha!*" I heard someone scream.

"Queechy!" screamed another voice, and two tall, thin black girls wearing leg warmers and their hair pulled back in tight buns ran to each other and hugged, jumping and squealing.

"You got taller!" "You lost weight!" and "How was your summer?" called random voices. It felt like everyone knew someone except me.

I looked back up at the familiar pretty girl on the top step of P.A. again. At that moment it suddenly came to me, and she turned around as if she knew I was going to say, "Didn't you go to Caitlin Braunstein's Bat Mitzvah?"

Last June, my friend Caitlin Braunstein had a Bat Mitzvah and she invited practically every kid from Riverdale, which was a school for rich kids. Her dad was a big lawyer and they lived in this huge apartment on Central Park West where Miss America used to live, Caitlin said. The front hallway and foyer had marble floors, and the bathroom off the study had a little gold door in the wall with a button. When you pushed it, the toilet paper popped out. I really liked Caitlin, but when I met her Riverdale friends at her Bat Mitzvah, they seemed cooler or older or something. They were all these pretty girls with expensive clothes and great hair and names like Alyssa, Jackie, Robin, and Elise. Oh, and Julie—one of them was named Julie. Like me.

"How did you remember me?" Julie said as she stepped down a couple of steps so we were both on the sidewalk. She smiled this big smile with her movie-star teeth and adjusted her canvas bag that I recognized from a store on the East Side called Chocolate Soup. It's a bag I always thought was really cool, but too expensive.

"I don't know," I said. "I remember people."

"I'm Julie. Julie Braverman. You're a friend of Caitlin's?" she said.

"Yeah. I'm Julie, too. Julie Prodsky."

"Oh, right! You went to elementary with Caitlin, right?"

"Yeah," was all I could say.

It turned out that Julie and I were on our way to the same homeroom, Mr. Werner's, room 301.

In room 301, Julie and I found seats next to each other in those chair-desks, and this big kid in the back with stringy black hair and an army jacket took out some drumsticks and started playing the desk in front of him. Other kids were filing in, and the room buzzed with so many conversations going on at once. Occasionally you could hear screaming in the hallway from more friends reuniting. The bell rang, an obnoxious high-pitched shriek.

"So, where do you live?" I asked Julie.

Her big brown eyes looked right into mine as she feathered her fingers through her bangs.

"On Ninety-Ninth Street and Riverside Drive," she said.

"No kidding! I live on a Hundred Sixth Street—hey we're practically neighbors!" I blurted back. Oh my God, I sounded like such a dork.

"Yeah," Julie said, seeming kind of distracted by all the

kids and noise. Then I started staring at her lips. They were perfect and full and heart-shaped. She was so pretty, I couldn't get over it. I mean, it wasn't like I *liked* her liked her—I just couldn't stop staring.

"Are you trying to figure out what lipstick I'm wearing?" Julie said. Oh my God. Caught in the act.

"Yes!" I said. "Where'd you get it?"

"It's Shiseido, my favorite brand. It's called Iridescent Baby Pink." Then she pulled the tube out of her purple LeSportsac makeup bag to show me.

"Here it is," she said, handing me a shiny black lipstick with curves in the plastic.

"Oh my God, Julie Braverman!" screamed a husky voice with a Brooklyn accent. Both of us spun around to see a short girl with thick eye makeup, her hair in a bun, and a huge Capezio dance bag, almost twice as big as her body. Anyone with a bun walked like a dancer, with her feet turned out. Even guy dancers had that walk.

"Natalie!" Julie said as she got out of her seat to hug her. "What are you doing here?"

"I got in!" Natalie screamed.

"I never heard from you after I got home," Julie said. "How was August?" The two of them hugged and giggled and whispered a little about something for a few minutes while I pretended to be interested in the contents of my fluorescent green pencil case.

Then suddenly Julie turned to me and said, "Oh my God, I'm sorry, this is Natalie Schaeffer. We went to camp together last summer. Buck's Rock. That's Julie."

"Hi. Another Julie!" Natalie said.

"Hi," I said.

"Are you in drama, too?" Natalie asked me.

"Uh-huh. You're in dance?"

"How could you tell?" she said sarcastically, slinging her huge dance bag under the chair next to Julie. At first I thought she was making fun of me, but then she laughed, and Julie looked at me and laughed, too.

"So you're in my homeroom?" Julie said to Natalie.

"Uh-huh." She cracked her gum.

Great. At first it seemed like Julie needed a friend, but in fact she already had one. I wouldn't be surprised if she knew other kids in our class, too. She was popular, and it wasn't even lunch yet.

Mr. Werner, a tall, white-haired man with little half-moon glasses on the end of his nose, came in and asked us all to simmer down. He took attendance, calling everyone by their last names.

"Auerbach? Barinni? Braverman?" he shouted, peering at us over his glasses.

"Here!" Julie said.

Normally, homeroom was going to be in the afternoon—it was only in the morning today because it was the first day of school. Mr. Werner explained how this would be an abnormal day, with shortened classes and orientation and special instructions, and then he told us about some rules, but I wasn't really paying attention. Then the bell rang again.

"Hey," Julie said, lightly touching my arm. "If we end up in different classes later, do you want to meet after school and take the subway uptown together?"

"Sure!" I said, trying not to sound too desperate, and I went off to find room 205, Mrs. Krawler's class, Voice and Diction.

Julie and I had acting and French class together. Acting was every day, but French was only on Mondays, Wednesdays, and Fridays. The schedules were confusing. There was so much to remember that by the end of the day, my brain hurt.

On the number 1 train going uptown, I noticed guys checking Julie out as they passed. Julie acted a little like she was used to that. I asked her if she had any siblings.

"I have four," she said. "Three sisters and a brother. But I only live with one of them—Mandy—she's just a year older than me. We're the only two that have the same dad. I mean, like, the same mom *and* dad. We all have the same mom. There are three dads among the five of us."

Well. I didn't know what to say. I've never known anyone who had such a big family, let alone with all those fathers. I've always wished I had brothers, older or younger—that my parents hadn't stopped with me. But I just had Ellie, who annoyed me and barely acted like a big sister. She never gave me advice about guys, 'cause she was totally in-experienced, which was completely pathetic. I mean, she was seventeen! One time I asked her what kind of birth control she would use if she needed it, and she got all flustered and made me get out of her room, saying she had too much homework.

I was still mulling over Julie's big family. "Uh-huh,"

was all I could muster. Should I have acted like three dads was no big deal?

"My parents got divorced when I was eight," Julie added.

"Uh-huh," I said again.

"Are your parents still together?" she asked me.

"Uh . . . yeah," I said, feeling so ordinary.

"Wow! That's kind of unusual, don't you think?" she said.

It was true. My old friend Kristin had divorced parents, and I could probably name at least five other kids I knew who lived with their moms and hardly ever saw their dads.

"Yeah, I guess so," I said. "But my parents fight all the time. Sometimes I wish they'd get a divorce!"

"No you don't," Julie said solemnly.

"No, I guess I don't, but my sister and I wonder sometimes if they might."

Then nobody said anything for a second as the train stopped at 66th Street and more kids got on, probably on their way home from school, too. My eyes wandered over to a set of subway doors where only one door opened; the other was stuck shut. This always surprised and annoyed the people on the platform. When the single door closed again I could read the giant silver spray-painted graffiti: CHRIS 217. Chris 217 really got around the West Side. He left his mark on the tile walls of the 103rd Street stop, too. I knew 'cause I walked by it about a thousand times a week.

"Does your mom have a boyfriend?" I asked.

"Yeah, Harvey," Julie said. "He's pretty cool. I probably see him more than my dad." She laughed. "My dad lives on Eighty-Eighth Street. But Mandy and I mostly like to stay at his place when he's out of town." She laughed again.

"Wow. Your mom lets you do that?" I asked.

"Well . . ." She smiled mischievously. "Let's just say she doesn't really know. If you know what I mean."

"Oh." I nodded, smiling back. "Where does the rest of your family live?"

"Well, Ruby's the oldest; she's an artist and lives in Tribeca. My brother, Hudson, and his wife, Renee, live on Eighth Street. And Liza lives with her boyfriend on a boat at the Seventh-Ninth Street boat basin."

"Wow," was all I could say again. I wondered if I would ever meet these people.

"I grew up with all of them around, so I don't consider any of them 'half,' even if we have different dads. Well, except Mandy and me," Julie said.

"So you're the youngest?" I asked.

"Uh-huh."

"Me, too. I just have one older sister. Ellie."

"Is that short for Eleanor?" she said.

"No," I said. "Eliza."

"Oh. Cool."

Then we stood there holding the pole not saying anything again, listening to the conductor say something over the PA system, but all it sounded like was really loud static. I was wondering if Julie liked me, which I knew was pretty stupid since she was totally spilling her guts. That must have meant she felt comfortable with me.

As we approached 96th Street, Julie's stop, she said, "Well. I'm next."

"Yeah," I said. "I guess I'll see you tomorrow."

"See you tomorrow," she said as the subway doors opened. She stepped onto the platform, and I watched her shiny, straight brown hair swing from side to side as she disappeared into the crowd.

2

Wasn't She Cross with You on Account of Your Fighting?

That first week of school I only saw Julie Braverman in acting or French or when passing her in the halls in the drama department. Though we talked a little bit, I thought I'd probably never really get to know her. She was too cool and exotic to be my friend and she always seemed to be with somebody. Everybody liked her, especially the boys. I once overheard Wally, this guy in my acting class, saying he had a huge crush on her.

In Mrs. Zeig's acting class we got our first assigned scenes. Mrs. Zeig was a tiny woman with beautiful dyed black hair that she kept pulled into an extremely tight ponytail at the back of her neck. This accentuated her big forehead. Mrs. Zeig sat in her chair very straight, kind of regal-like. She wore a lot of really tan foundation, and her eyeliner was always a little smudged, like she put it on without a mirror. She spoke in an almost British accent but not exactly—it

13

was just kind of proper-sounding. She said it was called "Eastern Regional Speech," and her goal was to get us all to sound like that. Good luck.

"Julie Prodsky and Max Friedberg. You will do a scene from a play called *Tomorrow the World.*" We were all spread out on the floor in our black leotards and tights or sweats, the required dress for acting class. Max was a few kids away from me, over by David Wine and Reggie Ramirez. I could tell the three of them were going to be friends. I remembered David Wine from my audition because he had such great hair (it was kind of like Scott Baio's, but blond), and he was kind of cute.

At the audition to get into P.A., there were like a thousand kids waiting in this big open area in the basement. They called it the basement even though it was on the first floor, near the lunchroom. The audition to get into the drama department had four parts, and you knew your chances were getting better if you kept moving on to the next part. The first part was the two contrasting contemporary monologues.

When I read the Performing Arts audition letter that said, "Please choose two *contrasting contemporary* monologues; for example, one dramatic, one comedic," I asked my dad, "What do they mean by 'contemporary'?"

"Something current, modern," Dad said. "They just don't want you to come in and perform Shakespeare or something too difficult."

"Oh, thank God," I said. Dad taught Speech and Drama at St. Andrew's College in New Jersey, so he was my drama coach; I was going to perform Anne from *The Diary of*

14

Anne Frank and Snoopy being the Red Baron from *You're a Good Man Charlie Brown.* Every time I even thought about my audition, I got nervous.

Then the big day arrived and I sat there in the basement near David Wine with the great hair, waiting for my name to be called. Dad looked funny sitting in a wooden school chair with his legs crossed reading the paper, and my stomach kept doing flip-flops. We had rehearsed my monologues a million times and I knew I was ready, but I had to keep running to the bathroom anyway. I probably had to go, like, four times. Thank God my monologues went pretty well. (One of the auditioners, a drama teacher, even laughed out loud at my Snoopy monologue.) By some miracle, I made it through all four parts of the audition, but I never stopped feeling nervous until Dad and I got on the subway to go home.

And now I couldn't believe I was actually sitting in my first acting class at P.A. When Max and I got picked to do our first scene together, he looked at me, gave me the thumbs-up sign, and murmured, "Julie . . ." I think we were both relieved to get each other. Max was a little bit of a hippie-druggie but also a pretty good actor. At least that's what I had heard. Sometimes he talked too softly, which annoyed me, but I could live with that. As far as scene partners went, I got lucky. Reputation was everything. You just kind of heard about people.

Then Mrs. Zeig announced the rest of the partners, and reminded us that we would perform our scenes on

15

Scene Day for the whole drama department.

"Scene Day for Freshman Acting is January nineteenth," she said, and I heard this kid William gasp. This redheaded girl named Donna sucked her teeth.

"We have plenty of rehearsal time," Mrs. Zeig said. "And if you mind your three Ps—if you're always prompt, present, and prepared—you'll do fine."

I hoped so.

The next Monday after school, sitting on the platform bench at the 50th Street subway station, I was thinking about how the hell I was going to make the first moment of my scene with Max work. We were playing a brother and sister, and Max's character, Emil, was always getting in trouble. My first line was, "Wasn't she cross with you on account of your fighting?" and it just seemed impossible to say without sounding totally fake and actory. But that's my job, Mrs. Zeig kept saying, "To make the words *your own*." Jesus.

Suddenly I looked up, and there was Julie Braverman standing in front of me.

"Hi," she said.

"Hi."

"How goes it?"

"Um, pretty good, I guess." I felt a little startled. "How 'bout you?"

"Just peachy," she said. "Hey, I tried calling you last night. I looked you up, but I guess I spelled your last name wrong."

She tried calling me? "Don't you have the class list?" I said.

"I left it in my locker," she said breathlessly, lightly smacking herself in the head. "Sometimes I'm a total space cadet."

She started to dig in the pockets of her bag, just as the train pulled in with a loud whoosh.

"I forgot to copy the French homework off the board!" she yelled over the noise. "Do you have it in your book?"

"No problem!" I nodded. Oh. That was all she called for—the homework. We got on the train and grabbed two seats next to each other. I took out my French notebook as Julie swung her dark blue bag into her lap, looking for a pen.

"Did you get that bag at Chocolate Soup?" I said.

"Yeah," she said.

"I love it. Wasn't it expensive?"

"Umm . . . no, I don't know. I don't think so. Everyone at Riverdale had them," she said, flipping through her notebook, looking for a blank page. "I think I have an extra one—you want it?"

"What?"

"I have an extra Chocolate Soup bag. Only it's light gray, not navy. I don't know why I got two, since I, like, never use the gray one, so you can have it."

Chocolate Soup bags were so cool. They were canvas shoulder bags with a big flap that covered over a huge inside pocket for all your books and then two outside pockets that snapped where you could keep pens or your makeup or whatever. Julie's was pretty worn in—part of the outside

17

flap was a little frayed, which made it even cooler.

"Really?" I said. "Thanks. That's so nice of you!" I couldn't believe she was going to give me a Chocolate Soup bag for free! I mean, she barely knew me.

"No biggie," she said. Then my eye wandered over to three kids about our age sitting two doors down from us. They were the ones I had seen hanging out outside of school on the first day smoking clove cigarettes. Julie looked where I was looking.

"Have you met them yet? They're in our class."

"They are?" I said. "I thought they were, like, juniors or something."

"Nope. They're freshmen—Daisy Curerri, Jennifer Smalls, and Gordon Pomeranian. They're in my dance class. I heard Daisy's been in an ABC Afterschool Special already. And she's got an agent," Julie said. At P.A. you weren't supposed to work professionally as an actor until you graduated, but plenty of kids did.

"Wow. Are they nice?" I asked. "They seem kind of tough."

"They're okay," Julie said absentmindedly. "A little cliquey." Then her face lit up like she got an idea. "Hey, what are you doing right now?"

"Just going home," I said.

"Wanna come over for a little while? For, like, a snack or something?"

"Right now?"

"Yeah. My mom won't be home yet. She gets home late on Mondays. And I could give you the bag."

"Okay, sure! Oh, but . . ." I hesitated. "I'll have to call

my parents when we get there to tell them when I'll be home. Okay?" I hoped she didn't think I was a total dork or something.

"No problem."

"Okay, then," I said.

"Great!" Julie said.

Her apartment on Riverside Drive was huge: three bedrooms, a living room with a view of the Hudson River, a dining room, and even a maid's room off the kitchen, but they didn't have a maid. They called it the sewing room 'cause it had a sewing machine in it, but it was also full of clothes. Like an extra giant closet. There were three bathrooms and Julie had her own nineteen-inch color TV *in her room* with a video cassette recorder! My parents were so behind the times, we *still* had a black-and-white set in the living room and no VCR. I tried to hide my awe and jealousy. Julie had her own vanity table sprinkled with little baskets of earrings and bags of makeup and perfume bottles and lipsticks, two closets stuffed with clothing and shoes and boots, and a dark purple bureau that looked crammed with more clothes.

"Sorry, as you can see, I'm kinda messy," she said as she scooped a couple of T-shirts and some underwear off her strewn-about rainbow comforter and tossed the clothes into a closet. On the walls were a Bruce Springsteen *Born to Run* poster, a Fiorucci poster of two angels (I had the same one), and a small painting of a squirrel in a square frame.

"My sister Ruby did that," she said pointing to the squirrel. "There's lots of her art all over the apartment. She's really good."

We left our jackets and bags in Julie's room, and she led me to the kitchen. I sat down at the table while Julie stood staring at the contents of the freezer. They had the fancy kind of fridge where the whole right side is the fridge and the whole left side is the freezer, which, by the way, was packed: bags of Zabar's fresh-ground coffee, frozen bagels and croissants, leftovers in Ziploc bags, and, like, five pints of Häagen-Dazs ice cream. She pulled out a pint of Swiss Almond Vanilla and showed it to me, raising her eyebrows.

"Yum," I said.

"So what do you think of Mrs. Zeig?" Julie asked as she put down some light blue ceramic bowls and spoons.

"She's pretty good," I said. "Kind of formal, I guess. But I like her."

"Yeah, me, too. You know that guy Reggie Ramirez? He was telling me that he heard Mrs. Zeig was the best of the freshman acting teachers."

"Cool," I said. "I thought I would recognize more kids that I met on my audition, but I only knew one guy—David Wine. Do you know him? He's pretty cute—I love his hair."

"Totally. I think he's friends with Reggie Ramirez. Who is *also* cute, by the way. I haven't seen anyone from my audition. Maybe that shows you how few kids actually get in," Julie said, smiling, like weren't we the coolest.

"Yeah, maybe," I said. "And isn't it cool that we have so many periods of drama classes each day?"

"Uh-huh. But I think it'll be better when we're juniors, because by then you can be in a play, and you can stay and rehearse after school. I heard some days when you're rehearsing you have to stay as late as six o'clock!"

"Wow. That'll be cool, to be juniors. It seems so far away," I said.

"I know," Julie said with her mouth full of Swiss Almond Vanilla.

Then we went through almost every other freshman drama student whose name we could think of: who we thought was probably a good actor; who would suck; who seemed like a druggie (Max, my scene partner); who'd be good to be friends with; who seemed cliquey, popular, slutty, conceited, materialistic; and so on. We started cracking up so much I totally relaxed and didn't notice that time had flown. Before we knew it, we had eaten the entire pint of ice cream and it was almost five o'clock. Then we heard the keys in Julie's front door.

"That's my sister Mandy," Julie said.

"Hello?" Mandy called from the living room.

"In here!" Julie shouted. I could hear Mandy walking down the hall to the kitchen. Her walk sounded slow and soft, like a saunter.

"Oh my God, Julie!" I gasped. "I never called my parents!"

She pointed to the phone on the wall and I picked up the receiver and quickly dialed my number. As I listened to the phone ringing, I looked up and saw Mandy in the doorway. She was loaded up with a Chocolate Soup book bag like Julie's but in dark brown, a guitar, and a big stack of mail. She was a little taller than Julie, and a little thinner, with shoulder-length dark blonde hair in tight, tight curls.

"That's Julie," Julie said.

"Hi," I said, checking out Mandy's vintage burgundy suede jacket. It had a ripped pocket hanging off one side. She dropped her jacket and stuff into a chair. I put my hand over the receiver and whispered, "I'm calling my parents."

"No sweat," she said, peering into our ice-cream pint. "Anything left?"

"In the freezer," Julie said.

"Hello?" said my dad's voice.

"Hi, Dad. I'm so sorry I forgot to call. I went home with a new girl I met at school, Julie Braverman. She lives on Ninety-Ninth Street. Actually, we met at Caitlin's Bat Mitzvah last year."

"All right," Dad said, but I could tell he wasn't really listening 'cause I heard Mom's shrieky voice in the background saying, "Is that Julie? Where is she?" Mom was always cranky when she got home from work. She was the book editor at *Ladies' Home Journal* magazine, and she hated her boss, Angela Woo, who was really mean and uptight. I thought *Ladies' Home Journal* was a totally stupid magazine, because it always had knitting or cookies on the cover.

Dad put his hand over the receiver and I heard a muffled, "Helene, relax, she's at her friend's." Then I heard my mother say something else that I couldn't make out, but it sounded angry.

"Hold on a sec, Jule," Dad said to me. Then loudly to my mother he said, *"Please!* I am on the phone! I can't hear her when you talk to me when I'm trying to talk to her!"

Then Mom screamed one more thing, but it sounded

like she was walking away. I rolled my eyes at Julie and mouthed, "My mother," and she smiled.

"Sorry, Julie," Dad said to me, sounding exasperated. "Are you coming home for dinner?"

"I'll be home by six or so."

"All right. It's your night to set the table, you know."

"I *know*. I'm not completely irresponsible!"

"No one thinks you are," he said calmly. "All right. See you later, pussy cat. Have fun." I hung up.

"I'm glad he's the one who answered," I said, breathing a small sigh of relief. "He's the more reasonable one. I think my mom had a cow."

"Does your mom freak out a lot?" Julie asked.

"All the time," I said.

"That's funny," she said, laughing.

"Our mom never freaks," Mandy said, opening a Fresca. "You could, like, call her from *jail*, and she'd be like, 'Well, when you get out, can you stop at the drugstore for some Apple Pectin conditioner? We're all out.'" Then Julie and Mandy started cracking up. "Speaking of Mom, where is she?" Mandy said.

"I think she's at a meeting," Julie said. "There's a note on the dining-room table."

"Oh," Mandy said. She opened the fridge and plucked a few grapes from a middle shelf. "So, Julie. Are you in drama, too?"

"Uh-huh," I said. "And you're at High School of Music and Art, right?" Julie had told me. "My sister's there, too. She's a senior in the art department." Music and Art (or M&A) was kind of like P.A. 'cause it had three arts majors: art, voice, and instrumental music. "Do you know Ellie Prodsky?" I asked.

"Don't know her," Mandy said without even thinking. "I only know musicians."

"Mandy's in voice; she's a singer," Julie said.

"And *composer*," Mandy said, slightly irritated. Julie smiled and rolled her eyes.

"Yeah," Julie said. "She's in a band. Fried X. Sometime we'll go hear her play—especially since there's this totally gorgeous British guy in the band, Oliver Moloney. Oh my God, I have such a crush on him. He plays guitar."

"Bass," Mandy corrected her. She took her soda and headed out of the kitchen, leaving all her junk in the chair.

"Sorry, *bass*." Julie rolled her eyes again. "Oh! Let me get the bag," she suddenly remembered, and ran back to her room.

"The only thing is," she said, coming back down the hall right away, "there's a blue ink stain on one of the pockets, but it's hardly noticeable."

"No, it's even cooler this way," I said. "I like it worn in–looking. Thanks so much!"

Walking home the seven blocks from Julie's, I was so excited just thinking about everything. What a day it had been. I had gotten a Chocolate Soup bag and a new friend! Not necessarily in that order.

By October, Julie and I were meeting to take the subway home after school pretty much every day—we planned it. And because we were always coming and going together, kids in our acting class started to call us Julie B. and Julie P.

One time Gordon said, "There go the Julies!" (There was a Julie L. in Freshman Acting, too, but we didn't hang out with her much.) We were Julie One and Julie Two. Julie and Julie Too. Or Julie and Julie Also. Somehow I was always introducing myself second, so I was Julie Also.

Most of the time Julie's mom, Mimi, was never home, but the first time I met her, she was wearing only a bra and a pleated skirt and I thought she was so much cooler and younger-seeming than my parents. She shook my hand with both of her hands, and I noticed her perfectly polished bright red nails.

"It's so nice to meet you, Julie!" she said with a big smile. "I've heard a lot about you!" Julie sucked her teeth a little.

"Don't worry," Julie said to me, "I haven't really told her that much."

"I think it's fabulous that you girls are aspiring actresses!" Mimi said, ignoring Julie's comment. She didn't seem to mind or even notice that she was standing there in her bra. "Well, I should finish getting dressed," she said. "I'm going to a meeting with Harvey." And in a little while we had the place to ourselves again.

Mimi was really beautiful, which made sense since all her kids were so good looking. And she was tall and thin, which made sense since she was a model. Her hair was a light chestnut color, like Julie's, and she wore it kind of short—very stylish. Julie showed me the coolest picture of her mom one day when she was telling me about Mimi's career. She walked me to the living room and pointed to the framed picture over the Indian bowl where they threw their keys.

"This is my favorite," Julie said. "It was a real magazine ad in, like, *People* and *Time*."

"Wow," I said. *It's Better in the Bahamas*, said the ad, and Mimi was laughing and showing her dazzling white teeth. She was wearing short shorts and a pink top that tied at the waist, and this handsome kind of older guy with salt-and-pepper hair was carrying her in his arms. They were both really tan and standing knee-deep in the most gorgeous blue water I'd ever seen. It was like paradise, and they looked so happy.

"She got to go to Florida for the shoot," Julie said, sounding cool for using the term "shoot."

3

How Could One Girl
Have So Much?

Julie and I were in her room picking out clothes and shoes and makeup because we were going to hear Mandy's band, Fried X, play at this bar downtown. You could be under eighteen and get in, and probably even get away with getting a drink. Julie said this bar didn't really care about carding. In New York City there were lots of bars like that, Mandy told us.

Julie had such great clothes—her stuff was so womanly—and she let me borrow whatever I wanted. She asked me to look in her closet and pick out a pair of jeans for her to wear while she was in the bathroom blow-drying her hair.

"So what time do we have to be home?" I shouted from the closet. I was going to sleep over that night.

"What do you mean?" she shouted back.

"What time's your curfew?"

"What curfew?"

"Don't you have a curfew?" I asked.

"Nope," she said.

"You're kidding!" I was shocked. "What about on school nights?" I started to sort through her jeans in the closet.

"Not really. My mom doesn't care. She just says to take a cab home from wherever we are whatever time it is."

Oh my God. I could not believe the luck! My over-protective parents wanted me home by ten on school nights and eleven thirty on weekend nights. *Man*, I couldn't help thinking, *it must be so great to have only one parent who was out a lot, like Mimi, and no curfew.*

As I was looking through Julie's closet it suddenly dawned on me that she had about sixty pairs of jeans in there! Well, maybe that was a bit of an exaggeration, but it was, like, *a lot of jeans.* And they were all designer brands like Fiorucci, Calvin Klein, Sassoon, and Girbaud. Not like my regular old Levi's from Morris Brothers. I felt like I was looking at the wardrobe of some princess of a foreign country, so I said, "How can you afford all these jeans?"

"Oh, most of them I didn't pay for," she shouted from the bathroom.

"You mean they were gifts?" I said.

"No. Not really."

I kept looking through her closet. Green-dyed Fio-ruccis with the lavender plastic tag around the belt loop, rust-colored Girbauds, stonewashed jeans, three pairs of blue denims in different shades, magenta jeans, baby pink corduroys. I was thinking, *What's it like to have all this clothing? How could one girl have so much?* Julie appeared at the doorway in a towel. She had a look on her face like the cat who ate the canary, as my mom would say.

"So . . . how did you . . . ?" Then slowly I started to get it. I gasped and whispered, "Oh shit! Julie, did you *steal* these?"

She nodded, grinning. "You don't have to whisper. My mom's not home. And Mandy does it, too. Mandy made up a code word for it, in fact. *Getting*. Like if you *got* something, it means you didn't pay for it." She smiled even bigger, like, isn't that clever?

"Oh my God." I wasn't sure if I should laugh or gasp again. "How?" I moved to her bed, holding the pair of Fioruccis I had picked, eager for the details. "How do you get away with it?"

"Well . . ." Julie exhaled like it was an old story. "You wouldn't believe how little security some places have. Even department stores." She sat down at her vanity to do her makeup. "What are you doing tomorrow? Saturdays are perfect at Fiorucci."

"I'm free," I said.

"Cool. We'll wear baggy pants. That way you can walk right out of the store wearing the jeans underneath."

"You're kidding!" I said.

"Nope. It's easy. You just walk right out; nobody says anything. Once I even tried walking out wearing just the jeans, no baggies over them, and nobody stopped me."

"Oh my God." I started to crack up and fell back on her bed. "How many times have you done this?" I said to the ceiling.

"Um . . . I'm not sure, maybe fifteen times?"

"Always at Fiorucci?" I asked.

"There, and certain department stores. Macy's, for one, is so easy," she said confidently. I didn't think I could look up to Julie any more than I already did, but this made her the coolest person I'd ever met.

"And you've never been caught?" I asked.

"Never," she said. She blotted her lipstick with a tissue.

Fiorucci was in the fancy neighborhood of East 59th Street, near Bloomingdale's. They sold lots of different kinds of designer jeans and corduroys there, in tons of colors—all Fiorucci brand, of course—and the best clothes, mostly kind of punk stuff and jewelry.

I felt this weird combination of excited and nervous. When I'd been to Fiorucci before, it was to buy stuff or get the free posters they gave out. I was collecting them. So far I had four: the two angels one that Julie had, the David Bowie–looking punk rocker one (his face was kind of severe), the big red lips one, and the one with the topless blonde woman in red leather Fiorucci pants hugging her knees so they covered her boobs.

In the dressing room I tried on a bunch of jeans, and then left the pair I wanted on the hook. Acting perfectly calm, I went back out to the guy in my red baggy overalls and my socks. I gave him the two pairs I didn't want and asked for three more. Julie was right; there was almost no security there—what a laugh. Nobody was counting what we took into the dressing room, and the clothes didn't even have those plastic sensor things on them. What was the catch? I tried on three more pairs of pants—a magenta, a green, and a dark brown—returned them, and asked for two more. This is what Julie had told me to do—by that point the guy didn't remember how many I had. On my way back to the dressing room, I heard Julie whispering to me.

"Jule! Juuu-lieee? Can you come here a sec, please?" I stepped into her dressing room and saw that she was red in the face and kind of sweating. Her jeans zipper was stuck.

"I can't get these off!" she whispered.

"Oh my God," I said, trying not to laugh.

"It's not funny," she said, trying not to laugh, too. "I can barely breathe in these things."

We tugged and tugged at the zipper, but it was totally stuck. I was wishing I had some of that EZ-Zipper wax crayon that Mom kept in the jewelry box on her bureau. "Are these the ones you want?" I whispered, feeling Julie's breath on my face as we pulled on the zipper and tried to hold back from laughing. It was like when you're supposed to be quiet 'cause you're in a church or library or something and you feel a huge attack of the giggles coming on. It was just a miracle no one knocked on the door to see what the fuss was about.

"Well, are these the ones you want?" I said.

"I hadn't decided yet," she said. "Don't you think they're too tight?"

"Yeah, kinda," I giggled, "but I don't think it really matters. Looks like these are the ones you're going home in!" Then we both started laughing so hard—silently—that tears welled up in Julie's eyes.

31

When we finally calmed down, Julie let out a big sigh and looked totally exasperated. The zipper still hadn't budged.

"I can't believe this," she said. "Okay, go back to your dressing room and put yours on before somebody notices us." I went back to my room, stifling my giggles, and I put on my jeans, and then my overalls over them.

We left any remaining pants on the counter, and the guy didn't even look at us. He was talking to this mother and daughter. The place was crawling with shoppers.

Back upstairs at accessories, and dressed in her pants over pants, Julie was walking like a robot and trying to hide her worried look that her new Fiorucci jeans might never come off. My hands were cold and sweaty at the same time. I didn't know how we were gonna get away with this. But I also kept thinking, *We just might*. Nobody seemed to be paying too much attention. The plan now was to actually buy something from accessories so we seemed less suspicious. We looked at the earrings. There was this really cool pair that had a little stack of fake pearls wrapped in shiny iridescent pink Saran Wrap—type stuff.

"Oh, I love these," I said.

"Me, too," Julie said, and I noticed she was glancing at the salesgirl behind the counter to see if she could just drop them in her pocket. They were $5.50. This made me nervous, so I took out my wallet and gave Julie a look. We each bought a pair.

Okay, we were ready to go, but the salesgirl was taking her time finding little plastic bags to put the earrings into, and I was getting antsy. I could feel my heart starting to

thump in my chest. *C'mon lady, hurry it up, it's time to go.*
I was willing her to hurry up by staring at her.

"Hey, Carla!" someone shouted to the salesgirl, and I turned around. It was the guy with the spiky green hair from downstairs. Julie and I glanced at each other, then looked at him. He didn't look at us. He stood there silently for a second waiting for Carla to notice him. Carla was crouched down still looking for plastic bags. I felt the sweat starting to form around my waist where the jeans under my overalls were hugging me.

Finally, Carla looked up at the guy and said, kind of annoyed, "What?" He threw a package of credit-card slips on her counter and said with a smirk, "Don't say I never gave you nothing!"

Ignoring the guy, Carla said, "Here they are!" She pulled out two bags and dropped our earrings in them. "Thanks for waiting," she mumbled, blowing some hair off her forehead.

As we got to the exit, Julie suddenly remembered the free Fiorucci posters and stopped at the poster counter.

"C'mon, Jule," I said, under my breath. That day's Fiorucci poster was of two topless women with their backs to the camera and their hands on their hips. One was white, the other black, and both were wearing black leather Fiorucci pants.

"I don't have this one," Julie said as she grabbed two and hurried out the door with me.

"Have a nice day, ladies!" the poster guy called after us.

"You, too!" we yelled, and then, trying not to sprint, we walked fast down the street, not really looking at each

33

other, sort of holding our breath. Julie kind of did a walk run, and once we were a few blocks away, she said, "Oh my God, we are so *good*!"

"I can't believe how easy that was," I said, and we headed for the nearest coffee shop. We went straight to the ladies room where miraculously we got Julie unzipped by rubbing some of my cantaloupe lip gloss on her zipper. Why didn't I think of that in the dressing room?

4

She Thinks She's the Queen of England

On October 20, Mom's forty-seventh birthday, she wanted to go to this really fancy restaurant, Café des Artistes. The waiters were all old men who had slicked-back hair and wore full tuxedos, and there were things on the menu like duck with raspberry sauce. Mom ordered a Stoli on the rocks and asked Ellie if she'd like to have her first drink, even though she was only seventeen. The drinking age in New York was eighteen, but it was in the news a lot that they might change it to nineteen or twenty-one. In New York City you could be fourteen and people thought you were eighteen. At least Julie and I could pass for being older; we hardly ever got carded. I thought it couldn't possibly really be Ellie's first drink, but she never told me anything, and since she hardly ever went *out* out, like to clubs with her friends or anything, maybe it was. I couldn't even count how many times I'd tried it. One time with my old friends Kristin and Olivia, we shared a bottle of red wine at Kristin's house and by mistake spilled most of it all over Kristin's Spanish textbook. Whenever we had Spanish after that, I could smell the red wine, 'cause I sat behind her. When Julie and I went to see Fried X, I tried a madras (which is orange and cranberry juice with vodka). It was so good!

"Why don't you have a fuzzy navel?" Dad suggested, and smirked like he knew one of us was gonna ask, "What's that?"

"What's that?" Ellie said.

"Just try it," Dad said. "I think you'll like it."

When the waiter came back, Ellie said, "A fuzzy navel, please," and then he looked at me.

"A Tom Collins," I said, and Mom shot Dad a look.

"Julie, when did you have a Tom Collins?" Dad said.

"Never," I lied, putting on my best innocent face. Then Ellie got really mad.

"Hey! I didn't get to have a drink when I was *fourteen*!" she said, emphasizing my age, probably to get me in trouble. "That's so unfair!" The waiter was trying not to smile and kept looking from Mom to Dad. I was kind of surprised he didn't ask us for ID. I guess he figured 'cause we were with our parents, it was okay.

"What do you care?" I asked her.

Ellie crossed her arms over her chest and got all huffy. "I can't believe it. It's so unbelievably not fair!" she said again, ignoring me.

"Well," Mom said cheerfully, "sometimes life is not fair." It annoyed me when parents said things like that. Like, "When you're the mother, *you* can decide." *Great*, I always thought, *that'll be in about a million years, so how does that help me now?*

As much as I hated Ellie sometimes, I kind of understood why she had a look on her face like she wanted to kill us all. Still, I was psyched about my Tom Collins—it was kind of like a lemonade with alcohol. My parents probably thought it was *my* first drink. Ha ha. Ellie cheered up when her fuzzy navel came with a blue paper umbrella, a plastic sword, and a maraschino cherry. Mine came with only a cherry, which I let her have 'cause she loves maraschino cherries and I hate them. She let me try a sip of her fuzzy navel. Totally yummy. It had a delicious thick syrupy peachy taste that went straight to my chest, and I got a warm fizzy feeling. I wished I'd ordered a fuzzy navel, too.

The whole night turned out pretty okay until we were leaving the restaurant and Dad was getting the coats. Mom and Dad started to make a scene with one of their fights, totally bugging out the coat-check girl, and it continued as we got outside on the sidewalk in front of the restaurant. I thought it was about the coat-check girl, 'cause Mom muttered something about an "insufficient tip."

Mom and Dad's voices were getting louder and angrier, and it was like they just didn't care that people on the street were looking at us. Ellie and I were trying to act like we didn't know them, and I felt this horrible lump in my throat forming. I knew the tears would be next, but I kept swallowing hard to stop them.

"Bernie, would you just get us a cab!" Mom snapped.

"Helene," Dad said, his voice angry. "Please don't start. We are two blocks from the subway. We'll hop on the train

37

and get home much quicker." *Please, Dad,* I was thinking. *Please don't have the subway versus taxi argument now.* My nice buzzy feeling from my Tom Collins was slipping away.

Mom's face was getting red, and I thought she might cry, too. "Bernie!" she screamed, and my chest tightened. "It's my birthday, goddamnit! We're taking a taxi! Here's one!" She stepped into the street, but the cab drove right by her.

"Listen!" Dad said loudly. "That dinner cost me a fortune, and the subway is right around the corner—do you think I'm made of money, Helene?"

"*I'll* pay for it!" she cut him off like he was just so stupid. I looked around for Ellie, but she was now halfway down the block reading the plaque on the gate of this church like she was fascinated. I knew she was listening. What a faker.

Then Dad said something that maybe was meant for me, but it was like he was talking to himself: "*Your mother*"—he always started sentences like that when he was mad at Mom—"she thinks she's the Queen of England and has to do everything top-of-the-line! Has to stay in five-star hotels, has to eat at fancy restaurants on her birthday, has to take cabs everywh—"

"*And what is so goddamned wrong with that?!*" Mom yelled.

Then he shouted back as if they were in our living room, something about Ellie's tuition and going to college and how we can barely afford it. People were still passing and looking, and I was wishing the collar of my jacket would just swallow me up.

I wondered if I should join Ellie down by the church. How could she have just left me there with these two? What was I supposed to do? I glared at Dad, like, *Please can we just get out of here? Is that so much to ask?*

Then Mom said the worst thing she could ever say to Dad.

"Bernie, you're just so goddamned *cheap!*" Oh my God, I've never seen him get so mad as when she said that. Dad was the kind of dad who never yelled except when he really meant it. It was pretty scary.

"GODDAMNIT, HELENE! IT IS NOT A QUESTION OF CHEAP!" Then Mom started crying. "JESUS CHRIST, WHAT CAN I DO TO JUST GET YOU TO BE A LITTLE PRACTICAL? WE ARE NOT RICH! STOP ACTING LIKE THE SPOILED LITTLE GIRL FROM PRINCETON." That's where Mom grew up— Princeton, New Jersey—in a big house where my grandparents still lived. Dad grew up in the South Bronx with parents from Russia, and he was the first one in his family to go to college. He had to go to City College instead of Columbia, 'cause his family "didn't have two nickels to rub together."

Just then a cab pulled up in front of the restaurant and Dad flagged it down.

"Girls! Get in!" he barked. "Ellie!" he called down the street. "What are you doing? Stop wandering off. Would you get in the taxi, please?"

"Thanks a lot, Bernie, for a wonderful birthday!" Mom sob-yelled, and I noticed the cabdriver's head whip around as she got in the backseat. She began digging through her purse for her Kleenex pack. Ellie and I got in, and I tried to look Ellie in the eyes, but she kept her head down. Mom just sat in between us with the tears coming down her cheeks, and I thought Ellie was gonna roll down her window and jump out of it.

Dad got in the front and told the driver our address. "On the corner of Broadway," he said.

"Tell him to take Amsterdam all the way up," Mom said through the glass divider.

"Helene! Stop," Dad almost shouted. "I *know* how to get us home!" I could tell he was trying not to yell again. Mom leaned back against the seat and was quiet. I just sat there feeling the lump in my throat, the warm tears now sliding down the sides of my face, wishing I could say the one thing to make Mom stop crying, but even though I searched and searched my brain I couldn't come up with it. Mom took my hand even though she was holding a balled-up Kleenex, and took Ellie's with her other hand.

"You kids are so terrific," Mom said softly and sniffled. She handed me one of her Kleenex.

I knew that Mom and Dad were seeing a counselor, Joyce Kazlick at Mt. Sinai, but I guessed it wasn't helping *at all*.

The next day at school I walked to the lunchroom with Natalie, the dancer. She, Julie, and I always talked in home-room, and we all sat together at lunch, too.

"Ugh! I have the *hugest* crush!" Natalie said dramatically. "Do you know Reggie Ramirez? He's in drama, I think?"

"Yeah," I said. "He's in my acting class. He's friends with David Wine."

"What I would do to lose my virginity to him!" Natalie

blurted out. "Oh, that would be, like, a dream come true!" Then, lowering her voice, she said, "You're a virgin, right?"

"Yes!" I said, feeling totally embarrassed. "Are you kidding?" I lowered my voice too. "I haven't even *made out* with anyone yet! It's totally pathetic!" I looked around to see if other kids were watching us, but luckily no one was. Students were being noisy and running through the halls, up and down the stairs.

"Oh," Natalie said. "That's not such a big deal. But doesn't it just drive you crazy?" Natalie asked.

"What?"

Then she kind of half-whispered again, "Being a virgin! Ugh, what I would do to lose my virginity! I just want to get it over with, already!"

"Yeah, but you don't want it to happen with just anyone, right? I mean, dontcha want to love the guy?" I said.

"I don't know," Natalie said. "Sometimes I think having a *huge* crush is enough. It's just so annoying to *still* be a virgin!" She lowered her voice again. "Do you think Julie B. is a virgin?"

"She is," I said. "But just barely. She's done *a lot*."

"Lucky," Natalie said. We got to the lunchroom, and there was Julie waiting for us. Before Natalie could continue with this whole virginity conversation, I launched into telling them about my mom's annoying birthday dinner last night, my parents' fight, and how horrified I was. Julie suggested that a little shopping after school would cheer me up. We spotted Daisy Curerri, Jennifer Smalls, and Gordon Pomeranian sitting on the floor in the corner looking at something secretly. The three of them were hunched around someone's backpack. The backs of Jennifer's and Daisy's jean jackets faced us, but we could tell from Gordon's face they were all laughing. We saw Gordon hold up a frilly red sleeve and Jennifer let out an "Uh-oh!" and they all cracked up, and Julie and I looked at each other and we just knew.

"They're looking at someone's clothes," Julie said in a low voice.

"Uh-huh," I said.

"I know that shirt," Julie said. "I saw it at French Connection. It's like forty-nine dollars or something!"

"Wow," Natalie said. We wolfed down our lunches because the bell was going to ring in a few minutes. We headed for the stairs; Julie and I had French, and Natalie had algebra.

"I don't think they bought that stuff," Julie said, smiling.

"I guess we're not the only ones," I said.

After school Julie and I went to Bloomingdale's, where we bought some Borghese magenta lipstick and plum-colored eyeliner. On our way to the bus stop to catch the 59th Street crosstown, Julie said, "Let's just go in here for a sec."

It was this little accessories store called Whoopsie! or something stupid like that. The name was written in script on the canopy over the door. The window was full of these really cool hats and bags—kind of flashy and colorful. There was only one guy who worked there, standing at the cash register in the middle of the store. He had a moustache and a really hairy chest, which I could see 'cause his brown polyester shirt was almost totally open to his belly button.

Gross. I'd never touched a hairy chest—I doubted if the freshman guys in my class even had any hair on their chests at all.

"Good afternoon, ladies," he said with some kind of accent, and we said hi back.

Then, like a flock of chirpy birds, these three women about our moms' age came in, looking so rich and Park Avenue. They were in navy and tan and looked like they were going boating. The moustache man got really flirty with the ladies and they were giggling, and I started checking out these really expensive knee-highs. I was thinking, *Jesus, twenty dollars for a pair of knee-highs just because somebody painted some swirly colors on them?* I mean, come on. Julie was near the window inspecting this opalescent white purse with tiny beads on it. She called me over.

"Check this out," she said under her breath. She opened and closed the purse a few times and the snap was kind of magnetic. It was fancy. Sixty-five dollars.

"Very cool," I said.

"Yeah," she said, and then suddenly, with her back to the guy at the register, she stuck the purse in the waist of her jeans, pulled her shirt over it, and whispered, "Let's go!"

The next thing I knew we were running down the street, my Chocolate Soup bag thumping against my side and the swirly-colored pair of knee-highs balled up in my fist.

5

Miss Silk Skirt

Sometimes when I went to Julie's after school and her mom was out, Julie said Mimi was at a meeting, and I didn't really think much about it. Then one day, in early November, Julie and I were standing in her kitchen making popcorn with melted butter in the air popper and she said out of nowhere, "I have to tell you something that you can't tell anyone."

"Okay," I said. "What?" I was totally thinking she was gonna tell me she stole, like, a TV or something huge.

"You promise? I'm serious, you really can't tell anyone," she said.

"I swear to God. Cross my heart," I said.

"Okay. . . ." Julie said slowly. "My mom's a recovering alcoholic. So usually when she's not here it's 'cause she goes to Alcoholics Anonymous meetings. I just wanted to tell you 'cause I'm sure you're wondering where my mom is all the time. I'm not supposed to tell anyone 'cause that's called

'Breaking Her Anonymity.' But seeing as we're practically best friends it seems so stupid to keep it from you. So please don't tell anyone."

"I won't tell a soul," I said softly. "Wow." *We're practically best friends,* Julie said. A part of me suddenly felt like jumping up and screaming, *"Oh my God, Julie's my best friend!"* I wanted to hug her, to dance around, to tell her she was my best friend, too. It was almost like the same feeling I had when I got into P.A.

But what did she mean by "practically"?

"It's not a big deal, really," Julie was saying. "My mom hasn't had a drink in, like, seventeen years or something. But once you're an alcoholic, you have to go to meetings for the rest of your life."

"Uh-huh," was all I could think to say. And now, knowing Mimi was a recovering alcoholic only added to her so-much-cooler-than-my-parents appeal. I mean, I always thought she was cooler than my mom 'cause she dressed so much better and didn't seem so old-fashioned. Like, Julie's mom met us one time at CBGB's to see Mandy's band. I couldn't believe it; she could totally hang out with teenagers and not even seem like somebody's mom or something.

The Saturday before Thanksgiving it got cold. We went to Macy's to see what we could *get*. We wore our puffy winter coats, which Julie pointed out gave you more places to hide stuff. We hooked up with Daisy Curerri, Jennifer Smalls, and Gordon Pomeranian. Julie and I had come to realize they were actually nice, not too cool or cliquey. Gordon was the only guy we knew who was into shopping. He usually smelled like coffee and clove cigarettes, and he was a really sharp dresser. The three of them were pretty experienced at stealing, Julie told me.

Daisy said that Macy's was the best of all the department stores in New York 'cause there were, like, hardly ever any salespeople around. Daisy and Julie agreed that what you had to do was bring a big Macy's shopping bag from home with your sweater in it or something so you could walk around looking like a shopper. Or you could buy something small like some socks and ask for a big shopping bag and some tissue paper to hide whatever you were going to steal.

So we headed to the junior girls' department, and Gordon went to the guys' department; we planned to meet him later. It was about eleven o'clock in the morning, and it was so true: You couldn't find a salesperson to save your life. We grabbed various tops, skirts, pants, belts, and whatever else, and headed for the dressing room where this older lady sat reading.

Just in case she was gonna count what we took in, I rolled up a skirt in its hanger and squeezed it between several sweaters and shirts. Usually they just counted the tops of the hangers, Julie said. The skirt was totally hidden and my heart was racing. *This is so strange,* I thought. Kind of like watching yourself in a movie but you're not really you, you're someone else. Stealing was kind of like acting.

The old lady waved us off to separate rooms *without counting our stuff.* Oh man, it was too good to be true. I was in a little room across from Jennifer, and the old lady barely got up from her stool and her *National Enquirer.*

Now we could come and go several times with different clothes like at Fiorucci, 'cause she didn't know how much stuff we had.

Inside my dressing room, I tried on the skirt. It was charcoal gray, kind of shiny, almost silklike, with mother-of-pearl buttons down the front. It made a swishy sound when you moved, and the shape of it was very 1950s, like you'd wear to a sock hop. I totally loved it. I strutted out to the mirror to show someone. Jennifer Smalls was examining her chest in a tight angora sweater. At that moment, her name seemed pretty ironic.

"Does this make my tits look square?" she asked me.

"Um . . . a little. What do you think of this skirt?" I said, twirling.

"Groovy," she said. Nobody I knew said "groovy" like they did in the 1960s, except Jennifer Smalls. She examined the price tag at my hip and her eyes got big. Two hundred and fifty dollars. She smiled and nodded knowingly, and we went back to our dressing rooms. I neatly folded up the skirt in the extra tissue paper I brought from home, then I put it underneath my sweater in the bottom of my shopping bag. I brought the other clothes back to the old lady. Without even looking at me, she waved toward a rack and said, "Put it there, please."

I rapped lightly on Julie's dressing room door. "Jule?"

"Uh-huh?"

"How ya doin'?"

"Done!" she said triumphantly, and flung her door open. She was fully dressed, shopping bag in hand, Chocolate Soup bag over her shoulder. Daisy and Jennifer said they'd meet us down at the Sixth Avenue entrance where Gordon would be.

As we walked outside, I felt the cold air on my face, and I listened hard for an alarm or something to go off, or someone to come running after us. But no one did.

At Aristotle's Coffee Shop a few blocks away, we found a big booth in the back. As Gordon slid into the red vinyl seat, he asked for an ashtray. The waiter was putting down paper placemats.

I ordered a tuna-fish sandwich on toast and a chocolate ice-cream soda. I just had to have something sweet to celebrate. Julie ordered turkey and cheese and a big order of fries for the table.

The waiter had greased-back hair and a pencil-thin moustache. As soon as he took our order and headed to the kitchen, I said, "I can't believe we just walked right out of the store like it was no big deal. Jesus, the people there are, like, totally asleep!"

"I know, right?" Jennifer said as Daisy was saying, "I told you Macy's is the easiest." She unwrapped a straw as the waiter put a Tab in front of her.

"Did you get that sweater?" I asked Jennifer, lowering my voice.

"Nah, I got a different one. Orange and blue cableknit," she said, half pulling it out of the bag to show us. "It fit much better. I think it was like fifty dollars or something." She grinned and took a slice of pickle from the dish on the table.

"Oh my God!" I said, giggling. "That is so cool!"

"Check you out, missy!" Gordon said. "Miss Silk Skirt."

"Mr. Leather Gloves!" Julie and I said in unison.

"Shut up!" Gordon said, looking around, trying not to laugh. "You're gonna make me paranoid."

"What else didja get?" I asked Gordon, who took a long drag from his clove cigarette.

"Calvin's . . ." he said through his nose, then exhaling. He pointed to the pack of cigarettes on the table, as if to say, anyone who wants, take. Daisy took one and Gordon put a pack of matches in her open palm.

"He collects them," she said. "You're up to thirty-three now, right?"

"Thirty-four!" Gordon said, smiling big.

"Oh my God," Julie said. "I thought I had a lot."

"Do you collect Calvin Klein jeans, too?" Gordon asked.

"No, Fioruccis," Julie said, chewing on her straw. "Well, I don't really *collect* them, I just have a bunch."

"Ooh, *Fiorucci*," Jennifer said. "I've never been. How is it there?"

"So easy!" I said. Then I realized I might be acting like this big professional when I'd really only gone stealing a few times. But no one seemed to notice.

"Yeah," Julie said. "No one counts the stuff you take into the dressing rooms there. It's really good."

"Hey, are you guys doing 'sense memory' in Mrs. Zeig's class?" Jennifer said. Jennifer, Daisy, and Gordon were all in Mr. Marat's acting class, and so far they didn't really like him. Sense memory was this acting exercise where you had to recall something like eating an orange or smelling your grandmother's house and kind of act it out. The homework was to bring in some sense memory experience and perform it in front of the class.

"I have no idea what to do!" Jennifer whined.

"Totally!" Julie said. "Do you guys know what you're doing?"

"I think I'm gonna do opening this jewelry box I got for Christmas when I was eight," Daisy said.

"Ooh, good one, Daze," Gordon said. "Do you think I could do smoking a clove cigarette?" he asked, exhaling smoke rings, and we all cracked up.

Then Jennifer had us cracking up even more because she did an imitation of this guy in their class, Mark Wilder, who thought he was God's Gift to Acting. She made this totally serious face with her eyebrows all knitted together and recited some Oscar Wilde piece he did in, like, a fake British accent. And she imitated Mr. Marat telling him how great he was; meanwhile everyone in the class was, like, rolling their eyes. Gordon laughed so hard, he spit a big mouthful of coffee down his front and onto the table. Then we all cracked up about *that.*

"So. Are we ever going to get to meet this famous Julie Braverman?" Mom asked me that afternoon as I was putting away the groceries. That was one of my jobs for my allowance. She was chopping parsley on the cutting board. It was almost dinnertime. I knew this would eventually come up.

"Um," was all I could say at first.

"You've had a sleepover at Julie's practically every Saturday night since school started," Mom pointed out.

"Why don't you invite her over sometime?" Dad called from the living room.

"I mean, we don't even know what her parents do," Mom said.

"Her mom's a model and her dad's in the music business," I said kind of under my breath.

"What?" Mom said.

"I don't know," I said. "I like going to her house." I thought about our family eating dinner like we did every night. What if Julie found us ordinary and boring? Dinner at Julie's meant we were free to make whatever we wanted or order pizza. Sometimes we ate with Mandy if she was around but hardly ever with Mimi. Mimi was at Harvey's a lot. It was so great.

"Besides, you met her, Dad, when you picked me up at Caitlin's Bat Mitzvah," I said.

"Oh, Julie, I don't remember. There were so many girls there," he said.

"Let's have her over for dinner next weekend," Mom said. "I'll make Peachy Chicken. . . ." she said temptingly. Chicken with peaches was my favorite dinner that Mom made, and when I was little I called it Peachy Chicken and the name stuck. Mom always made it for special occasions like my birthday. The sauce was made from Campbell's cream of mushroom soup and canned peaches. It was the most delicious dish ever.

"I'll think about it," I told my mother.

I wasn't sure why I didn't want to invite Julie over. I

mean, part of me did and part of me didn't. Maybe it was 'cause she seemed so much more experienced and mature than me, and I thought my parents would think she was a bad influence or something. Or that they wouldn't like that she just had a single mom who was a recovering alcoholic, and almost never home, not that they'd ever know those things. I was also scared my parents might get into one of their fights right in front of Julie, and I'd die of embarrassment. Then maybe Julie would think I come from a really screwed-up family and she would think *I* was really screwed-up.

Or maybe there was something about Julie and me that felt private, and I didn't want to share it.

"I can't believe you got that skirt," Julie said later during our nightly phone conversation. "It's amazing!"

"It's probably the most expensive thing I will ever get," I said quietly, getting comfy in my dad's big easy chair in my parents' bedroom. The other phone was in the kitchen, so their bedroom was the only place you could get any privacy at all. How I wished for an extension in my room! I closed the door and turned the clock radio on just in case anyone was listening, but my parents were busy watching TV, and Ellie was in her room.

"You could wear it to Kahti Fearon's Christmas party," Julie said.

Oh my God, *yes*! Kahti was a popular junior in the drama department who we barely knew, but we were totally psyched to get invited to her party. When she asked us in the hall on Monday after French, we said, "Of course we'll come!" and then Julie dug her nails into my palm trying not to scream. She was especially excited because she had a crush on Rick DiBiassi—also a junior in drama and *so* Julie's type. Dark hair, tall and skinny, leather jacket with lots of zippers. Total rocker look. Since he was in Kahti's class, it seemed like a sure thing that he'd be at the party.

"What kind of tights should I wear with that skirt?" I asked Julie.

"Do you have any fishnets?"

"No."

"Oh my God, have you ever been to Betsey Johnson?" she asked.

"No, what's that?"

"It's a store on Columbus Avenue. I have to take you there! They have the best stuff, and they have a really good selection of fishnets," Julie said.

"Should I *get* a pair of fishnets?" I whispered. I was so paranoid that my parents or Ellie might be listening.

"Of course!"

"Okay! When should we go?"

"I don't know, after school sometime? Or next Saturday?"

"Totally," I said, and then we got into a conversation about Daisy and Jennifer Smalls and how at the beginning of the school year we didn't really like them but now we did. When Daisy told us about her agent and the commercial she did, she wasn't all conceited about it.

"Did your parents go to the parent-teacher conferences on Friday?" Julie asked.

"Of course," I said, rolling my eyes. "Both of them did. They always go to my sister's, too; they've never missed one. It's so embarrassing."

"No, it's good, I think," Julie said, her voice getting soft. "My mom forgot."

"She didn't go?"

"Nope."

"What about your dad?"

"Are you kidding? He doesn't even know what grade I'm in."

"Oh," I said. I didn't know what to say. "Well, they're just dumb meetings with the teachers. It's not like anything important happens, really." I didn't know why I said that, 'cause I actually liked that my parents wanted to meet my teachers. They always came back making jokes like, "All your teachers say you're not very bright, and you don't work hard enough!" But then they would tell me they were proud of me. "Yeah." Julie sounded kind of sad, and I couldn't believe that there could be anything about my family that would seem cool to her.

"Listen," I said, deciding to change the subject. "My parents think it's weird that I've never invited you over, so . . . um . . . would you want to come over for dinner sometime?"

"Of course," Julie said, brightening.

"Really?" I said. There. That wasn't so hard. Hearing Julie sound into it surprised me, and I felt relieved.

"Sure," she said. "Did you think I would say no or something?"

"I don't know. We just always have so much fun at your

place 'cause your mom's not around. I didn't think you'd really want to meet my parents, let alone spend an evening with them. And my sister."

"Are you kidding? It'll be fun. So when am I coming over?"

"How 'bout next Friday? Maybe we could go to a movie afterwards."

"Okay," Julie said.

Then Julie and I got absorbed in conversation again, and before we knew it we went through the entire junior class of guys in drama and could not find one who was cuter than Rick DiBiassi.

"What about Josh Heller?" I said. I always noticed Josh Heller in French. He had intense blue eyes and black hair.

"From French?" she said.

"Yeah, he's always with that guy Tim Haas? I think he's Josh's best friend. Don't you think he's cute?" I said.

"Hmmm . . ." She thought for a second. "I suppose . . . but he's short."

Not for me. I was only four-foot-eleven.

6

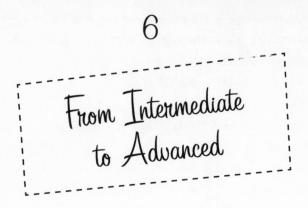

From Intermediate
to Advanced

It was totally blustery out the day Julie and I went to Betsey
Johnson on Columbus Avenue. The style of the store was
semi-punk. There were two floors, and the dressing rooms
were up on the second level, on a balcony. It seemed like
everything in the store came in only two colors: black and hot
pink. In fact, the salesgirl who greeted us at the door wore
hot-pink lipstick, a pink shirt tied at the waist, a black ruffly
petticoat as a skirt, black fishnets, and combat boots.

There were black lacy body stockings—these one-piece
leotards that you wore with a shirt and skirt or jeans over
them. Probably too sexy for me to pull off, I thought, but
Julie said, "C'mon, you gotta try one on." There was also
this hot-pink cotton dress with a low scoop neck and flowy
skirt that I liked. I tried that on first but decided my stomach was too fat for it. Julie was always telling me I wasn't

fat, but I was self-conscious about my stomach anyway.

Julie came out of the dressing room giggling in her black bra, body stocking, and a hot-pink miniskirt.

"That looks amazing!" I said.

"You think?" she said.

"Yes, definitely, but maybe you should have like a white button-down shirt or something on top. Like tied around the waist maybe? With a wide black belt?"

"Oh, totally. Good idea," she said. She threw her T-shirt over her top and went downstairs to find some vintage white men's dress shirts and belts. Girls wearing big men's shirts was really in, especially if they were cotton-soft and really worn-looking.

I changed from the pink dress to the body stocking and put my Fiorucci jeans over them to see how that looked. I was right—it wasn't really me. Julie came back up wearing a white shirt unbuttoned over her bodysuit and carrying a few belts and three more white shirts. There were only two dressing rooms up on the balcony, and we were the only ones up there.

"Ta-da!" she whispered as she pulled out a pair of black fishnets she had hidden between two shirts. "Size A, right?"

"Yeah, thanks!" I squealed.

"Shh! Put them in your bag," Julie said, tying the bottom parts of the white shirt around her waist. She faced the mirror, and I noticed something rectangular sticking out from under her shirt at her shoulder.

I gasped quietly. "Uh-oh, Jule."

"What?" she whispered.

"I guess you didn't feel this, did you?" I said, reaching

down her back and pulling up the white plastic sensor thing that was attached to the body stocking. It was like two pieces of whitish-grayish plastic hinged together like a clamp or rectangular jaws or something. It would set the alarm off at the front door.

She thought for a second but didn't seem to bug out. I was thinking, *Oh well, we'll just leave empty-handed, who really cares?* Then Julie said, "Come in here a sec." So we both went into her dressing room and pulled the pink velvet curtain shut. Fishing through her bag, she pulled out her purple LeSportsac makeup bag and found a tiny nail scissors. We sat on the pink carpet and Julie stretched the back of the bodysuit around her waist so the plastic sensor was almost in her lap.

"Look, it's on a seam," she whispered. She cut a tiny hole and slipped it off. "Piece of cake." Dropping the plastic sensor on the floor, she told me to turn around and she'd do mine.

"How's it going up there, girls? Those shirts okay?" It was the salesgirl shouting up from downstairs. Julie gave me a look like, *You go,* and I said, "Fine," leaning on the railing of the balcony.

"Fabulous!" the girl said. "You wanna try any other belts?"

I looked back toward Julie. "No, I think we're good!" I shouted.

"All right!" she said.

I went back into Julie's dressing room and took a deep breath. "We just could have been so dead! What if she had come up here?" I said.

"C'mon. Let me get your plastic thing," Julie whispered, seeming unfazed.

"Nah, it's okay," I said, taking the body stocking off. "I don't want it; it's not really me."

"Do you want a white shirt?"

"Well, yeah. . . ." I hesitated.

She started searching for the plastic tag on one of the white shirts. Down at the waist, again on a seam, there it was. Turning the shirt inside out a little, with two snips, off it came.

"See that?" Julie said. "Because it's on a seam, it'll be easy to fix that hole."

"Or I could even leave the hole," I said. "Then my mom will believe me if I say it cost me five dollars at the flea market."

"Oh, you're a genius. But your mom never asks where you get stuff," Julie said.

"True," I said. How could my mom be so oblivious? "So you're gonna get the body stocking?"

"Yup and I think that pink dress you don't want."

"Oh my God, that dress is, like, seventy-eight dollars!" I started giggling.

"I know!" Julie giggled back. *What courage she has,* I thought. Then again, who was I to talk? I got a 250-dollar skirt last month.

She snipped the plastic sensor off the pink dress.

"I'll meet you downstairs, Jule," I said, carrying the remaining two white shirts. I figured we'd just leave the belts in the dressing room.

"'Kay," she said.

The salesgirl greeted me on the ground floor. "How'd you make out?" she said.

"Fine," I said. "I think I'm gonna put these back, though, and look around a little more." *If only Mrs. Zeig could see this performance,* I thought, feeling pretty proud of myself.

"Okay, I'll take them," the girl said, taking the white shirts. She didn't notice that we had started with four and now there were only two. She turned away from me just as Julie came down with her Chocolate Soup bag, which looked a little fuller.

"All set?" Julie said.

"Yup," I said.

"Oh, girls!" the salesgirl suddenly called to us. "Did one of you leave this?" I looked up at her on the balcony and my heart did a somersault. She was holding Julie's purple LeSportsac makeup bag. I felt the blood rush to my face. How did she get up there so fast?

"Oh, Jesus," Julie said quietly, and then totally acting, said, "Yes! Thank you! Sometimes I'm such a spaz!" And she laughed at herself, meeting the salesgirl on the hot-pink-carpeted steps that went to the balcony.

"Not a problem," she said. "I'm always leaving my stuff places. Like, how many times have you ever left your umbrella in a cab? Or your sunglasses?"

"I know!" Julie said. *C'mon Jule, I can't take this. . . . We gotta go. We. Got. To. Go.*

Julie took her makeup bag back, but she was careful not to put it in her bag in front of the salesgirl. Who knew what was in there close to the surface?

"Thanks again!" Julie said, and we were out the door. There was no sound but our feet hitting the pavement.

Outside, we crossed Columbus Avenue. I could feel the warmth return to my hands as my nervousness subsided. We headed toward Central Park, where we sat on a bench outside the planetarium.

"Hey, can I ask you something?" I said. "The Chocolate Soup bags"—I touched hers—"did you steal them?"

"Of course! Those are expensive!" I don't know why, but I was kind of surprised.

"Why did you take two?" I asked.

"Because I didn't know which one I liked better, and it was really easy there. Crowded store, nobody really paying attention, no security . . ."

"Uh-huh," I said.

"Why?" she asked.

"I don't know, I've just been wondering."

"Are you mad at me for giving you something I stole?" she said.

"Not at all!" I said. "I love this bag." Suddenly I saw this side of her like I was important to her.

We gathered up our stuff off the bench and started walking toward Broadway. I noticed the leaves were really blowing around like crazy. Christmas was two weeks away; I loved this time of year.

"Hey," I said, stopping for a second.

"What?"

"What did you do with the white plastic things?" I asked.

"I pulled up a piece of the carpet in the dressing room and stuck them under there," she said, smiling.

"Oh my God," I said. We started walking again and I thought to myself, *I just went from intermediate to advanced.*

When Julie came over for dinner, she had on a new polka-dot top. I hadn't seen her wear it yet, but I knew she probably *got* it from Canal Jeans. I wore my green baggy jeans that I *got* from Unique Antique Boutique one day after school with Julie. She was being extra polite, saying "Yes, please" and "Thank you" to my parents, and I started to think I was stupid to be so worried. Of course she knew how to act in front of them. It's not like she was going to blurt out some klepto story of ours. Or describe for my family the graphic details of the last guy she made out with. And I was pretty psyched that she even liked the Peachy Chicken. She kept making yummy sounds and saying to my mom, "Mrs. Prodsky! This is so good!"

"I'm glad you like it," Mom said. "And please, call me Helene."

"So, Julie, has your family always lived on Ninety-Ninth Street?" Dad wanted to know.

"Since I was born," she said.

"I hear your dad is in the music business?" Mom said.

"Yeah, he produces some jazz singers like Judy Coles Harner," Julie said. "She sings at cabaret places."

"Is that right—Judy Coles Harner!" Dad said. "We love her music. We have several of her records!"

"Oh. Cool," Julie said politely.

Then my mom said that she was pretty sure Judy Coles

Harner played at the Algonquin once, this really fancy dinner club–type place, but Bernie was too cheap to take her there.

"Helene," Dad said, trying to stay calm. "Are you going to start?" This seemed to shut her up because she just glared at him over her forkful of chicken. Dad pretended not to see her expression, and I don't think Julie noticed. Then Dad launched into a long, boring story about one of the students in his speech class at St. Andrew's College. You wouldn't believe the problems with the New Jersey state school system and blah blah blah. I mean, like, did he think we cared? Didn't they realize my new best friend was sitting at their table eating with my great-grandmother's good silver?

Ellie barely said a word, but that was nothing new. We might as well have been watching Tom Brokaw during dinner, which we sometimes did. Why couldn't they be like other people's parents? When I went to Kristin's house for dinner the first time, her dad wanted to know all about my interest in acting and stuff. Kristin nearly died of embarrassment, but I didn't mind.

Finally, when Dad's story ended, Julie asked Ellie what clubs she and her friends liked to go to.

"What?" Ellie said with a mouth full of salad.

"What clubs do you like?" Julie repeated, "Like, the Roxy or Xenon, you know. . . ."

"Um . . . I'm not. . . . I don't. I don't really go to clubs," she said, looking down.

"Oh," Julie said cheerfully. "Well what do you like to

do?" And then there was this weird silence, and I tried to think of something to say. Julie gave me a shifty look like, *Sorry, did I say something wrong?*

"She likes to go to museums," I blurted out. "She doesn't really do normal teenage stuff."

"Shut up!" Ellie said, getting upset.

"What?" I said innocently. "It's true, isn't it?"

"You're just too stupid to understand museums!" she hissed.

"I'm not too stupid, just too bored! Besides, I like to do things with people in my age group, not with, like, fifty-year-olds!"

"Girls! Girls!" Mom raised her voice. "Come on now, we have a guest. Behave yourselves!" Then we were all quiet for a minute. "Bernie, pass the salad," Mom said.

Then I felt Ellie give me a hard kick under the table.

"Ow! Hey!" I threw my fork at her face, but I missed.

"All right! Enough!" Dad yelled.

"You deserved it," Ellie said. "Trying to act all high and mighty in front of your new friend! Who are you trying to impress? Please! Spare us, Miss Actress!" Then she threw her napkin in her chair, stormed off to her room, and slammed the door. I felt the tears welling up, but I swallowed hard. Julie, my parents, and I sat there in the weird silence again. Mom wiped her mouth with her napkin like nothing had happened.

"I'm sorry, Julie," I said under my breath.

"No, no, it's okay," she said, and touched my hand for a second.

"Honestly," my mom said, looking at Julie. "I don't know what we're going to do with them." She shook her head like, *What a pity.*

"Oh, my sisters and I fight all the time, too," Julie said, but I knew she was just saying that.

"Ellie's just jealous, 'cause she doesn't have any friends," I said.

"Julie, stop—" Mom said, but Dad interrupted her.

"How 'bout some dessert?" He stood up to clear his plate, taking Julie's. I stood, too, taking my plate and Mom's. "We've got some nice melon, cookies. . . . Julie? What do you like?" It was clear he was talking to the other Julie.

"Oh, I'm fine, Mr. Prodsky. I couldn't eat another thing."

"You sure?" he called from the kitchen.

"Yes. Dinner was delicious. I'm so full," she said.

"Really? It's no trouble," Mom said. "Honey! Will you bring me an apple?" she said to my dad. Then, to Julie, "I'm trying to stay away from the cookies. But you girls go ahead."

"An apple!" Dad sang from the kitchen.

"Would you like an apple?" Mom said to Julie.

"No, really, I'm fine."

"We should get going if we're gonna catch that movie. Is that all right, Mom? If we go now?" I said.

"Well, all right. Where are you going?"

"Loew's Eighty-Third. We're seeing *Arthur*."

"Okay," Mom said, seeming a little disappointed that dinner ended so abruptly. I went to the front hall closet to get our jackets.

"Thanks so much for dinner, Mrs. Prodsky," Julie said.

"Helene," Mom said, forcing a smile. She sucked on an ice cube from her empty glass of water.

"Oh . . . okay," Julie said, sounding a little uncomfortable.

"Bye! Have fun, girls!" Dad said from the kitchen doorway.

"Back by eleven thirty, right?" Mom said.

"*Yes*, I *know*," I said, not hiding my annoyance.

I locked the door behind us while Julie rang for the elevator.

"I am so sorry," I said to Julie. "I didn't think tonight would be such a nightmare."

"What are you talking about?" she said. "It wasn't that bad. Your parents are nice. They're funny. And it only got sticky there at the end with Ellie. I'm sorry if I caused that."

"No you didn't. . . . She's just . . . weird." Then I just couldn't hold my tears back anymore; they came sliding down my cheeks.

"Hey," Julie said, touching my arm, "it's no big deal, really."

"I just . . ." I said, trying to catch my tears and finding it difficult to look at her. "My family just gets me so upset!"

"I know," she said, putting her arm around me. "I guess that's what families are supposed to do—drive you crazy."

The elevator came, and I wiped off my face so Freddy, the elevator man who's known me forever, wouldn't ask what's wrong. He just nodded at us, and we pretty much rode silently down the twelve floors. When we got outside Julie stopped in front of my building and said, "Listen. I know you think I have this great family, but believe me, they're nuts. Completely nuts. Just like yours is nuts, only different." I just looked at her, not knowing what to say.

"Believe me, you'll see it, I promise." She put her arm through mine, and we started walking toward the subway. "And the dinner was good. I loved the Peachy Chicken."

"I'm sorry I'm being such a baby," I said, feeling more warm tears on my face. "I feel so stupid."

"Who better to cry in front of than your best friend?" Julie said.

7

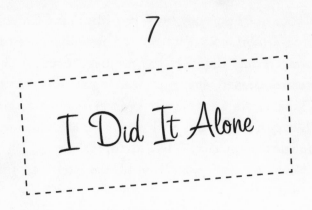

I Did It Alone

One weekend during Christmas season I went down to Canal Jeans by myself. Canal Jeans was in Soho and had excellent vintage clothes. There was also a great flea market nearby on Greene Street. I hadn't tried stealing there; I guess it felt too risky 'cause of it being outdoors and all out in the open. You never knew who was watching. It was a good excuse to use if Mom asked about any new stolen clothes—that I got them at the flea market. She knew things were cheaper there. But she never asked, which kind of bugged me out. I mean, how out of touch with your kids can you get?

At Canal Jeans I was looking for one more Christmas present for Ellie. Our family celebrated Christmas even though Dad was Jewish and Mom was Protestant. We weren't really any religion, which was okay with me.

As much as I hated Ellie sometimes, we always got

68

each other good presents, and we'd kept up a Christmas-morning tradition that we started when we were little. Since we weren't allowed to wake up Mom and Dad until eight thirty, and watching the yule log burn on TV got so boring, Ellie had the idea to give each other stockings using our toe socks. Rainbow toe socks were really popular when we were little—these knit socks with separate colored toes. Ellie and I stuffed them with little doodad kinds of presents. Stuff like makeup or bookmarks, pins, jewelry, or what-ever.

So when I went Christmas shopping at Canal Jeans, I was on the lookout for toe-sock stuff, but I also needed a few other presents. Ellie was easy to shop for 'cause she loved vintage clothes and I knew her taste exactly. I had every inten-tion of *buying only* that day, but I couldn't help notic-ing that the kind of dresses Ellie liked were on racks right outside the dressing rooms. Nobody seemed to be checking people into the rooms—it was just chaos because the store was so crowded. The dresses were only $9.99, but, *What the hell?* I thought. I grabbed three of them: one with purple flowers, one with gray and white triangles, and one with yellow squiggles. I thought Ellie would like the purple-flowered one the best—it was very 1940s, with shoulder pads and wide collars and covered buttons. I quickly checked for feet, opened a dressing-room door, and slipped in. Some painters pants and long underwear were already hanging there. *God, you could make out like a bandit in this place,* I thought. I held the purple flowered dress up against my body. It looked like it would be a little big on me, which was good 'cause Ellie was taller.

I heard a rap on my door. "Need any help in there?" a female voice called. I sucked in my breath.

"No thanks. I think I'm good," I said, sounding nonchalant.

"Okay, well if you need a different size or something just holler. I'm Bettina."

"Okay, thanks." I breathed out. Hmmm. Did she see the purple flowered dress from underneath the door? I hoped not. I stood there thinking for a few seconds, and then I pulled the tags off the dress and stuffed them in the pocket of the painters pants. Fortunately, the dress was very thin material so it rolled up to almost nothing, and I buried it deep in my Chocolate Soup bag. I took a deep breath, stepped out of the dressing room, and returned the other two dresses to the rack. I didn't see Bettina, or any salesperson for that matter—only shoppers everywhere. Julie was right; she always said that Christmas season was the best. I headed to the cashier, where I paid for a pair of navy gloves for my dad. My face felt a little flushed the whole time.

"Aren't these great?" the guy who rang me up asked. He had a turquoise mohawk. "I bought everyone in my family a pair of these." Mohawks totally creeped me out. I mean, I was all for self-expression and being true to yourself and all that, but I found it so weird to look at the shaved bald part of this guy's head.

"Yeah," I said, wishing he would just hurry up so I could get the hell out of the store.

"And did you see what they do?" the mohawk guy said. He took one of the gloves and turned it inside out to reveal a pale yellow color. "They're reversible!" He grinned a toothy grin at me.

"Cool!" I said, hoping I sounded enthusiastic enough. *C'mon Mohawk Guy, just ring me up, all right?*

"Of course," he added, "I think the blue is prettier." He turned the glove right-side in, and pulled out a Canal Jeans plastic bag from beneath the counter.

"Would you like a few buttons?" he asked, pointing out the free fluorescent Canal Jeans pins on the counter in a Lucite box. *Oh, yeah, good for Ellie's toe sock,* I suddenly remembered.

"Sure," I said, and he threw a fuchsia one and a green one in my bag.

"Merry Christmas, sugar. Happy New Year!" He handed me my change.

"You, too," I said, trying not to run out of the store.

I got outside, threw the drawstring Canal Jeans bag over my shoulder, shoved my fists in my pockets, and did not look up until I was at the subway entrance. *Oh my God, wait'll I tell Julie. Stolen Christmas presents, what next?* I couldn't stop thinking, *I did it alone, I can't believe I did it alone,* for, like, the whole train ride uptown.

That night on the phone with Julie, I asked if she ever thought about getting caught.

"What do you mean, have I imagined it?" she said.

"Yeah and, like, have you thought about what you'd do?"

Julie paused for a second. "Well, I guess I'd play totally

innocent. I'd say it was a dare, that somebody at school dared me. And that it was my first time."

"Uh-huh," I said. Then we were both quiet for a second.

"I heard from Jennifer Smalls that you should stay away from the Upper East Side, like fancy stores on Madison Avenue? It's pretty snooty there. Jennifer says some stores have two-way mirrors," Julie said.

"You're kidding!" I said. "That's gotta be against the law. Doesn't that infringe on our rights to privacy or something?"

"Who knows. . . ." Julie said, sounding like her mind was going somewhere else.

"What would you do if your mom found out?" I asked.

"I don't know—with me being the youngest of five, my mom's dealt with a lot worse from my brother. And my sisters. I bet she wouldn't care that much," Julie said.

"Oh my God, if my parents found out, I don't know what I'd do," I said, trying to imagine the scene. "I can't believe you've never been caught."

"'Cause I'm *good*," Julie said, laughing.

"And so modest!" I said sarcastically.

"Kidding," she said.

"Would you be scared if you did?" I asked.

"What? Got caught? Of course! I'd probably shit in my pants!" Julie said.

"Come on. No you wouldn't."

"No, but I'd cry for sure."

"Me, too," I said. Oh my God. I'd totally cry.

* * *

The next day was Monday, and Julie and I got to French before Josh Heller and Tim Haas. They were both juniors in drama, and I always saw them together; I figured they were best friends. They even dressed kind of alike. Every time I saw Josh I got a little nervous. I knew I had such a crush.

Julie and I usually sat by the window, but for some reason that day we sat in the back. I was writing in my notebook, copying the homework off the board, when I sensed Josh slide into the chair next to mine. I immediately recognized his white Adidas tennis sneakers. They made me think of this guy from my camp, Jeremy Schwab, who said that "ADIDAS" stood for "All Day I Dream About Sex."

From the corner of my eye, I looked at Josh. He was wearing a brown 1950s-style vintage cardigan sweater. It kinda felt like he had looked at me, too, and then looked away. *Oh shit,* I thought, *I hope I'm not blushing.* So I tried willing myself to not blush. *No blushing, Julie, no blushing,* I willed. Then a piece of his sweater got caught on a metal screw of the desk, and I don't know what came over me but I just reached out and unhooked it.

"Hi," he said to me, looking up. He had never said hi to me before.

"Hi," I said, and I couldn't help but laugh a little. "You were stuck." I smiled this huge smile, thinking, *Please God, don't let there be anything in my teeth.* I felt Julie's head look up, too.

"Oh. Thanks." He looked at his elbow. "I guess we haven't officially met," Josh said, and then he actually stuck his hand out for me to shake it! "I'm Josh."

"*I know!*" I wanted to blurt out, but instead I just said,

"Hi," again and shook his hand. Nice strong grip. Warm hand. Then I felt a little kick from Julie on my foot, but she kept looking straight ahead like she was reading the board. What an actress. I could see her totally trying not to crack up.

Then it looked like Josh was gonna say something else, but Madame Craig shouted, "*Alors! Alors!* Let's settle down now!" and began the lesson. Josh took out his notebook and pen and I faced the front, but it was all I could do not to turn my head and just stare at him the whole period.

The first time Madame Craig turned her back to us to write the verb *partir* on the blackboard, a tiny crumpled-up ball of notebook paper landed on my desk.

Written in the note was Julie's script: *Oh my God, Josh Heller said hi to you and shook your hand! Are you dying?*

I quickly glanced at Josh, who was scribbling something and didn't look up, so I just gave Julie a quick look back to say, *Yes! But be cool about it, okay?*

Then I saw Julie writing me another note. *Oh God,* I thought, *I don't know if my heart can take this.* I caught Julie's second note like I was catching a firefly cupped in my hands just as it hit my desk and Madame Craig turned back around to face us.

"*Excusez-moi.* Julie?" Madame Craig said. We both looked up and my chest tightened. "*Pardon.* Julie B.," she said, and I exhaled.

"*Oui?*" Julie said, and I stopped listening to read my note as secretly as I possibly could. Madame Craig asked Julie to conjugate *partir.* The note said, *What would you do if JH asked you out????!!!!!* Oh my God, I was going to have to kill her. How could I be expected to concentrate on French verbs?

Then another balled-up note landed on my desk, only this time it came from my other side. *WHAT ARE YOU GUYS WRITING NOTES ABOUT?* it said in Josh Heller's block-lettered-all-capitals penmanship. But thank God I heard what Madame Craig was asking just in time so that as she said, "*L'autre* Julie,"—even in French, I'm the other Julie—by some miracle I knew the answer. First person plural: *nous partons.*

I looked over at Josh, who was smiling at me and clearly waiting for my response. First I scribbled on a little piece of paper, balled it up, and threw it to Julie. It said, *Josh wants to know what we're writing about!*

Julie wrote back, *Tell him, HIM!*

Then I wrote, *You must be high. I can't do that!*

Then Julie wrote, *Yes you can, I dare you.* So I ripped off a tiny new piece of paper and wrote on it *YOU*, and I passed it to Josh. I couldn't believe I actually wrote that. I must have gone crazy. I caught the tail end of the two seconds it took him to open the note, and I saw him read it and laugh quietly. Oh my God, I loved his teeth.

He wrote back, *I had a feeling. Do you like coffee?* It was the last note before the most annoying thing happened. Madame Craig caught us and made Josh move his seat to the front of the classroom.

"*Monsieur Heller!*" she said angrily. Then she said some more stuff in French that I didn't really understand, but I think it was something like, did we think she was born yesterday, and she pointed to an empty chair in the front row.

Poor Josh gathered up his stuff and slunk off to the front before I could tell him my answer. *Yes, I love coffee. With lots of milk and sugar.*

I obsessed about what I would wear on Wednesday. Was he going to ask me out for coffee? I finally decided on my regular Fioruccis with my cutoff white sweatshirt and the earrings that Natalie gave me that were made out of chandelier parts. I had the clothes all laid out on my orange pillow chair.

But on Wednesday, Josh wasn't in French. He wasn't there on Friday, either. Where *was* he?

8

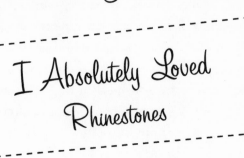

I Absolutely Loved Rhinestones

The Sunday before Christmas, Mom said from behind the Lord & Taylor catalogue, "I know just the thing for Marty." Aunt Marty was Mom's younger sister, and she had "fun jewelry" on her Christmas list. Mom was lounging in bed with the Book Review and various other sections of *The New York Times*, as she always did on Sunday mornings. This was her Sunday morning routine: get out of bed, wash her face and brush her teeth, eat some Wheaties with half-and-half in the kitchen (she didn't like milk) and maybe some Branola bread toast, get back in bed, and read the paper.

Marty and Mom were not particularly close—probably because Mom picked fights with her sometimes—but they talked almost every Sunday morning. I could always tell it was Marty on the phone 'cause Mom said, "Hi ya!" (Which, by the way, were Ellie's first words: "Hi ya!" So the story goes.)

"Would you like to come with me to Lord and Taylor, Julie?" Mom said. "There's a good holiday jewelry sale."

I figured, sure, what the hell. I thought for a second about what it would be like to be in a department store with Mom, after all my recent escapades in department stores, but then I put any thought of stealing out of my mind. I wasn't a complete idiot; I knew I would never do anything stupid with my Mom *right there*. Maybe I'd actually buy something.

As soon as we got to Lord & Taylor, we browsed through the "costume jewelry," as Mom called it, on the first floor. I didn't see anything too exciting. Mom said to the salesgirl, "Where are these?" and pointed to the ripped-out page from the catalogue. The photo was of some long necklaces that I thought were pretty ugly. What made grown-ups choose the fashions they did? Mom had so much clothing that I hated; I wished she would dress more young and stylish like Mimi. Some of Mom's clothes seemed so old-ladyish. She had blouses with these wide ribbon-tie things at the neck that made a big loose bow and were made of material that was so itchy I didn't know how she could stand it.

"Mom, that shirt is, like, so out of style," I said one time when she was getting dressed for work.

"So?" she said, blinking at me. "What do you care? You don't have to wear it." She had a point.

"So, people are gonna think you're really old-fashioned."

"What do I care what people think?" she said, almost laughing, like, what a crazy idea. What other people think.

"You mean to tell me," I said, "that you *really* don't care what other people think about you?"

"Nope," she said, and smiled at me.

I was thinking about this conversation as Mom took out her coral lipstick and reapplied it, using the mirror on the jewelry counter where the salesgirl had directed us.

I looked at her reflection in the mirror on the counter. Thank God she had *finally* updated her hairstyle. For my whole life my mom had worn her hair in this totally embarrassing, *sprayed* way that was so incredibly 1960s, like a bouffant. Ellie finally got her to cut it and get a perm and look like a normal person who was of this decade.

Mom was examining the multicolored beaded necklaces on the counter, and my eye was suddenly drawn to some glittering rhinestone bracelets one counter over. I absolutely loved rhinestones. Mandy had a really cool rhinestone bracelet that I was dying for. She wore it when she played gigs with her band, and it totally added to her rockstar look. I always stared at it on her wrist as her hand moved along the strings of her electric guitar and wished I had one. As the lady was taking out necklaces for Mom, I said, "I'll be over there."

"All right," Mom said, not really looking at me.

The rhinestone bracelets cost $12.50 and were like those stretchy watch bands. They were so cool, I was practically salivating. I tried one on. Oh man, it looked so good on my wrist. There were a few other customers around the counter, but no salesperson that I could see. Just then, a thin blonde woman popped up out of nowhere and said, "Can I help you?"

"No thanks, just looking," I said.

"All right, let me know if you need anything," she said kind of distractedly as she went to deal with some customers on the other side. A middle-aged couple looked aggravated, like, excuse *us*, we were here first. I put back the rhinestone bracelet and tried on another one, a little wider—$15.50. It looked even better than the first one! *My hand is made for this bracelet,* I thought. I rotated my wrist a few times, watching how it flickered sparkly specks of light.

"Julie!" my mother called, and I jumped a little, catching my breath. I turned around to look at her at the opposite counter.

"Come here. Tell me what you think of this," she said. She was holding up two long strands of turquoise beads and examining them from over her half-moon reading glasses.

"Just a sec," I said. Then I looked down at my wrist, and my winter coat had neatly slid right over the bracelet. It was completely hidden. I walked over to Mom's counter.

"Um," I said, touching the necklaces with my other hand—the one with no rhinestones. "I think the one with the smaller beads is more Marty."

"Yeah. I agree." Mom thought for a second, then said to the salesgirl, "Okay, we'll take one of these, please."

"Will this be cash or charge?" the salesgirl said.

"Charge," Mom said, taking out her Lord & Taylor card.

I looked back at the rhinestone counter, and there were new customers standing where I had been, looking through the cases and at the stuff on the counter. This was too perfect for words. No one saw me put that bracelet on my wrist. Very slowly, I scanned the whole floor, kind of acting like I was trying to find someone. Was there anyone who could have seen me? How could I be sure? Did I risk it? I felt the bracelet through my sleeve and found the small paper price tag, which I pulled off and stuck in my pocket. I moved the bracelet up a bit closer toward my elbow, in case my sleeve moved or something.

"Let's go upstairs and have lunch," Mom said. She closed her wallet and took the small shopping bag with Marty's present inside, and we headed to the up escalators.

At the Birdcage Restaurant, we ordered BLTs on toast and a Tab with lemon for me and a tomato juice for Mom. Gross, I hated tomato juice. Right away, I excused myself to go to the ladies' room. Luckily, Mom didn't say, "Why don't you take your coat off first?" or something, like I thought she might. Sometimes, the fact that Mom was oblivious was good.

The sign said LADIES' LOUNGE, and the room was totally pink—pink sinks, pink tiles, pink soap, pink stalls. Everyone in there seemed over sixty-five. There was a lady with a gray sprayed hairdo and big thick glasses in a pink-and-white maid's outfit mopping up around the sinks. She handed people a paper towel after they washed their hands. I went into the pink stall at the end of the row, shut the door, and took off the bracelet. I wrapped it in some toilet paper, stuck it inside one of my gloves, and put it in my coat pocket. The weird thing was, I didn't feel nervous at all. I didn't know what had come over me; I was usually so nervous until I got out of the store. I just had this totally confident feeling. I flushed the little paper price tag down the toilet.

On my way out of the ladies' lounge I noticed a pay phone and immediately called Julie. I mean, I just had to tell her about my bracelet. Maybe she'd have some tips for me or something. We hadn't really covered Getting Out of a Department Store with Stolen Jewelry and Your Mother. Her phone rang about seven times. No answer. Bummer.

When I got back to the table, Mom was reading her *New Yorker* magazine, but she put it away when I sat down.

"I liked your friend Julie," she said, which totally bugged me out.

"Really?" I said.

"Of course, why wouldn't I like her?"

"I don't know. I just didn't think that dinner had gone so well."

"It was fine. She seems like a lovely girl." A *lovely* girl. Why did I hate that? "Lovely" sounded so, I don't know, fake or something. The waitress brought our sandwiches just as I was thinking my mom was so stupid. I mean, how could she be so out of it? How could she not know about the fifteen-dollar bracelet stuffed in my glove? Then I got paranoid. Maybe she did know, I thought. Maybe Mom saw me do it and was acting like she didn't. Maybe she was waiting for the right moment to catch me.

"What was wrong with the dinner? Didn't Julie have a nice time?" Mom said.

"Yeah, I guess so," I said. "But did you have to start a fight with Dad?"

"I most certainly did not start a fight with Dad," Mom

said, pressing her hand to the center of her chest defensively, like, *Who, me?* "What makes you think that?"

"Oh, only that comment about his being cheap or something."

"Well, he is," Mom said, sighing. "I married a man who's cheap. When you get married one day, Julie, be sure to have your own money. I wouldn't be able to do half the things I want to if I relied on *your father* for everything." I didn't know what she was talking about. Getting married was, like, an impossible thing to imagine. I was only fourteen!

"How's your friend Olivia? Do you still talk to her?" Mom changed the subject. Olivia Howe and I had gone to school together from kindergarten through eighth grade. She was the funniest person I ever met—she made up tons of hilarious songs that I could never get out of my head. When we were, like, ten or something, she got the idea to create a magazine called *Galore* that we drew with Magic Markers on white paper and stapled together for Ellie, who was the only subscriber. Inside we drew advertisements for fake Bonnie Bell lip gloss flavors like aspirin and brussels sprouts and we laughed about that for hours. But now we were in different high schools. I had a new best friend and Olivia probably did, too.

"No, I don't talk to her much," I said. I took a big bite of my BLT, and caught a falling piece of bacon. "She's at Dalton now, and it's just kinda weird with us being at different schools."

"Why is it weird?"

"I don't know, it just is."

"I don't understand you kids today," Mom said. "Everything's so complicated."

"You mean it wasn't complicated when you were a kid?" I asked.

"Well, I don't think I had all these stop-start friendships like you and Ellie do—"

"Ellie!" I said. "You can't compare my friendships to Ellie's; she barely has any friends!"

"Now that's not true, Julie, you know that's not true. There's Katie Rockwood, and who's that other girl—"

"Please!" I interrupted. "You know how I know Ellie has no friends? 'Cause all she ever does is hang out alone in her room! I mean, what is she doing in there? She couldn't be painting all the time. Don't you think she should be spending time with kids her own age?"

Then Mom just stared at me blankly for a second. "I don't know what you're getting yourself all worked up about," she said as she took a bite of her sandwich. Then we didn't say anything for a little bit.

When the waitress came to take our dirty plates away, Mom said, "Would you like dessert?"

"Nah," I said.

"You sure? Have whatever you want."

"No thanks," I said, sipping from my Tab even though it was empty. I started poking the lemon with my straw and Mom got the picture, 'cause she took out her Lord & Taylor charge card and waved it at the waitress.

As we went down the escalator to the ground floor, had my hands in my pockets and felt my bracelet safely tucked away. The walk toward the exit doors on Fifth Ave nue seemed so slow, I almost couldn't bear it, and Mom was not a fast walker. She was still kind of half looking at the jewelry we passed as we headed for the exit. *C'mon, Mom,* I was willing her, *let's get out of here.* Instead I said, "Marty's really gonna like that present, Mom." I was trying to be nice since lunch had been tense. Why was I feeling so irritated at Mom for not noticing things? It wasn't like I wanted to get caught.

"Yeah, I think so, too," Mom said. We finally reached the revolving doors, and I waited a second to let Mom go in front of me, but she stopped to pull up the furry-rimmed hood of her down maxi-coat. I knew she was gonna tell me to bundle up so I wrapped my scarf around my neck and zippered up my coat as Mom, looking like a little Eskimo from behind, went through the revolving door. I followed and I was actually not surprised to suddenly be out on the sidewalk, the cold air on my face, my precious bracelet safe in the glove. A tiny part of me wondered if the rhinestone saleslady would come running out. But nothing happened.

After dinner that night I asked if I could be excused because I just had to call Julie. Thank God it was Ellie's night to load the dishwasher. I went to my parents' bedroom to use the phone and closed the door.

"Julie!" I said, trying to contain my excitement and keep my voice down. "Guess where I went today?"

"Where?" Julie said, whispering, too.

"I went to Lord and Taylor with my mom to get my aunt Marty's Christmas present, and . . . are you ready for this?"

I paused for dramatic effect. "Are you sitting down?"

"Yes! What?"

"You won't believe it. . . ."

"Just tell me already, what?" Julie said.

"I got. A rhinestone bracelet. With my mom standing one counter away," I whispered.

Julie gasped. "Hold on a sec," she said, "I gotta close my door." Julie had her own phone in her room. Well, she and Mandy shared a phone number, but it was a different number from Mimi's. There was a phone in both Julie's and Mandy's bedrooms.

I told Julie the whole story, and she said, "Wow. That's so cool. We'll have to go back there together next weekend or something."

"Totally," I said. "It's kind of a store for old ladies, so there's, like, no security."

"And Christmas season is key. I'm telling you," Julie said.

"Totally," I said.

"I can't believe your mom didn't notice!" Julie said. Then, it was so weird. Just at that moment in our conversation, as if my mother had ESP, she picked up the extension in the kitchen.

"Julie!" she said in her angry voice. "Please come get the shoes you left lying on the living-room floor and all the other stuff you left on the couch!"

I heard Julie go "Oop—" and then try not to laugh.

"Mom! I am on the phone! God!"

"Well, your father and I are going to watch *Masterpiece*

Theatre, and I don't want to always have to clean up after you—"

"All right! Can you wait one damn minute? Can I have a little privacy, for Chrissakes!" Mom didn't seem to care when Ellie or I cursed. That was one good thing.

Click went the kitchen phone. She'd hung up. It was official, my mother was nuts. Julie started laughing out loud.

"Oh my God, that was so embarrassing," I said. Part of me wanted to laugh, too, but I was so mad. "Do you think he heard us?" I could feel my heart beating and my cheeks were hot.

"Probably not," said Julie.

"Frankly, I don't give a shit. I just want to strangle her with this phone cord," I said, winding my hands up in it.

"Yeah," Julie said. "Well, don't let her get you all riled up. That's what they, like, totally try to do."

"You don't know how lucky you are to have the mother you do," I said.

"Yeah, well, she's a nut-job, too," Julie said, sounding sympathetic. "Do you want to know what my mother said to me last night?"

"What?" I said.

Julie paused for a second. Then she lowered her voice and said, "She asked me if I'd ever had an . . . an *orgasm*."

"What?!" I half-screamed.

"Shhhh!" Julie said. "Keep it down! You don't want your mom picking up again, do you?"

"Sorry," I said, giggling and holding my mouth. "Why

did she ask you that? Just, like, out of nowhere?"

"Totally. I mean she's completely crazy. She wanted to know if I knew how to 'take care of myself.'"

"What does that mean?" I asked.

"I had no idea, until my mother explained it. 'Taking care of yourself' is, you know, *masturbating*. Or 'pleasuring yourself,' she said. I mean, ewwww! Then, are you ready for this? She said if I didn't learn how to 'take care of myself,' I could never expect a man to."

I gasped. "Oh my God. Julie, you have *got* to be kidding me!"

"Nope, I swear. How could I possibly make this up?"

"So what did you say to her?"

"I told her to please shut up because she was completely grossing me out. That even if I wanted to talk about that stuff, she was, like, the last person on earth I would talk to about it."

"Totally," I said. "I can't even imagine my mom saying something like that. She's too uptight."

"Or maybe it's just 'cause she's not as crazy as my mom," Julie said. Then she paused and said, "Nah . . . your mom's nuts, too!" And we both started cracking up.

"I know!" I said, laughing and starting to feel better. "So, wait." I was thinking about the orgasm stuff. "How did she say you're supposed to learn?"

"Oh. From this book," Julie said, sounding annoyed. *"When Women Explore."*

"She gave it to you?"

"Yes!" Julie said, laughing.

"Ewwwww!" I said, and then we paused for a second

like, kind of giggling, kind of not knowing what to say. I had this image of Julie under her covers with no underpants on holding *When Women Explore* and a flashlight.

"Gross!" she screamed when I told her, and we got totally hysterical. Julie was laughing so hard I knew there were tears streaming down her cheeks. She was a crier-laugher. When we finally started to quiet down, Julie said, "Have you ever had one?"

"What?" I asked.

"An orgasm," she said.

"No! Are you kidding? I haven't even *made out* with anybody, remember?" I said, a little offended that she forgot this important fact.

"Oh, right. Sorry. You will. It'll happen soon, I'm sure of it," she said.

"Have you?" I said.

"Have I ever masturbated? Or ever had an orgasm?"

"Well, both," I said.

She giggled a little. "I mean, I've felt around down here, you know. . . ."

"Well sure, me, too. . . ." I said.

"But I don't think I've ever had an orgasm. I'm not sure," she said.

"Has Mandy?" I asked.

"I don't know. I never asked her. I bet she has. She's already slept with a few guys. She's pretty experienced. What about Ellie?" Julie said.

"I have no idea. I could never ask her *that*!" I said, thinking about the impossibility of a sex talk with my sister. "It's pretty unlikely."

"Right," Julie said, a little lost in thought. We paused again, mulling all of this over. "Let's talk about something else, okay? I am starting to get creeped out."

"Okay," I said, thinking. "My mom told me she liked you today when we had lunch at Lord and Taylor. She said you were *lovely*."

"Oh. Cool," Julie said, sounding flattered.

"No it's not!" I protested. "I mean, what does that mean, 'lovely'? It's, like, so pretentious or something."

"You're just mad at your mom 'cause she interrupted our phone call. Which totally makes sense; I'd be mad, too. Why don't you go clean up your stuff and we'll talk tomorrow?"

"All right," I said, feeling kind of depressed.

"Talk to you later," she said. "And congratulations on that good score!"

"Thanks," I said. I was glad she said that. I stomped into the living room and scooped up my stuff. I could feel my parents look at each other, but no one said a word.

9

This Is What Everyone's
Raving About?

The next Monday in French, Tim Haas told me Josh Heller had strep throat. He had already missed three days of school. So that's why he wasn't in class last week. When I heard this, I felt so relieved, but I couldn't help thinking, *Why is Tim Haas telling me? Did Josh Heller tell him to?* It was kind of a big deal since Tim and I had never really spoken before.

"He might be back tomorrow," Tim said.

Two days later, the last day before Christmas vacation, the school was buzzing with excitement. You could just feel it. Kids and teachers noisily passed me in the halls as I made my way to French. I overheard conversations about various New Year's Eve plans—the rich kids' ski trips and the guidance counselor, Mr. Silver's, plans to sleep until the morning of January 2, 1982.

Then all of a sudden, there was Josh Heller walking in step with me up the stairs to the third floor.

"Hello," Josh said. He was wearing his knapsack on one shoulder and holding a small paper bag.

"Hi," I said, without a second even to hide my surprise. "You're back."

"I'm back." He grinned his gorgeous grin at me.

"I heard you had strep. I guess you're better now?" I said. That sounded like such a boring thing to say. *Think, Julie, think! Say something smart or funny.*

"Yeah, thanks, I feel much better," Josh said.

"Good," I said, realizing I sounded too relieved. "It would be such a bummer to be sick during vacation," came out of my mouth next.

"No kidding," he said. We got to the French classroom entrance and just stood there awkwardly for a second, with other kids walking around us.

"Well," Josh said, looking a little self-conscious. He was about to say something else when Madame Craig pushed passed us, saying, *"Entrez-vous! Entrez-vous! Vite!"* and some other French that I think meant, "Take your seats and hurry up." Josh and I sat down next to each other. I noticed Julie wasn't there yet, and it wasn't like her to be late.

Madame Craig started class by telling us to turn our desks to the person on our right and begin a conversation in French. This meant I was assigned to Josh! Madame Craig went around the room telling everyone the assignment was that we were two old friends who hadn't seen each other in years. As Josh settled into his desk, putting his school bag and small paper bag under his desk, he said, "Uh . . . should I start?"

"En français!" Madame Craig shouted. *"Seulement en français!"* "In French," she was saying.

"Uh, *bonjour!*" Josh said and we both cracked up. Most of the class was laughing 'cause of course *"bonjour"* was all anyone could think to say at first.

"Bonjour," I said back. *"Comment . . ."* —I had to think— *"Vas-tu? Um . . . Il y a longtemps, non?"* "How goes it with you?" I was saying. "It's been a long time, right?" At least that's what I was trying to say.

"Oui," Josh said, smiling, and I was psyched he understood me. *"Uh, très, très longtemps. Cinq ans?"* he added carefully. *"Peut-être?"* "Yes, it's been a very long time, five years maybe?" he was saying.

"Oui, oui," I giggled. Saying "wee wee" sounded so funny. *"Vous . . . uh, tu . . ."* I always mixed up the formal "you" and the informal "you," and I was searching for the verb "to live." *"Tu habites à Paris, non?"* I asked him if he lived in Paris now, thinking I probably said it wrong. I was just making stuff up.

"En fait," Josh responded slowly. *"Je ne . . . vais . . . pas à Paris. Je habite à* New York." I thought he was trying to say that he never went to Paris and lives in New York.

"Vraiment?" I said, impressing myself that I remembered the word for "really."

"Vraiment," Josh repeated. Then he reached under his chair and pulled out the small paper bag. He looked around

a little like he was trying to hide what he was doing.

"*Alors, voilà! Café pour toi!*" he said, seeming proud of himself. "Well, here it is! Coffee for you!"

"Wow," I said. "Uh...*comment dit-on,* 'cool'?" "*Comment dit-on*" meant "How do you say?" It was, like, the first thing we learned. "*Merci!*" I continued, feeling kind of stunned. "*Vous êtes ... très ... gentile.*" "You are so nice," I said, wishing I knew how to say, "*That* is so nice." "*You* are so nice" sounded really stupid.

"*De rien,*" he said, which means, "It's nothing." Then we both looked at each other and cracked up again, realizing that most of the other students were spending a lot of time laughing, too. None of us spoke French very well. Then I could tell Josh was trying to tell me to hide the coffee under my chair, but he just pointed and said, "*Ici, ici!*" meaning "Here, here!"

"Oh, right," I said in English. "I mean, *oui.*" I put the coffee under my seat. I could feel it was still hot.

Then Madame Craig saved us all by clapping her hands to get our attention and telling us to turn our desks back to their original positions.

"Hey," Josh said, in English, as the class made a lot of noise with their desks. "Are you going to Kahti Fearon's party tonight?"

"Yeah. I am," I said.

"Great," Josh said, smiling again. "Me, too." Then I caught him sort of scanning my face. He looked at my hair and my earrings. I happened to be wearing the chandelier ones.

"Cool earrings," he said.

94

"Alors! Alors!" shouted Madame Craig, then she said something else about our conversations and the homework.

The bell rang, and Josh said, "See you later." As soon as he was out of sight, I had the urge to scream. I was dying to scream, but I couldn't; I had to rush to my next class. I barely had a minute to take in all that had just happened between Josh and me. And where the hell was Julie?

At the beginning of acting class everyone was talking, so Mrs. Zeig shouted over the noise. "Hello, hello! Let us begin! Find your rehearsal spots! Get with your scene partners! If your partner is absent, please see me." Everyone took their spots in some corner or area of the basement while I thought to myself, *How will I ever be able to concentrate when I can't stop thinking about Josh? Am I gonna see him at Kahti's party tonight? Josh and I just kind of flirted in another language!* Julie was absent, it turned out, because I saw her scene partner, Liliana, go up to Mrs. Zeig. How would I last the whole day without talking to Julie?

My scene partner, Max, was dragging an army duffel bag toward our spot. We had been bringing in props from home and leaving them in our lockers. He took out a blanket that we threw over two chairs to make a bed, some old books for the night table, a plastic vase, some clothes, and a pair of old-fashioned lace-up shoes that I hadn't seen before.

"Wow, those are cool," I said, picking up one of the shoes—actually, it was more like a boot.

"Yeah," Max said in his slow stoner voice. "Aren't they? They were my great uncle's."

95

"Are you gonna wear them? Do they fit you? Or are they just a prop?" I said.

"No, I'm gonna wear them. They're a little small, but you know, 'The clothes make you feel,'" he said, and laughed a breathy laugh.

We were learning from this book called *An Actor Prepares* by Stanislavski—he was this Russian guy who developed a method of acting—that specific clothes or shoes that make up your costume could make you feel like a different person, like older or younger or fatter or whatever. Kind of like if you start chewing gum, you feel like a character who chews gum. It was a totally cool acting trick. One time for an improv, I had to be an old lady, and I put about ten marbles in each of my Keds sneakers and it made me walk really slow and uneasy like an old person. Not to mention, it actually killed my feet.

Mrs. Zeig came over to us and wanted to know where my rehearsal skirt was. I had left it in my locker, having temporarily lost my mind after I drank Josh's coffee practically in one swallow on the way to class. It was the last rehearsal before Christmas vacation, so I didn't think it really mattered.

"Go and get it, Julie! You are a professional actress, and you must always be prepared for every rehearsal! The skirt will affect how you feel!" Mrs. Zeig said. She didn't sound mad, just, like, teachery. Max sort of laughed under his breath. I went and got the skirt, then pulled it on over my leotard and tights. Mrs. Zeig watched us do some of our scene, and it went pretty well, even though I could barely get the picture of Josh's smile out of my head.

For homework over Christmas break she loaded us up with six chapters of reading from *An Actor Prepares*.

When the bell rang for lunch, I ran to the phone booth in the basement to try to beat the line. Luckily, I got there first. I sat down inside and closed the door.

"Ugh, I had the *worst* cramps," Julie said from home, where she had been lying around all morning. "It was unbelievable. I'm sorry I wasn't there this morning."

"It's okay," I said, keeping my eye on the kids passing by the phone booth, "but you'll never believe what happened in French this morning!" I told her about my conversation with Josh and the coffee.

Julie screamed. *"Oh my God!* Josh-fucking-Heller bought you coffee? You're kidding me!"

"Shhhhh! Oh my God, my ear! He was so sweet, oh my God, Julie. He asked me if I was going to Kahti's party— we're still going, right?"

"Of course! We wouldn't miss it! Rick DiBiassi'll be there—who cares about a few little cramps? You're coming over after school, right?"

"Yeah. Well, I have to go home first and get my stuff. And Julie, guess what else?" I said, unable to contain my big fat stupid smile.

"What?"

"He said my earrings were cool."

"Get outta town!"

* * *

After school, I raced home and rushed through folding and putting away the laundry. Mom did the laundry so I never put in more than one or two "new" articles of clothing at a time. Not that Mom noticed, but I was being careful. I took a shower and packed up my gray silk skirt from Macy's with the mother-of-pearl buttons that I'd saved to wear for Kahti's party. I had planned to dress and do my makeup at Julie's, so in my bag I added black fishnets, a red sweater, a pair of low black boots, my LeSportsac makeup bag, and my toothbrush, since I was staying over. Julie always loaned me one of her nightshirts to sleep in, so I didn't have to bring one.

I found my dad reading the paper in the big green chair in my parents' bedroom. Dad got home from teaching early, and Mom was still out.

"Okay, bye, Dad!" I said.

"Uh . . ." Dad said, looking over his paper. "Where ya headed?"

"To Julie's. I'm staying over there tonight. Mom knows."

"Well, all right," he said hesitatingly, like he was gonna say something else. I waited, feeling annoyed and antsy.

"What, Dad?" I said finally.

"You girls got big plans tonight?" he said.

"We're going to a Christmas party. This girl at school is having a party."

"Oh, okay. Will her parents be there?"

"Of course," I lied, rolling my eyes, like *duh*.

"All right, pussy cat. Well, have a good time! We'll see you tomorrow, then!"

"Yeah, see you tomorrow!" I said, and I was out the

door, down the elevator, across the seven blocks to Julie's, up to apartment 3A, ringing the bell.

Julie answered the door in a bra, tights, and black suede miniskirt. Her hair was piled up on her head, and one eye was made up with eyeliner and mascara. We kissed on the cheek hello.

"Good evening," she said in a funny Dracula voice.

"Hi, cutter. How are your cramps?" I said.

"All gone!" she said.

"What a miracle, just in time!" I said.

We got dressed in our party outfits, and Julie said my skirt looked amazing with the black fishnets. I had to admit, my legs looked pretty good in them.

Finally, after three different combinations of rubber bangles, suede boots, tops, jackets, and scarves, Julie's outfit was complete. We put on our winter coats and checked our bags and pockets for the essentials. "Wallet, keys, cigarettes, lipstick," Julie said.

"Let's go!" we said in unison, and headed for the subway up to Riverdale, where Kahti lived.

It turned out practically the whole freshman drama department was invited to the party, which was pretty annoying, because Julie and I thought we'd been singled out. But I got about eight compliments on my new skirt, just in, like, the first hour we were there, which made me feel good. When anybody asked how much it cost I said, "Oh, I don't remember, I think it was on sale!" Kahti's parents were out of town and she lived in a penthouse apartment. You could just feel everyone's readiness to party, now that school was out for three weeks.

I noticed Josh Heller right when we got there, and although he waved to me and Julie from the corner of the living room, he didn't come over to talk to me. I was too scared to go over to his group of juniors—Rick DiBiassi, Tim Haas, and Charlie Myerson.

After we'd been at the party about an hour and mingled a lot, I still hadn't talked to Josh, and I felt like he didn't even care that I was there. I had started to bum out, then Julie said that David Wine had pot, so we went into Kahti's bedroom with him and Reggie Ramirez and got high! I was pretty excited 'cause I hadn't tried it that much. The couple of times I had smoked pot, it totally made me laugh my head off. I rationalized that if I did have an encounter with Josh, I'd do much better if I was stoned.

Then Julie and I got the munchies so we stood at the food table eating M&M Christmas cookies and Doritos for what seemed like a whole hour. As we stood there munching, I watched Josh talking to this pretty blonde girl in his class, Leah Reemer. I couldn't tell if they were acting like friends or more than friends. I was feeling jealous and obsessed with staring at them but trying not to. They seemed to be laughing a lot. Julie said it was just the pot making me paranoid. "Don't let your imagination get carried away," she said.

Then Julie decided our mission was to find someone for me to make out with, if only just for getting it over with and for the practice. It was true. I mean, I was closing in on fifteen and I wasn't getting any younger. Julie was so much more experienced than me; I could never catch up.

"When you do get the opportunity to kiss Josh," Julie reasoned as she licked the orange Dorito crumbs from her fingers, "you don't want him to think you've never kissed anyone before, right?" This was such a good point.

So I totally started flirting with David Wine, which I didn't expect; it must have been the pot. Suddenly I was laughing at everything he said, and I grabbed his arm a couple of times like I was gonna fall over from laughing. Julie gave me a look like, *Perfect! David could be your make-out guy!*

Fortunately, David was totally flirting with me, too, like telling me he liked my skirt and stuff. Suddenly I just blurted out, "I think you're probably the funniest guy in our class."

"Really?" David said, looking flattered. "You're pretty funny, too, you know, and not a lot of girls are funny. I mean, don't take that the wrong way, I mean, I think a lot of girls don't think it's cool to be funny."

"Totally," I said. "I know exactly what you mean."

When he said he'd go get us some punch, I grabbed Julie—I had to talk fast 'cause I was so nervous.

"If it happens, how will I know what to do?" I asked her.

"You'll know," she said. "Just do whatever *he* does."

"What if he leans in to kiss me and his mouth doesn't open?"

"It'll open, don't worry."

"How will I know what to do with my tongue?"

"Just do whatever he does with his—I promise you, you'll know. You'll see how easy it is." Even though it was fun to flirt with David and I was starting to loosen up, I kept half an eye on the party crowd to see where Josh was.

So David and I were standing there drinking our raspberry-flavored punch that somebody had totally spiked, because I tasted it and felt this strong twinge between my eyes, and he turned to me and said, "Wanna go out on the terrace?"

"Sure," I said. I saw Julie's eyebrows go up as we passed her, and I could feel the rapid thumping in my chest. We got out on the terrace, and it was pretty chilly. I wished I had grabbed my coat. David put down his drink and leaned against the brick wall of the apartment building. He looked me up and down. I was a little surprised that I actually liked being checked out like that. He smiled. I smiled back.

"Are you cold?" David said.

"Um. A little," I said, cupping my drink. Then he took the drink out of my hand and put it on the ground next to his. He took my hand, and our fingers interlaced and swung a little back and forth. Then he pulled me to him and it was like I fell gently into his chest. I couldn't believe it, but we started kissing! I was making out with somebody! But all I could think about was Josh Heller and Leah Reemer and if they were still talking and laughing. Were they making out on some other part of the terrace, maybe? David and I kept kissing and I tried to keep my eyes closed, but for one instant I opened them. It was weird to see how he looked up close— I could see he had a few zits. Luckily he didn't see me looking at him. I hoped my breath wasn't too bad.

David's tongue was making rhythmic circles around mine so I moved my tongue in rhythmic circles around his.

How did he even know I wanted to make out? Was it written all over me? Did Julie tell him? Our tongues were circling wildly. We were breathing through our noses and I was thinking, *This is what everyone's raving about?* It wasn't such a big deal. It was a little boring, even. His tongue against mine felt like what I thought it would feel like—like if you had two tongues in your mouth instead of one. His hands were around my back and stuck in one place. *They must be getting cold back there,* I thought. It felt like we were trapped in those tongue circles for about five minutes when finally, I think 'cause we were both shivering a little, we came up for air. Oh my God. I did it. My head was spinning. We were smiling at each other like a couple of goofballs. I felt so totally corny in that moment, like it was a scene from a soap opera.

Then, out of the corner of my eye, I saw the French doors to the terrace open and out came Josh Heller and Rick DiBiassi, holding their cups of punch. Where was Leah Reemer? Josh and Rick had their winter coats on and walked down the terrace away from us. I was kind of bummed that Josh hadn't arrived one second sooner to see me kissing David. I didn't think he saw me at all. Oh, who was I kidding? So Josh bought me a coffee; it didn't really *mean* anything. He probably had no interest in a dumb little freshman like me.

"What?" David said, 'cause I probably looked like I was zoning out.

"Nothing," I said. "Let's go back inside. It's cold." My hands were freezing, and I could see Julie in the kitchen looking for me. I smiled at her, and she knew something had happened. She was so connected to me, it was unbeliev-able. Somehow I lost David on the way to the kitchen, which was just as well 'cause Julie grabbed my arm and pulled me into a corner.

"So?! What happened? Tell me everything!"

"We made out," I said, like it was an obvious and simple fact. Like, I have brown hair and brown eyes. "I did it! I actually did it! Oh my God, Julie! Am I blushing like crazy?"

"Not too bad. You look rosy; it's good. I knew it! I knew he'd be the guy!" she said.

Then I sighed and took a sip from Julie's cup of punch. I had left mine out on the terrace.

"What?" she said. "Was he really gross or something?"

"No. I mean, I don't know, I think he was okay." Then I lowered my voice, and felt a small lump forming in my throat. I took a deep breath again. "I was just wishing it had been Josh."

"I know," Julie said, brushing a piece of hair off my cheek. "But that was your little dress rehearsal. For when you get to kiss Josh."

"Yeah, right," I said. "Like that's really gonna happen."

10

Christmas totally stressed Mom out. She got cranky about having our relatives come over for a big dinner because she didn't really like to cook. Dad took me or Ellie to get the Christmas tree, and the three of us decorated it.

Every year my parents had the same fight:

"Helene! You don't have to do everything. The girls and I will help!"

"I know, Bernie, you always say that, but the fact is I always end up doing everything while you sit around taking pictures and enjoying everybody. I get stuck in the kitchen and don't get to see anybody open any presents!" It was true. Mom's presents were always the last ones left under the tree 'cause she was in the kitchen.

Then she'd say, "Let's just order everything from Zabar's so I don't have to cook!" Then Dad would try to sweet talk her a little: "But you make such a terrific ham,

honey, everybody loves your ham," and Ellie would roll
her eyes at me to say, *Dad just thinks Zabar's is too expensive.*
Then I'd usually chime in, 'cause I hated cooked ham. I
think it was the cloves or something.

"I don't!" I said. "I hate ham. No offense, Mom, but how
about roast beef or something? Let's make that!"

"You see?" Mom said, gesturing to Dad. Then she turned
back to me. "And who's gonna cook this roast beef? Your
father?"

The fight never solved anything, and Mom was right—
she ended up doing most of the cooking, even though Aunt
Marty always made soup and dessert.

Christmas morning, though, was just us four Prodskys.
Ellie and I woke up first and opened our toe socks. Ellie
got me some cool pens with lips on them, a funny notepad
in the shape of a foot, a mood ring, new playing cards with
rainbow unicorns on them, bath salts, chocolate cigarettes,
purple eye shadow, and a porcelain Garfield pin for my
jean jacket. I got her a small bag of pistachios, a lipstick, a
tiny tin of watercolors, some fish magnets, watermelon
bubble gum, plastic jangly earrings with hearts on them,
some perfume samples, and a Kliban Cat washcloth. Oh,
and the fluorescent-colored Canal Jeans pins. I only stole
the earrings and the lipstick; everything else I paid for.
She was pretty psyched to open all that stuff.

Then we woke up Mom and Dad, who were in good
moods. They didn't usually fight first thing in the morning.
Mom had to do her same old morning bathroom routine—
first she washed her face with cold, cold water. "To wake
me up," she said when I asked why it had to be so *cold*.

Then she brushed her teeth vigorously, for what seemed like fifteen minutes. It was a wonder she still had teeth at all, she scrubbed them so hard.

Then finally, we dug into the *pain au chocolat* (which was a fancy way of saying chocolate croissant) that Mom bought us as a treat for Christmas breakfast. She had her orange juice like always, first thing, before she could "put two sentences together."

As soon as Dad emerged fully dressed and showered, camera loaded, Ellie and I began to devour the loot. No matter what I did, I always managed to unwrap all my gifts before Ellie, making me think Ellie got more. It was so dumb, but I just couldn't linger and pause over each present like she could. I was too impatient. Ellie got me some good stuff—like this cool necklace from Savage, a jewelry store on Eighth Street she knew I loved, and a shirt from Reminiscence.

I was excited to see her open the purple-flowered antique dress I got her at Canal Jeans.

"Ooooh . . . Julie!" she said as she took it out of the tissue paper. "It's beautiful! You spent too much!"

"Nah," I said, "don't worry about that." If she only knew.

"Let's see, Ellie," Mom said. Ellie held it up to her chest.

"Hey, nice," Dad said, snapping a picture. Then Ellie examined the sides of the dress where I had pulled the tags off. I felt my heart skip a little.

"There are no tags," she said. "Where'd you get it?"

"I had to pull the price off, silly," I said, trying to sound nonchalant. "It's from Canal Jeans. You love the dresses there, right?" *Reminding her of what a great sister I am will distract her from anything suspicious,* I thought.

"Oh, Julie, thank you so much," she said, kissing me on the cheek. Whew. I was ready to switch the focus to somebody else's present, but Ellie leapt up and said, "I'm gonna try it on!" She ran to her room, pulled off her pajamas, and came back in seconds, modeling the dress.

"I could wear it today when everyone comes," Ellie said.

"It's kind of summery," I said. "You might be cold if we go out to the movies." Going to the movies on Christmas night was our tradition.

"It looks a little big, doesn't it?" Mom said.

"Yeah, I guess," Ellie said, pinching the extra material at her sides. She was so damn skinny, my sister.

"But it's the right length," I pointed out. Please God, can we get off the subject, before someone asks if I saved the receipt? Taking back and exchanging gifts was a given in our family. And then, she said it.

"Would you mind terribly, Julie, if I go to Canal Jeans just to see what else they have?"

"No, not at all," I said, sounding like it was no biggie. "But I think that one looks great on you." Please just shut up about the dress, already.

"Yeah. . . ." Ellie said.

"Okay," I said. "I just thought that one was so you."

"I think it's a lovely dress, Julie," Mom said. "All you have to do is have the sides taken in a little. You could take it to a tailor."

"I don't know," Ellie said. "I'll see." She went back to

her room to change out of it. Then, just as I was rooting around under the tree for a present for somebody else, Dad said, "Julie, did you keep the receipt?"

"Uh-huh," I lied, feeling glad I was hidden by branches.

"Good girl. Always get a receipt!" Words to live by, according to my dad. "I hope you girls didn't spend all your hard-earned money on Christmas. Don't do what your mother does," he continued, sort of under his breath, but of course we all heard him. "You know your mother, she goes crazy every year, has to get you girls everything. I'm in debt to my eyeballs!" Ellie came back in dressed in her pajamas.

"Dad! You're not supposed to say that on Christmas!" she reprimanded him.

"Really, Bernie, what's the matter with you?" my mother said. "It's Christmas! Can't you say anything nice?"

"What?" Dad said. "What did I say? Was it untrue?"

"Well you don't have to make the girls feel guilty about it!" Mom said.

"I'm not making anyone feel guilty!" Dad shot back.

Ellie and I just sat there on the living-room floor surrounded by balled-up wrapping paper and ribbons, staring at them. Why did they have to do this? Just then, Ellie touched me on my hand and said, "By the way, I'm gonna keep the dress."

I found a present marked "To Julie, Love Santa. So you can talk all night long." Mom always put little clues in the to/from cards on the presents. Most of the time the clue made it so obvious to figure out what the present was before you opened it, but this one stumped me. I just had no idea. It was a medium square box. It was heavy, like it could have been a cement block or something. When I opened it I let out such a scream because it was a bright red phone!

By the time my aunt Marty's family came, everybody was in a better mood again and we ate way too much dinner and dessert. Everyone opened more presents, and then we went out to see the movie *Only When I Laugh*, which I thought was pretty funny, and Kristy McNichol was good. We got home around nine o'clock and I called Julie right away.

"Merry Christmas!" she answered without saying hello.

"Merry Christmas!" I said back.

"Hey!" I could tell she recognized my voice. "How was it?" she asked.

"It was pretty good," I said. "Even though my parents had a stupid fight. And I ate too much, as always." I lay down on my bed.

"Me, too. Whatdja get?" I could hear a lot of noise in the background, and I pictured Julie's big living room full of strewn-about presents, ripped wrapping paper, and bits of food on plates scattered around on the floor or on top of the piano or wherever. I kept hearing her brother Hudson's booming voice and Mimi laughing in a high pitch.

"Well, funny you should ask," I said, "'cause I'm talking to you from the best present I got! My own phone!"

She gasped. "Oh my God! That's so great! What color is it?" she asked.

"It's bright red! And . . ." I said, pausing to be suspenseful. "It's my own number! Can you believe it?"

"Wow! Wait, give me the number later, I don't have a pen. But I thought you only asked for an extension in your room," she said.

"I know! They surprised me! I can't believe it, they've never been this cool! The only bummer part is that I have to pay the bill. Some bullshit about how it'll teach me about money, they said. But my dad said it'll only be like eight or nine dollars a month."

"That's not so much. No biggie," Julie said.

"What did you get?" I asked.

"Oh man! Are you ready? Mom got me a hundred-dollar gift certificate to Parachute—which, by the way, is my new favorite store—*the* most gorgeous suede Kenneth Cole boots you have ever seen, um . . . let's see . . . a subscription to *Rolling Stone* . . . a gift certificate to Disc-O-Mat, oh, um . . . Hudson and Renee got me this amazing leather bomber jacket, you can totally borrow it, it's the coolest. . . . Oh, and I'm sure there's some other stuff; I can't remember right now."

"That's great," I said, trying not to sound too deflated.

"You got other stuff besides the phone, right? I mean, the phone is the best present ever!" Julie said, backpedaling a little.

"Yeah. . . ." I said, thinking about the books I got from Aunt Marty and the cassette of *Zenyatta Mondatta* by The Police from my cousins. Mom and Dad also got me a flannel nightshirt, a winter hat, and a 1982 calendar of Broadway shows. Nothing as cool-sounding as what Julie got. My parents would never have gotten me Kenneth Cole boots. Or a leather bomber jacket.

"Oh my God!" Julie practically screamed. "I almost forgot to tell you!"

"What?" I said.

"Guess who called me today?" I never would have guessed. "*Oliver Moloney!* You know the totally gorgeous guitarist in Mandy's band?"

"The British one? From Fried X?" I said. I could not believe this.

"Yes!" Julie squeaked.

"What did he say? How come he called?" I asked, feeling both excited and jealous.

"He called to say Merry Christmas. And . . . to . . . *ask me out on a date!*"

"You're kidding!" I gasped.

"Nope! He's taking me dancing at the Palace next Wednesday night!"

"The Palace? Wait—that's not New Year's Eve, is it? I thought we were gonna spend New Year's Eve together, go to Gordon's party or something. . . ." I said, trying to stop my voice from getting high and squeaky. A lump was forming in my throat, and I could feel tears coming. God, what was wrong with me? Why couldn't I just be happy for her?

"Of course not! New Year's Eve is *Thursday* night. Don't worry, I would never do that to you! We're definitely going to Gordon's party."

Suddenly there was a burst of noise from Julie's living room. It sounded like someone went, "*Hey-hey!* Look at this! Wow!"

"Oh, that was Harvey," Julie said, lowering her voice. "He just opened a present—it's this totally ugly sweater. I might have to go soon, Jule, I think I have to help with dessert. But I just had to tell you about Oliver, I mean, can you *believe* that he called?" I could tell she was out-of-her-mind excited about him. I tried to feel happy for her, but I was having trouble mustering it up. It wasn't so much that I was jealous it was Oliver—I mean, he was gorgeous and eighteen and had the sexiest accent, but I didn't really want him. I just wanted to be asked out.

"Yeah, it's pretty cool," I said, forcing my voice to sound normal, wondering if she could tell. Then I heard Hudson in the background shout, "Merry Christmas, Julie P.! Now get off the goddamned phone!"

"Whoops, did you hear that?" Julie said, laughing. "They're starting dessert. I better go."

"Yeah, okay," I said.

"I promise I'll call you later. But it sounds like your Christmas was good, right?" she said.

"Yeah. It was good," I said. I hung up the phone and wondered what was wrong with me. Why was I crying?

New Year's Eve day came all of a sudden, and Julie and I realized it was our last chance to find some cool new outfits for the party. So we went to Unique Antique Boutique downtown where the selection of vintage clothing was amazing. We discovered a new variation to *getting*: switching price tags. It was really easy to do on bowling shirts 'cause the material was so soft. You could maneuver the plastic stick thing out of its hole. I was kind of collecting bowling shirts—I had two already, one turquoise, one kelly green.

We did our usual routine of taking four or five different things into the dressing room. I had my eye on a red-and-black bowling shirt that said "Nick" in script over the breast pocket. The body of the shirt was red and the sleeves and pocket were black. Oh, I loved it. It was $19.99, but I slipped the plastic tag out of its hole and replaced it with one I took off of a $6.99 shirt. Were we geniuses or what? I also had my eye on a black 1950s taffeta dress. Julie had brought a bigger bag than I had and she managed to roll it up in there for me. So I went to pay $6.99 for the shirt—that's what the price tag said, after all. They couldn't argue with that. If they did, I was all ready with my innocent act: "Um. I found it on that rack of bowling shirts"—then I'd point—"over there," I'd say, like, oh well, I'm just an innocent shopper. But the redhead at the cash register just rang me up and didn't say anything. That wasn't really stealing, was it?

Aside from the bowling shirts, we got some sparkly pink tights and suddenly it was getting to be about five o'clock we had to get back to Julie's to shower and get dressed up.

We were pretty psyched about Gordon's New Year's Eve party, because it was at his dad's apartment and he was out of town. Ever since Oliver called Julie, he was all she could talk about. Oliver, Oliver, Oliver. Did I think he would like her New Year's outfit? She had given him Gordon's address and told him to stop by; didn't I hope he would? Or maybe we'd hook up with him after the party? I was too busy thinking about Josh Heller. Would he be at Gordon's party? Probably not. I had heard the juniors were having their own party somewhere.

Gordon's dad lived in a skanky neighborhood called Alphabet City a couple of blocks from CBGB's where Fried X played. All the buildings there seemed identical and kind of dark and spooky. When we got to the party, people were already spread out all over the living room and kitchen. There were empty Budweiser beer cans lying around, and big bowls of chips on the coffee table. The living-room couches were frayed and covered with these hippie-looking bedspreads. My first thought was, *Gordon's dad must be young,* because his place seemed like a college student bachelor pad. In spite of how beat-up the furniture was, there was the coolest sound system. This guy in our class in the music department, Wally, was an excellent mixer/DJ, so he started pulling out records and blending one song into another. A bunch of us started dancing, which was totally fun. He mixed the Jackson 5's "ABC" into "Physical" by Olivia Newton-John, which totally cracked us up and was really fun to dance to.

Julie, Natalie, and I danced for a while until we were totally sweaty and dying of thirst. It was about eleven o'clock when who walks in the front door but Oliver! Damn, he must really like Julie, 'cause I didn't think this older guy would show up to hang out with freshmen like us. Well it took about two minutes before Julie and Oliver disappeared off to some bedroom, and I thought, *Shit*. I had gone to the bathroom for two seconds to redo my lipstick, so Julie didn't even have a chance to tell me where she was going.

I looked around for Natalie and almost jumped back when I saw her and Reggie Ramirez curled up in this big rust-colored armchair totally making out! People were sitting right next to them on the couch and they were just going at it like no one was even there! Reggie's hand was going up Natalie's dress a little bit, and she wasn't even trying to stop him. I didn't know what to do, not just 'cause I had no one to hang out with (let alone *make out* with) but I couldn't stop staring at Natalie and Reggie groping each other, even though I knew that was sick.

The music coming out of the room where I thought Oliver and Julie went was really loud. It was "Everytime I Think of You" by the Babys, and totally different music was playing in the living room, like Adam and the Ants or something. Oliver and Julie had to be fooling around in there. I wondered if they were naked. I knew I'd get the full scoop later. So I looked around, and the only other person who was not talking to anyone else was Wally, who was super skinny and had greasy hair. Poor Wally, I mean he was a really nice guy, but he wasn't exactly popular. People just liked him 'cause he could DJ. Anyway, Wally was pretty much ignoring me, and I wasn't sure if that was good or bad. He seemed obsessed with peeling off the label of his Heineken in one piece in between spinning two turntables.

Now Natalie and Reggie had also gone off somewhere; the chair they had been making out in was empty. Where were Jennifer, Gordon, and Daze? The people on the couch must have been friends of Gordon's who didn't go to P.A. The thought that Wally and I were the big losers of this party made me want to cry, and I had to work hard to fight back tears. I went into the dark kitchen, where some people were talking and dancing and kissing. They didn't even notice I entered the room. How could I interrupt Julie and Oliver to tell them I wanted to go home? They would think I was such a dork; it wasn't even midnight yet. My watch said 11:47. I looked out the window at the creepy neighborhood and felt scared. I saw a couple with party hats stumbling around and a group of, like, eight people laughing and singing. I didn't really want to leave the party by myself, and I thought a cab all the way uptown would be expensive. What would I do if Julie stayed in that room with Oliver all night? What if she didn't actually want to be in there and I was supposed to save her?

I opened the fridge. Inside there were some bottles of Heineken, a few wine coolers, an open can of 9 Lives, and a saucepan with a lid on it that I didn't dare touch. I suddenly thought of my fridge at home on Fridays after Mom went shopping, when it was stocked with lunch meats, snack-pack puddings, cans of V8, Yodels, Granny Smith apples, carrot sticks, and whatever else. Then my mind drifted to the fight Mom and Dad had had just a couple of nights ago.

"I just don't know how we're going to swing it," Dad said, sounding angry.

"We'll find a way, Bernie, we always do," Mom said. "Ellie will qualify for a student loan. RISD is her first choice. We'll find a way." RISD was Rhode Island School of Design and Ellie really wanted to go there. It was pronounced like RIZ-dee.

"We're not Rockefellers, Helene, or hadn't you noticed?" Dad said, holding up the grocery receipt. "How you manage to spend this much on groceries for a family of four is just beyond me—"

"Bernie, please stop talking to me in that tone of voice," my mother said. "You want to do the shopping? You do it! You'll see what it costs!"

"Helene! Stop already!" was his response, and he stormed off to the bedroom muttering something about what would be the harm in going to a state school; after all, he went to City College and turned out fine.

The music switched from Adam and the Ants to the Hall and Oates song "Kiss on My List." I took a bottle of Heineken and opened it with the sticky opener lying on the counter. Heineken tasted like a metal railing to me. When I went back to the living room, some heavy guy I didn't recognize was in the rust-colored chair smoking. I looked around for a place to sit, thinking, *I got all dressed up for this?* Everyone was off losing their virginity, and I was sitting on the arm of an ugly couch with people I didn't know.

I decided the only thing to do was to go look through Gordon's dad's extensive music collection. I was an actress

fter all; I could act like I wasn't bugging out. There was
his really tall black painted bookshelf full of records and
apes. Looking at the tapes with my back to everyone, I
ould fight back my tears or even let a few slip in semi-
rivacy. *C'mon, Julie,* I willed my best friend, *come out of
here. Please don't lose it tonight, I'll just die if you do. I'll
e, like, the only virgin in our class.* I made myself take big
wallows of my Heineken. This seemed to help a little. I
potted a brand-new cassette of the Split Enz called *True
olours* with "colours" spelled the British way. It still had
he plastic on it.

I don't know why, but taking this Split Enz tape sud-
enly seemed like the most important thing. And the eas-
st. It was dark and smoky and noisy, and no one was even
ware of my presence. I mean no one. I slipped the cassette
nder the skirt of my dress and, pinching it there in place
ith my hand, walked a little awkwardly to the bathroom.
he bathroom was at the end of this short unlit hallway,
ut the doorknob wouldn't turn—it was occupied. *Shit.*
hen I realized no one could see me in the hallway, so I
uickly pulled up the skirt of my dress and stuck the tape
1 the hip of my tights. It just barely fit there and you could
nly see the shape of the box if you were looking.

Then the phone rang and I couldn't believe anyone even
eard it, but the music went off where Oliver and Julie were
nd Oliver came out barefoot wearing jeans and his white
iirt unbuttoned. I could see his chest hair. He went right
the kitchen without seeing me and I heard him pop the
ps off a couple of beers.

I looked at the door he left slightly open. "Jule?" I said

kind of loudly over the music coming from the living room. She saw me and waved me in, excitedly. She was half naked under a comforter, pulling her bra back on, grinning ear to ear. Oh my God. No, this wasn't really happening.

"Julie," she said, smiling, "it's true what they say. It was kinda painful."

This had to be, hands down, the absolute worst night Of my life.

"What?" I said, noticing how shaky my voice sounded, hoping Julie didn't.

"I did it!" she said, her face shiny and smiling. I had this urge to just run out of there, but instead I sat on the edge of the bed and felt frozen. What was Josh Heller doing that very moment? I wondered. Not thinking about me, that was for sure.

"I did it," Julie said again, almost to herself. "I can't believe it."

Then we heard a group of people in the living room counting down. Suddenly the music went off and Dick Clark came on the TV.

"Six, five, four, three, two, ONE! HAPPY NEW YEAR!" everyone yelled. We heard various screams, noise makers, and horns from people on the street. People in the living room were hugging and kissing with continuous "Happy New Year's" that overlapped each other. Julie sat up, still partially under the comforter, and opened her arms to hug me.

"Happy nineteen eighty-two, Jule!" she said, and we hugged. "This is gonna be the best year ever."

"Happy nineteen eighty-two," I said, and watched m

tears fall into Julie's hair. I could feel the plastic cassette box pinching me in my stomach.

At about two o'clock in the morning, Julie, Natalie, and I left the party in a cab. Natalie immediately launched into the story of how she didn't go all the way with Reggie but he did go up her shirt and he had *amazing* hands. I just sat there feeling like the inexperienced idiot I was, thinking that I couldn't even imagine what it would feel like to be felt up, and the tears came running silently down my face again into my dress. Nobody noticed for a while—Julie and Natalie just kept talking about Oliver and Reggie—until finally Julie said I was being really quiet.

"Did you have a good time?" she asked me, which had to be the dumbest question of the century. Before I even answered, she saw me crying and said, "Oh no! What's the matter?" She took my hand, and Natalie swung her head around and said, "What's wrong? Are you okay?"

"I don't know," I sobbed. "I just—feel—like—I'm never gonna—have a boyfriend—" I stammered, trying to breathe. "Or do—half the things you guys have done—" More sobbing and breathing, and I wanted to say, "No guys will ever like me, I'll be a virgin for the rest of my life!" which I knew was really dramatic, but I couldn't get it out anyway because of the huge gulpy breaths I had to take through my ears. Julie and Natalie jumped right into, "That's not true!" and "Are you crazy?" and "Of course you'll have a boyfriend!" and other comfort-me words.

"Of course you'll have a boyfriend!" Julie said again.

"You are, like, such a catch!" Now she had her arm around me so I was leaning into her, crying into her shirt, and Natalie was pushing hair out of my face.

"Totally," Natalie chimed in. "I bet you anything Josh Heller will ask you out."

"He doesn't even know I exist!" I sobbed.

"Oh, that's not true!" Julie said. "He brought you coffee!"

"He what?" Natalie said, and Julie told her about that day in French class.

"Oh my God! That is, like, such a sign! He must like you, Julie!" Natalie said.

"Yeah, but he totally ignored me at Kahti Fearon's party," I argued, sounding like a baby.

"But so what?" Julie said. "You were making out with David Wine!"

"You what?" Natalie said. "I can't believe you didn't tell me! You creepy slut!" This kind of made me laugh and catch my breath a little.

"You can't tell anyone, Nat," I said. "I didn't tell you 'cause Jennifer Smalls likes David, and I didn't want her to find out."

"I won't tell her, I promise." Natalie crossed her heart.

"You see?" Julie said. "If you were an inexperienced loser, would David Wine, who is totally cute, by the way, and the funniest guy in our class, want to make out with you?"

I didn't say anything; I just looked down at the wet spot on my dress.

"No!" Julie and Natalie said together.

"I'm hungry," Julie said all of a sudden. We were just getting to the McDonald's near 72nd Street.

"Let's get some fries," she said. "You could use some fries and a chocolate shake, right, Julie?" Julie told the driver to pull over.

"Yeah," I said.

"It'll be the first chocolate shake of the New Year," she said.

11

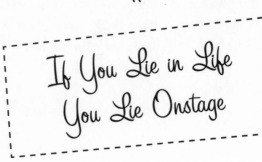

*If You Lie in Life
You Lie Onstage*

Christmas break was over just like that. A couple of day
into the new semester, Mom and Dad went to their ap
pointment with their marriage counselor and then out t
dinner. Whenever they went out, Ellie and I made Hungr
Man TV dinners for ourselves. Or frozen fish sticks wit
tartar sauce. For some reason, Ellie and I got along bette
when our parents weren't around.

I got home after six o'clock 'cause I went to Sak's afte
school. By myself. I got a really cool pair of green Girbau
jeans. There was a little hole at one of the ankles where
cut off the plastic thing, and though I wanted to show ther
to Ellie I didn't dare 'cause they were, like, fifty-dollar jean
and she would wonder where I got the money. I was wear
ing them underneath my painters pants, so when I g
home, I made a beeline for my room. I tried to keep m
new stolen clothes hidden from Ellie. Whenever she aske

about something, I said I had borrowed it from Julie.

"Hi," I said to Ellie, who was on the couch, surrounded by books, drawing paper, and pencils, watching *Family Feud*.

"Hi," she said, not looking up. "Mom and Dad said to make salads with our TV dinners—do you want to do that or load the dishwasher later?"

"I'll load the dishwasher," I said, hurrying into my room and closing the door.

"Geez! What's the rush?" I heard Ellie call after me.

I threw my book bag and coat onto my bed and took off the top layer of pants. I was so excited; I couldn't wait to wear the Girbauds tomorrow. I examined my lower body in the mirror. The jeans made my butt look great, and I even felt almost not fat in them. Just then, Ellie opened my door. I screamed.

"Oh! Did I scare you?" she said.

"Yes!" I said holding my heart, "Could you *knock* please? Jesus, you get so mad at me if I don't knock on *your* door!" I subtly sat down on my bed Indian-style and pulled my bag into my lap like I was looking for a book. I tried to cover the jeans with my bag as much as I could. It was maybe a Tony Award–winning moment.

"I'm sorry. I just wanted to say, dinner's in about twenty minutes. You want milk?"

"Okay. Thank you. Good-*bye!*" I said. How irritating.

"*Okay*. You don't have to be so touchy." She closed the door. Did she notice the jeans? That whole exchange was too quick for her to notice, right? I changed back into my painters pants.

We ate dinner watching reruns of *I Dream of Jeannie*

and *The Partridge Family*—our love of reruns was one of the few things we had in common.

"What'll you do if you don't get into RISD?" I asked Ellie during a commercial.

"I don't know, it'll totally suck. I'll have to go to one of my safety schools."

"I heard Mom and Dad fighting about the cost of tuition the other day. I mean, I probably shouldn't tell you, 'cause you shouldn't feel guilty or anything. . . ." I said.

"No, I already know. But they fight about everything. Their marriage is, like, totally on the rocks," Ellie said, eating a forkful of mashed potatoes.

"Yeah," I said. Then we watched a Pine-Sol commercial without saying anything.

"What do you think would happen if they got a divorce?" I said.

"I don't know," Ellie said. "They'd stop fighting, I guess."

Before bed, I was washing my face in the bathroom that Ellie and I shared. You had to walk through Ellie's room to get to it, which was okay, 'cause Ellie was a pretty deep sleeper—she didn't wake up if I came in to pee in the middle of the night.

"Jule?" she said from her bed, her lap covered with different-sized paintbrushes. She was doing a small watercolor painting of her bedroom windows.

"Yeah?" I poked my head through the bathroom doorway, my mouth full of foamy toothpaste.

"Where were you after school today?"

"What?" I gargled.

"Did you have something after school today? How come you came home so late?"

I spit out and rinsed. This gave me a few seconds to think.

"I stayed after to rehearse with Max, my scene partner."

"Oh," she said. I waited a few seconds. She seemed to buy it.

"Jule?" she asked again, and I held my breath a little.

"Yeah," I said, burying my face in a towel.

"I promise I'll knock next time," she said, looking at me.

"Okay, thanks," I said.

"Sleep tight," she said.

I got in bed and stared up at the ceiling for a while, thinking about what a liar I was. I lied to Ellie. I couldn't tell her I went to Sak's after school 'cause she'd want to know if I got anything and then I'd have to lie about that. I wondered if it was really bad of me to lie so much. My acting teacher, Mrs. Zeig, always said, "If you lie in life, you lie onstage." I lay there thinking as long as I was a dishonest person I'd always be a dishonest actress. A bad actress.

Then I thought about my new Girbaud jeans and got excited. *What top should I wear with them tomorrow?* I wondered. *Or should I wait and save them for a special occasion?* I went through my wardrobe in my head. Maybe my white long-sleeved shirt with the tiny dancing cartoon guys and musical notes in purple and green and black would go good with the jeans. It was the shirt I was wearing one time when Julie pointed out I dress more cute than sexy. She didn't mean it in a bad way, I could tell, but it kind of hurt my feelings. Julie could pull off dressing sexy 'cause she was pretty big-chested. I didn't even start to have a chest until, like, a year ago. Anyway, I liked my musical notes shirt in spite of what Julie said, and it would look great with my new jeans. I'd tell Ellie that I borrowed the jeans from Julie. But I wouldn't say anything unless she asked.

Ugh. Scene Day finally arrived, and I was so unbelievably nervous even though Max and I had rehearsed and rehearsed and we knew we were ready.

"The purpose of Scene Day," Mrs. Zeig tried to convince us, "is to determine which part of the *craft* each of you needs to work on."

Yeah, right. What it really felt like was the whole drama department watching and judging if you were a good actor or not, based on this one stupid scene.

In the auditorium there was a big stage with movable audience seats. So for Scene Day we created a "theater in the round"—a space on the floor in the middle of the room where we performed, surrounded by chairs on all four sides. Mrs. Zeig sat in a chair a little bit off the stage announcing our names and each scene before we went on. Max and I were third, thank God. I don't think I could have stood it if we went last or near the end.

So we did our scene. Somehow that first line—"Wasn't she cross with you on account of your fighting?"—came out of my mouth and it didn't sound weird. I just said it like of course I say stuff like that all the time. Max responded, and I thought we were playing off each other well. And then, before I knew it, we had done the whole scene. Once it was over, I didn't really remember it. Julie said that was a good sign, that that meant I was really in it, that I wasn't self-conscious or watching myself. Julie said I was really good but she was biased, of course. All I knew was that I was so nervous that my hands were freezing, but once I was out there onstage, all my nervousness went away. It was the best feeling of relief when we were done and everyone applauded. Mrs. Zeig gave me a warm smile and squeezed my shoulder as I passed her on my way to the bathroom to change out of my costume.

On my way back to the auditorium, I ran into Josh.

"Wow," he said, just looking at me. "You were, like, so *real*."

"Thanks," I said, like it was no biggie, but I could not stop smiling the hugest smile.

12

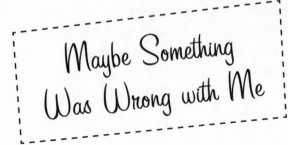

Maybe Something Was Wrong with Me

February was freezing, but that didn't stop Julie and me from going to the outdoor flea market on Greene Street where I saw this gorgeous vintage cigarette holder. It was a long black plastic tube with a white stripe around the middle and rhinestones, like from the 1920s. I imagined a flapper girl in a red fringe dress and red satin gloves smoking with it. I suddenly felt like I just had to have it—not that I was really gonna use it, it was just so pretty.

This lady was selling all kinds of tchotchkes like cigarette holders and cases, old-fashioned tins, hair stuff, and old hats that were, like, part veil. She had long, silvery-white hair in a ponytail, but her face was young-looking. She wore a big man's checked wool shirt.

Julie was opening and closing this silver cigarette case, and I was eyeing the holder with rhinestones, and the ponytail lady said to Julie, "That's sterling silver." She had a Southern accent, and you could see little puffs of her breath in the cold. "And an antique."

"Uh-huh," Julie said.

"Could use some shining up; just needs a little silver polish." Her eyes were an intense dark blue and crinkly when she smiled.

"Yeah," Julie said, flipping it over to see the price: thirty-five dollars.

"That's an excellent price for an antique," said the pony-tail lady, lightly hopping from one foot to the other and hugging her gloved hands under her armpits.

"Uh-huh," Julie said again. She kept opening and closing it; I couldn't figure out what she was doing. Inside the case was a little piece of purple felt. Then the lady answered some other customer's questions about a set of wineglasses or something and when she came back to us, Julie said, "Would you sell it for twenty-five dollars?" The ponytail lady frowned and thought a minute.

"I'd go to thirty, but I can't go lower than that. It was my great-grandmother's. See those initials there in the corner? SSB? That was my great-grandmother, Stella Schuman Brandt."

"Wow," Julie said. "Cool."

"You girls aren't smokers are you?" the ponytail lady said. "Don't smoke, it's bad for you. What are you, sixteen?"

"Yes," I said. Sometimes I couldn't help lying. I had just turned fifteen the weekend before, and Julie and I celebrated at Serendipity, this amazing ice-cream and dessert place. Julie would turn fifteen in October, so we actually wouldn't be sixteen till next year.

131

"It's a present for my older brother," Julie explained. "He smokes—he's twenty-four."

"Ah," the ponytail lady said. "Just a moment." And she went down to the other end of her long rectangular table to open some matching canisters for a guy. I was still eyeing the black cigarette holder with the rhinestones.

"Do you want that?" Julie asked me under her breath. I nodded. Very slowly she turned around, so her back was to the table. Then she said in a very low voice, "Stick it up your sleeve . . . ready?" She looked around some more. "Now." And I did. I put my glove back on so the cigarette holder wouldn't fall out. I had pulled the holder from a coffee can full of plastic cigarette holders in different colors. You couldn't really tell one was missing. Just then the lady came back to us.

"Decided?" she said to Julie. I put my hands in my coat pockets.

"I don't know, thirty dollars is kind of a lot. . . ."

"I'm sorry, darlin', I can't go lower than that. Like I said, it was in my family. I'm just broken up to have to sell it."

"Okay," Julie said, taking out her wallet. "I'll take it. It really is beautiful."

"I'm sure your brother will love it," said the lady, putting it in a plastic bag. "You have silver polish at home?"

"I think so," Julie said, handing her cash.

"Just a little bit'll shine it right up." She handed the case in a little baggie to Julie. "Thank you, darlin'. Stay warm!"

"Thank you," Julie said, and we were out of there.

*　　*　　*

132

Walking to the subway on Canal Street, I had so many thoughts buzzing around my head. Mostly just, *Oh my God, oh my God, oh my God,* over and over like that. *I never stole at the flea market before*. It always seemed so out-in-the-open and more risky than a store. When we got a few blocks away, I pulled the black cigarette holder out of my sleeve and slipped it into my Chocolate Soup bag. I felt kind of out of breath, but I couldn't tell if it was the excitement or the cold or because we were walking fast. Then I remembered I had a new vintage scarf to wear in my hair that I had stolen from Unique Antique Boutique after school last week. It matched the cigarette holder exactly, 'cause it was black with white dots. Usually knowing I had new stuff to wear to school the next day made me feel happy. But this time, I had a sick feeling. I started to wonder if that cigarette holder I stole also belonged to the ponytail lady's family. Maybe Stella Schuman Brandt was a flapper back in the 1920s, and when she was twenty-five (that was the coolest age—I couldn't wait to be twenty-five) she flipped her cigarettes out of her monogrammed silver case and popped them into her rhinestone holder, and her handsome boyfriend with slicked-back hair dressed in a tuxedo lit them for her.

I suddenly had this urge to turn around and go back. I wanted to inconspicuously stick the cigarette holder back in the coffee can. I could do it without the ponytail lady seeing me. I'd wait for just the right moment. But we kept walking to the subway. Just before we got to Canal Street, it actually occurred to me that we could go to Canal Jeans and look through the bowling shirts. How could I think about returning my cigarette holder one second and stealing something else the next?

When I got home from the flea market that day, I closed my bedroom door and sat on my bed holding the cigarette holder in my lap for a little while. Then I hid it in my underwear and sock drawer. I'd probably never use it. Why did I even want it in the first place? Maybe something was wrong with me. Was this really bad, what we were doing? Was something bad gonna happen to us? How long could we get away with it?

The next day I went over to Olivia Howe's house on Central Park West. She just called me up out of nowhere and invited me over for lunch, which I thought was pretty cool. We made tuna-fish salad on whole-wheat bread like we used to all the years we were growing up together.

"So how do you like P.A.?" Olivia asked me.

"It's pretty good. But it's hard. There's a ton of work," I said, taking a bite of my sandwich. Whole-wheat bread sandwiches tasted so different from what I was used to. My mom always bought Pepperidge Farm white.

"Us, too," Olivia said. "Dalton is *known* for its demanding homework. Like, it's almost like *college-level*. I think it was even written up in some magazine, my dad said, as, like, one of the hardest schools in the city." Suddenly our conversation felt tense.

"Yeah. Studying acting is really hard. We're, like, always in rehearsal and stuff, I'm always memorizing lines—"

"Oh," Olivia said, looking kind of put off. Was I being

competitive? I didn't mean to be; I was just trying to tell her about school. And anyway, all I heard about Dalton was that it was a school for celebrity rich kids.

"Are there any celebrity's kids in your class?" I said brightly, hoping this would ease the tension.

"Yeah, Tom Brokaw's daughter. And I think Bette Midler's kid is a few years behind me."

"Cool!" I said, trying to act impressed. But it still felt weird.

We hung out in Olivia's room looking at our old eighth-grade yearbook and talking about our new friends. I tried to tell her about Julie without sounding like I was bragging about how cool she was. I wanted to tell her about my crush on Josh Heller, but the timing never seemed right. I waited for Olivia to talk about the boys in her school, but she never did. Then the phone rang, and Olivia went to answer it in the kitchen. When she was gone for a while, I started to poke around her desk. I found this really cool little tin box with hot-pink elephants painted on it. It was empty. Without even thinking really, I dropped it into my bag.

13

Shoplifting Is Not
a Game

"I don't think you should have said yes," I complained to Julie as we waited in the cold the next Saturday morning on the corner of 59th and Lexington. We were going to Bloomingdale's to see what we could get. "Three people is too conspicuous."

Julie had told Jennifer Smalls she could join us that morning at Bloomingdale's.

"It'll be fine," Julie said. "Jennifer's experienced."

"I know, I just think it would have been better with just you and me."

"What about that time we all went to Macy's? That was, like, five of us," Julie pointed out.

"That was different," I said. "Besides, it's like eleven fifteen. She's late. Where the hell is she?"

"How was that different?" Julie said, and just then Jennifer came running up to us.

136

"Am I late?" she said, slightly out of breath, and gave us each a kiss on the cheek.

"Don't worry about it," Julie said. "Let's go in. It's freezing."

We browsed through the angora scarves and gloves on the first floor, near B-WAY, the cosmetics part of Bloomingdale's. When no one was looking, I slipped a lavender scarf under my armpit inside my coat. I had to move a little stiffly after that, but I didn't think it was noticeable. We all stood at different racks and shelves a few feet from each other, acting like we weren't together. Jennifer, I noticed, had been holding a lime-green hat in her hands, and when I looked back at her again, the hat had disappeared and she was trying on gloves. *God, she's good,* I thought. Her face was kind of hidden behind her long, permed blonde hair. Julie was wearing her big black puffer coat—perfect for hiding stuff. She discreetly held up a mohair magenta scarf, looked over at me, and raised her eyebrows, as if to say, *Do you like it?* I shrugged, meaning, *It's okay.* She put it back. I really wanted the lavender angora gloves that matched the scarf under my armpit. I felt a little nervous, but I was sure I was acting calm. B-WAY was pretty busy; lots of people were around the cosmetics counters, no one really looking at us. It was my perfect opportunity. I quickly put the gloves in my outside pocket. *Nobody saw,* I thought, looking around slowly. There were some ladies browsing around the hats and gloves, but they seemed too far away to see us. Okay, we all glanced at one another—time to go. For some reason we all just knew this by our glances—this was going to be a quickie. We had other stores to get to.

I stepped into one of the revolving doors and felt a hand on my shoulder. I tried to push the door but somebody's foot was stuck in the way, stopping it from moving. It took me a second to figure out what was happening. A blonde lady dressed in regular clothes flashed a badge at us and said, "Excuse me, can I see what's in your coat?" I froze and stared at her. She stared back at me. Julie and Jennifer were standing a little to the side, and they were frozen, too. Oh my God. I had heard of people called "plainclothes cops" who acted like shoppers; I think I saw it in a movie once. Shit. A cop with no uniform. Just a badge. She had flicked it so fast in my face, it was just a blur of silver.

"Did you hear me?" the blonde lady said. "Please unzip your jacket." Still semifrozen, I slowly opened my coat and handed her the scarf.

"Come with me please," the lady cop said.

Then she motioned for the three of us to walk in front of her down one of the aisles of B-WAY. It went Julie, Jennifer, then me, and I could have sworn we were all walking in slow motion. That's what it felt like. No one said anything. It was like there was no sound except the pounding in my chest. All I could think was, *What do I do with the pair of gloves stuffed in my pocket?* Should I have told her right away or waited to see if she knew they were there? We solemnly marched down the aisle, past all the cosmetics counters like Borghese, Shiseido, and Lancôme. I looked down at the black-and-white-checked floor the whole way. Where was she taking us? She opened a heavy black door that you'd never even know was there, and we went down one flight to the basement. We sat on a bench in a room that was as tiny as a fitting room, and she sat on a metal folding chair in the doorway. She began to question us and never smiled. I thought she looked fortyish. Her blonde hair had a little gray in it, and it was kind of sprayed. She was wearing a white cotton blouse and a tan Members Only jacket.

I looked at these Polaroid mug shots and handcuffs hanging on the wall behind her head. Were they gonna take our pictures, too? Oh my God, if my parents found out about this they'd *kill* me. I'd never hear the end of it. Aunt Marty would find out, and I'd die of shame and embarrassment. What if I got expelled from school? Would this mean I couldn't go to college?

Was this lady gonna arrest us? I could tell Julie and Jennifer were trying not to cry, just like I was. The cop had a clipboard with forms on it, and she asked us our names and addresses. Oh shit, this was really happening.

Julie went first—thank God 'cause I needed a minute to think of a fake address. There was *no way* I could tell her my real address; if they'd sent something home to my parents or called them, that would've been it. My life would've been over.

"Julie Braverman," Julie said, "Two Sixty-Five Riverside Drive." She could give her real name and address because she had a mailbox key and got home in the afternoon before Mimi. I was not so lucky; I did not have a mailbox key.

"And you," the lady cop said to Jennifer.

"Jennifer Gibson, One Eighty-Six Franklin Street," she said, still hidden behind her hair. Oh man, she gave Julie's sister Ruby's address in Tribeca! Ruby was twenty-six and lived in a big loft. *Way to go, Jennifer,* I thought. I wished I had thought of that. And how did she think of that fake last name so fast? The lady cop finished writing and looked at me. All I could think of was that building where Olivia Howe's dad moved for a brief period when her parents almost got divorced. Was it 115 Central Park West? One Fifteen Central Park West was the only building I could think of that I knew exactly where it was. What if she quizzed me about the cross street or something? I had to force myself to speak.

"Julie Howe," I said, "One Fifteen Central Park West." Julie and Jennifer did not even flinch. I amazed myself. I knew I was keeping a straight face, but the tears were getting harder and harder to hold back.

"How old are you girls?" the lady cop asked.

"Fifteen," we said.

"Well, it's a good thing you're not sixteen or I could arrest you as adults. You could be sent to a correctional juvenile home. Shoplifting is not a *game*, you know that?" She looked at us like this was the most serious thing ever. Then I heard this small squeaking sound coming from Julie. Oh Jesus, was she cracking up? From the corner of my eye I saw tears falling into her lap. We didn't know what to say. We could barely hold our heads up 'cause we were so scared. Jennifer kept sniffing to keep her nose from running and my eyes spilled over, too. It was impossible to hold it in.

"Would you like to explain yourselves?"

We stared at the lady cop and the mug shots on the wall

hanging behind her. One guy in a mug shot was black and he had a huge blond Afro. I wondered what that guy did. Nobody was saying anything.

Finally, Julie said through her tears, "It was a dare. . . . Some other kids in our class dared us. We've never done this before. I swear." Jennifer and I just sat there totally silent except for our crying.

The lady cop looked at each of us for a second. "Uh-huh," she said. Man, was she mad. "Well, you should know better than to accept such a stupid dare. And you're never going to do it again. At least not here. Now stand up," she said bossily, and reached for the Polaroid camera on the shelf. She pointed it at Julie and clicked. Oh, shit. This couldn't be happening. Julie's picture slid out of the camera and the lady cop put it on a chair, where it sat developing. Then she snapped the camera in Jennifer's face. And then mine. I couldn't even imagine what we all must have looked like sobbing like that.

Our three pictures sat on the chair, slowly revealing who we were, while the lady cop took out some forms and more clipboards and pens. She motioned for us to sit back down on the bench, then handed each of us a pen and a clipboard and made us all sign the form on it. We were agreeing to never again set foot in Bloomingdale's for the rest of our lives. Oh . . . my . . . God. How would I avoid Bloomingdale's for the rest of my life? I imagined Christmas morning and Mom has bought me a shirt from Bloomingdale's and it's the wrong color and I have to exchange it. How would I finish collecting all the different "Bloomies" undies, with the *O*s like tennis rackets or hearts or wreaths? What if I ran out of Shiseido Iridescent Baby Pink lipstick—did they even have a Shiseido at Macy's?

We sat in this little basement room for maybe fifteen minutes and we had our winter coats on, and I was sweating. We signed the forms and suddenly we were free to go. The walk back up the stairs, through B-WAY and out the revolving doors, was much faster this time.

Jennifer, Julie, and I could not look one another in the eye. We got outside onto Lexington Avenue and exhaled. It was cold out. The three of us started walking toward the subway, and I stuck my hand in my pockets.

"You guys," I said. I pulled out the lavender angora gloves.

"Oh my God," Julie said. We all burst out laughing. But it was weird; it was kind of like we were crying-laughing. It felt like what it must feel like to be crazy. Pretty soon it was just laughing-laughing—we were practically doubled over right there on the sidewalk.

"What an idiot! Do you think she was even a real cop?" Jennifer said.

"She must have been! I've never been so scared in my entire life!" I said, trying to catch my breath. "How did I get away with this?" I waved the gloves in the air.

"Shhh! Shhhh!" Julie said. "Put them away." And she looped her arms through mine and Jennifer's and led us to the Lexington Avenue subway.

On the train, my head was spinning. Julie and Jennifer seemed fine, but I felt this hollow feeling in my chest. Would we ever stop doing this? What if we never stopped?

                    *   *   *

Sunday morning Mom and I were in the kitchen getting breakfast. Ellie was still asleep and Dad was in the shower.

"Mom, can I ask you a question?" I said out of nowhere. She'd had a few sips of orange juice and was pouring Wheaties into a bowl. I was waiting for my English muffin to finish toasting.

"Of course," she said.

"What if I told you I wanted to go see . . . um . . . like . . . a professional?"

Then she thought for a second, and I wasn't sure if it was too early in the morning for her to talk about stuff like this or if she was gonna ask me why or what.

"What kind of professional?" she said.

"Um. Like that lady you and Dad go to sometimes at Mt. Sinai. Joyce What's-her-name?"

"Joyce Kazlick?"

"Yeah. Joyce Kazlick. Like her."

"You mean, you want to see a therapist?"

"Yeah," I said, not really looking at her. My mother was looking at me over her reading glasses, about to open *The New York Times*.

"Well, I suppose we could find you someone. Or you could see Joyce. I'll call Mt. Sinai on Monday, okay?"

"Okay," I said, and the toaster oven popped open.

"Okay," she said, and that was that. She didn't ask why or pry any further. I couldn't believe it. I mean, part of me kind of wanted her to, but part of me was glad she didn't.

"And Mom?"

143

"Mm-hmm?" she said, pouring half-and-half on her cereal.

"Don't tell anyone, okay? Don't tell Ellie."

Mom made the motion for zipping her lips. I left the kitchen feeling kind of bummed out, and I didn't know why.

14

*Thank God I Was
Seeking Professional Help*

I got to Joyce Kazlick's office at Mt. Sinai early, which was a good thing since I had to pee. The plaque on her door said OYCE KAZLICK, C.S.W., but I didn't know what "C.S.W." meant. I loved the smell of the liquid soap in the bathroom; it reminded me of Dr. Beaumont, my pediatrician, and I always liked him. I thought the smell of the soap and my liking it was a good sign. As I sat there on the tan vinyl waiting chair in Joyce Kazlick's hallway, I tried to concentrate on reading *The Crucible* for Dr. Deutsch's English class, but I kept smelling my hands instead. An older balding black man sat snoozing a few chairs away. He held his cheek in his hand and his elbow kept sliding off the armrest, but he didn't wake up. Finally, Joyce Kazlick's door opened.

"Julie?" she said. I expected her to be young, thin, and stylish with blonde shoulder-length hair. In fact, she was a

bit chubby, had short brown hair in, like, a Dorothy Hamil
haircut, and she was wearing a royal blue dress with breas
pockets and a red plastic belt. I was impressed that sh
chose such a dress in spite of her round figure. I almos
always wore my shirt untucked so that no one could see m
stomach.

"Yes," I said, and she held open her office door for me
As I walked past her, I got a whiff of her shampoo—
brand called Gee Your Hair Smells Terrific. Another goo
smell.

"Have a seat," she said, and smiled. I sat. "Excuse hov
small this office is. It's only temporary." Her office was tin
It just about fit a desk and two chairs and a set of bookshelve
over the desk.

"Oh," I said.

She sat in a chair and swiveled to reach for a clipboar
behind her on her desk. "I just have to ask you a few question
before we get started, okay?"

"Okay," I said. She asked me my address, my age, m
school, how my grades were, a little about Ellie and m
friends. Then she told me that everything I talked to he
about stayed in this room—it was all one-hundred-percer
confidential.

"So what made you want to come here today?" Joyc
asked. She had a kind face.

"Umm. Wait. Whatever I tell you, you can't tell m
parents, right?" I asked.

"That's correct. I can't tell anyone. Completely conf
dential."

"Okay," I said, and took a deep breath. "I . . . steal . .

clothes. And stuff." I looked at her face to see her reaction, but she just sat in her vinyl chair staring back at me like I was supposed to continue. She sat with her hands folded over the clipboard in her lap and her stubby legs crossed.

"Uh-huh," she finally said.

"And I'm afraid . . . I'm thinking . . . I think it's gotten really out of control."

"What do you mean, 'out of control'?" Joyce said.

"Well, my best friend, Julie, and me? She's the one who taught me how? Well, we've gotten so good that we could go just about anywhere and get away with it. Well, almost anywhere." I paused for a second, but Joyce didn't look like she was going to say anything so I continued.

"I've gotten so much stuff, like hundreds or thousands of dollars' worth of stuff by now, I'm not sure."

"Mm-hmm," she said. I couldn't believe she didn't act more surprised. I knew she wasn't gonna, like, call the police or something, but I didn't expect her to be so calm.

"Your best friend's name is Julie?" she asked, writing in her clipboard.

"Yeah, I know, two Julies," I said.

"Just clarifying." She inhaled and recrossed her legs. "When you steal clothes, are you always with Julie?" she asked.

"Most of the time," I said. "I've done it by myself, too. There's lots of kids in my school who do it." Joyce let me just sit there for a few seconds. I wondered what she was thinking, just watching me like that.

"Tell me more about your friend Julie," Joyce said.

"Well, she's totally beautiful. And popular. Most of the

147

boys in our class have a crush on her. But it's not like she'
stuck-up or anything—I mean, you'd think maybe a gir
who was beautiful and popular would be stuck-up or ob
noxious or whatever, but she totally isn't." Then I though
for a second, and Joyce didn't say anything. She just looke
at me.

"And she has the coolest family," I said.

"What do you mean?" Joyce asked.

"Well, her mom? She's beautiful, too, of course, and
doesn't really act like a mom. I mean, she dresses really cool
like really stylish, and she's a model and she's never hom
so Julie and I get to hang out alone in their huge apartmen
all the time. It's the best. And Julie has all these older sibling
who she can hang out with like they're her friends, yo
know? Like her old sister Mandy? She actually *likes* he
and they hang out together!"

"Don't you like to hang out with your sister?" Joyce said
"Ellie, right?"

"Yeah, Ellie. No. I mean, no we don't really hang ou
I can't really talk to her. . . ." My voice cracked when I sai
that, and I stopped talking so I wouldn't cry. "I'm sorry,
don't want to cry," I said.

"Why not?" Joyce said. "This is the place to cry. N
need to apologize for it." Joyce looked at me sympathe
ically. "But I'm afraid our time is up. Do you think you'
like to come back and see me? Does this time work fo
you?"

I nodded.

"Okay, see you next Wednesday at four thirty, then
she said. "Do you want to take some tissues with you?"

148

I took a few from the box on her desk and left. I wondered if I was the biggest teenage nutcase she had ever seen.

By March it was still really cold out, and I was dying for spring. Everyone at school was wearing layers and big bulky sweaters (some stolen) even though the radiators blasted at P.A. so strong you could practically walk around in a tube top.

Julie and I were talking in the lunchroom, and I said kind of out of nowhere that I was feeling really nervous about all the stuff we were *getting* lately.

"What do you mean, nervous?" Julie said.

"I don't know," I said, then I just made myself say what I was scared to say. "I don't think I can do it anymore."

She didn't say anything; she just looked like she was thinking.

"I think we're . . ." I started to say. "We're . . ."

"We're what?" Julie said, not really angry, but weird or something. Like, irritated.

"I think we're kleptomaniacs," I blurted out. Then I paused, and we just looked at each other. "And it really scares me." I felt like I could cry, but the tears were too far down in the pit of my chest. I just took another bite of my rice and gravy that we got from Cubana and swallowed hard.

"Are you kidding?" Julie said, smiling. She took a sip of her Tab.

"No." I lowered my voice. "I think this is serious. Isn't kleptomania, like, an addiction? I mean, being a kleptomaniac is a real thing," I said. Julie leaned in toward me to hear 'cause some kids in the corner were singing "Happy Birthday" to someone at the top of their lungs.

"We're not *kleptomaniacs*," she said. "Stop saying that. It's just shoplifting. It's not an addiction. We can stop anytime we want."

"That's just it, Jule, I don't feel like I can. I keep telling myself, 'This time will be the last time,' and then I do it again."

Then she didn't know what to say. I bet it was 'cause she felt like she couldn't stop, either. Every day, when I got to school, as soon as I saw Julie in the morning, the first thing I did was check out her clothes from head to toe. I immediately knew what was stolen and what wasn't. Even her accessories and bag. And before I saw her, I prayed maybe this morning, please God, maybe this morning she'd be wearing bought things instead of stolen things. But she never was. Never. Like today she was wearing Fiorucci jeans that she *got*, a Canal Jeans top she *got,* and a stolen jacket from Parachute. Even her earrings I knew she *got* at Savage. I was also wearing stolen jeans from Sak's, but at least I had on my favorite sweater that wasn't stolen—it was my grandfather's old 1950s green cardigan that zipped up. I loved it.

I couldn't even remember the last time Julie was wearing an entire outfit of bought stuff. God, did her mother ever notice? She was as oblivious as my mother.

"Doesn't your mom wonder about all your new clothes?" I said.

"Maybe. I'm not sure. But if she does, I'm sure she

thinks I buy them with my own money."

"I'm scared my mom's gonna find out," I said, still speaking softly. "Didn't Bloomingdale's *bug you out*?"

"Yeah, a little bit. But you can't let these things get to you," she said.

"It was only, like, a few weeks ago," I said. "I can't stop thinking about it!"

"I know," she said. "You worry too much. Trust me, it's not that big a deal. Think of all the kids we know who do it. It's not that serious."

Maybe Julie and me (and Jennifer, Daisy, Gordon, and whoever else) should be going to Kleptomaniacs Anonymous meetings, like Mimi went to A.A. Did they even have that? Maybe we'd have to go for the rest of our lives. Well, at least there'd be people there I knew.

All of sudden Julie acted like this talk was a big joke and she started laughing.

"Come on, Jule!" she said, grabbing my knee a little. "Don't look so serious! That Bloomies thing was, like, totally unusual. We're so good, and we've gotten so much great stuff. How could you want to stop now?"

Because I'm scared, I wanted to say again, but I couldn't. Like if I said anything more she'd get angry at me or maybe even drop me as a friend and then what would I do? I wanted so badly to tell her that every time we went stealing now, I was terrified of getting caught, of my heart racing so fast I'd have a heart attack, of my parents finding out everything.

The next Wednesday at four thirty I sat down in Joyce Kazlick's office and felt like I couldn't stop bouncing my leg. It was my fifth visit and I wasn't sure if Joyce was helping me, but I liked coming.

"Are you feeling nervous?" she asked after a few seconds of watching my bouncing leg go. I was getting the sense that she actually cared. I was thinking about Bloomingdale's and getting caught and whether they had actually sent something to 115 Central Park West addressed to me—or the fake me. All that was making me jittery, but for some reason I couldn't make the words come out.

"What's up?" Joyce said finally.

"My mother always says if Julie or whoever jumped off the Brooklyn Bridge, would I? Like, even though I know a lot of kids who steal, I know that doesn't make it right or okay, but I just can't seem to stop doing it and it really scares me. . . ." I said, and looked down at my hands. Suddenly my fingernails were fascinating. I couldn't seem to look at them and talk at the same time, so I sat quietly for a minute.

"Does anyone in your family know? Have you told your sister?"

"Are you kidding? No way would I tell my sister! I can't really talk to her about anything!" I said, realizing I sounded angry. I was thinking, *Didn't I already tell her that?*

Joyce shifted forward in her seat a little, like now this was getting interesting. "Why not, why can't you tell your sister?" she asked.

"'Cause we're so totally *different*, she wouldn't understand."

"How are you different?" Joyce said.

"Well, I don't know, she's, like, always in her room. I don't know what she's doing, really, but she doesn't seem to want to do teenage-type stuff, like me and my friends. She doesn't really ever go to clubs or anything. She's totally shy. She doesn't have a lot of friends. I mean, I don't even know if Ellie's kissed a boy yet, and she just turned eighteen! She doesn't tell me anything, either."

Joyce waited for me to continue.

"The truth is, I wish I could talk to her about boys and stuff, but whenever I try, she gets kind of weird. Thank God I have Julie and her older sisters to talk to about that stuff."

"How do you think Ellie would respond if you told her about the stealing?"

"I think she would think I was totally fucked-up and weird," I said.

"Do you think she'd tell your mother?" Joyce asked.

"Probably," I said, then thought again. "Well, no, I mean, not if I asked her not to, she wouldn't, but I can't imagine ever telling her."

"What would you do if you mother found out?"

I inhaled. "Oh my God, I don't know. I'd die. She'd probably scream and yell at me like she does at my dad. I'd probably get seriously punished."

"How?" Joyce said.

"I'm not sure," I said. "I guess they could take away my allowance. Maybe no sleepovers at Julie's for months or something like that? But anyway, I don't think my parents will ever find out. When I told my mom I wanted to see a therapist, she didn't even ask why or anything. She didn' seem surprised or curious, or I don't know. . . ." My voice trailed off.

"Did you want her to?" Joyce asked.

"Want her to what?" I said.

"Ask why, seem interested?"

I couldn't really answer her, 'cause I had a lump in my throat and honestly, I didn't know.

My next session with Joyce was a few weeks later because Joyce had gone on vacation. I had kind of missed seeing her and for some reason sat down in the chair with a loud thump and immediately started biting a hangnail on my thumb.

"Hello," Joyce said, taking me in.

"Hi," I said grumpily.

"How are you?"

"I don't know," I said. I really didn't know what to say. didn't know how I felt.

"You seem angry," Joyce said.

I felt my jaw stiffen when she said that, and a little headache started in the middle of my forehead. My face felt frozen in a frown.

"I don't know if I'm angry," I said. "I don't know."

"Did something happen?"

"No. I don't know. I haven't stopped stealing, if that what you mean."

"Did you think you would stop after talking to me fo

a couple of months?" Joyce said, putting down her pen. I liked her. I wasn't exactly sure why but I did. I zoned out a little until I realized she was waiting for me to say something.

"I don't know," I said.

"Did you want to tell me about a particular incident?"

"I don't know."

"Okay," she said, sighing. "What do you say we leave 'I don't know' out there in the hallway." She gestured toward the door. I just blinked at her. "Because you do know, Julie. You know why you came here, why you wanted to start talking to me. To 'a professional'—isn't that what you told your mother?"

"Yeah. . . ." I said, kind of wishing I hadn't.

"So tell me what's going on." Joyce's chair squeaked as she readjusted her position.

"I don't know," I said, then realized I was supposed to leave "I don't know" out in the hall, so I laughed a little. Joyce smiled.

"I just think something's really wrong with me. . . ." My voice trailed off, and I fell into a really good zone-out on Joyce Kazlick's chubby knee.

"Because?"

"Because I'm a kleptomaniac," I said, snapping back to look Joyce square in the eyes. "Isn't that what I am? Isn't that what a kleptomaniac is? Someone who steals uncontrollably and can't stop?"

Joyce waited again.

"I mean, I think about stopping all the time, but the thing

is, I never do. I never do stop." I took a deep breath. "And
I'm starting to get scared that I can't even talk to Julie about
it. I mean, I tried to talk to her about it."

"Uh-huh," Joyce said.

"Julie doesn't seem to want to stop. She seems so okay
with it all. Like it's just no biggie to her. So it's hard to talk
about it."

"What's no biggie to her?" Joyce asked.

"All the stealing we do!" God! Was she even listening?

Again, she sat back in her chair and waited. She was
thinking. Looking at her notes, she said, "You told me that
you're usually with Julie when you go shopping."

"Yeah," I said.

"Is it always Julie's idea, when you go?" Joyce asked.

"I don't know. Oops, I mean, I guess so," I said, worrying
that this was telling on Julie. Maybe Joyce sensed my
uneasiness, 'cause she reminded me that everything we
talked about was confidential and no one would ever know
what went on in this room.

"Do you always want to go with her?" Joyce asked.

"Yeah, usually," I said, starting to swing my legs in my
chair. "I mean, at first I was really into it, like Julie always is.
And she didn't pressure me or anything, if that's what you're
asking."

"Okay. And now?" Joyce said.

"Now?" I said, crossing my arms over my chest. My head
was starting to pound. I bit at my thumb again—I just
couldn't get that hangnail off. "Now . . . . I mean, like, lately
I just feel like it's so bad what we're doing, even though I
want to do it. I mean I want to do it, *and* I don't want to do

t. I only take things because I want them. Even though I know I shouldn't do it, I mean, I know better. My mother would say that." I imitated my mother's voice, *"You should know better!"*

Then Joyce Kazlick and I stared at each other again.

"The thing is," I said, "I don't even really think about stealing until I go shopping. Like, if I'm in a store, I do it. I mean, there are times when I go to stores with the intention to steal but I wouldn't be stealing if I wasn't there, do you know what I mean? This is so hard to put into words, what I mean."

"You're doing all right," Joyce said.

"It's like . . . I mean, I can control myself if I just stay at home or do something else. Like I saw this movie on TV once where this dizzy blonde girl steals all this stuff, like scarves and makeup and lipsticks and stuff, and then gets home and dumps it all out of her purse and says, like a total airhead, 'Where did I get all this stuff?'—like she didn't know she did it! I mean, give me a break! Well, it's not like that with me. It's not like I'm a klepto and don't know it, 'cause I do. I know what I'm doing. That's what's so weird."

Joyce thought about this for a second.

"And you think knowing you steal or being aware of it means something?" she asked.

"Well, shouldn't it?" I asked, wiping my sweaty hands on the thighs of my jeans. My stolen magenta Fiorucci jeans. "Shouldn't it mean I could control myself and stop?"

"What do you think?" she said. How totally annoying. Why couldn't she just answer my question?

"What will happen if you get caught?" Joyce asked,

which I didn't expect, but I just looked down and picked at the hangnail on my thumb. *I did get caught,* I was thinking, but I just couldn't make my mouth say it. Joyce kept looking at me.

"It would be really bad," I said finally, thinking about Bloomingdales. "Our friend Jennifer Smalls got caught, and she talked her way out of it. She told them some other girls dared her and it was her first time and she'd never do it again. And she made up a fake name and address because they made her sign these forms that she'd never go into that store ever again!" Joyce just blinked and wrote something down.

"Well, of course she was really freaked out," I continued.

"So what did you think when Jennifer Smalls told you that story?"

"It freaked me out, too." I thought about that little fitting room where we sat sweating in the basement of Blooming-dale's, the blonde lady cop's sprayed hair and Members Only jacket, and the fuzzy lavender angora gloves, now hidden at the top of my closet.

"Mm-hmm," Joyce said.

I remembered thinking after we left Bloomingdale's that if getting caught didn't make me stop stealing forever, I didn't know what would. But it didn't.

Joyce was looking at me kind of sympathetically, and I thought she could probably tell I felt frustrated and weird, 'cause then she said softly, "What?"

"I just feel like I'm so fucked-up, and I don't know what to do." I finally yanked that hangnail off my thumb and it bled a little. It hurt.

Joyce Kazlick asked me what I thought would happen if I told Julie more about how I felt. I said I did kind of tell her, but she didn't really care and I worried she might not be my friend anymore, even though I knew that was stupid—Julie wasn't really like that. She was open-minded. I had told her that I went to see a therapist and she said, "Cool." Everybody in her family had been to a therapist at one time or another, so she didn't think I was crazy or anything. She even asked me sometimes how it went with Joyce.

"What?" I said. Joyce sighed and we sat there quietly for a few seconds.

"Is there any part of you that might want your mother to find out?" she asked. I didn't know what to say. Joyce glanced at the clock and said, "I'm afraid we have to stop for today, but I'll leave you with that to think about. I don't have the answers, Julie. But I believe you do. Somewhere inside you, you do. Together we'll find them." She clipped her pen to her clipboard.

How could I have the answers when my life was totally out of control?

15

I Will Not Get a Thing

One Saturday in the middle of March, Julie and Jennifer Smalls dragged me to Patricia Fields. Patricia Fields was known for being kind of a punk-rock store. They sold fluorescent pink and orange and green wigs, and spiky dog collars that people wore as chokers. The salespeople who worked there wore combat boots and plaid miniskirts and red or black lipstick. They also sold some non-punk stuff like silk shirts, turquoise fishnet stockings, black rubber bracelets, and makeup.

We had gone to see *Tootsie* at the Waverly, which was this small movie theater in Greenwich Village that was kind of run-down. Sometimes it smelled like pee in the lobby. I loved *Tootsie*—it was so funny, and such a good love story.

I didn't think we'd end up shopping that day. When Jennifer said, "Let's swing by Patricia Fields," I just stopped walking and said, "No, let's not. I can't do it anymore."

I amazed myself. Julie and Jennifer both stopped for a second, but they didn't seem surprised or even annoyed. Then we all started walking again.

"Just come with us; you don't have to get anything," Jennifer said. A part of me couldn't believe that they weren't gonna be mad at me if I didn't steal. So what was the harm in just going with them, I thought.

"All right," I said. "But all I'm gonna do is *browse*. I'm not touching a *thing*." Maybe I'd just wait in the doorway like the lookout girl. I swore to myself, *I will not get. I will not get a thing.* But as soon as I entered Patricia Fields, I immediately thought, *So here I am again,* and I had this feeling like, *How can I not get something?* Maybe this would be my last time for real.

After about ten minutes, I could tell Julie had something hidden inside her jacket from the way she pressed her elbow to her side. I felt kind of like I was outside of myself, looking down from the ceiling watching everything. Then I noticed a pair of blue sparkly stockings and a rhinestone belt. Jennifer saw me notice the stockings. "Beautiful," she whispered, fingering a pair. "I just have to have these."

"Me, too," I whispered back, and Jennifer giggled a little. *Oh my God, I'm a psycho,* I thought. I was waiting for one of them to say, "I thought you were just going to browse." I was so glad they didn't.

Suddenly I felt really tired. Then both sweaty and chilly. I wondered if I was having a nervous breakdown. I didn't think that was even possible at my age. Nervous breakdowns only happened to people in their forties. Then I overheard the conversation this punk-rock guy was having with the

161

people behind the counter. I wasn't totally sure, but I thought he was doing an imitation of his father when he was drunk. "You blasted kids!" or something, he said in a Cockney accent, and he did this funny walk with his belly out, and this just cracked up everybody at the counter. Right when the laughter got really loud, I slid the stockings in between two shirts and slipped into the dressing room with my stuff and nobody even looked in my direction. Jennifer was already in the dressing room next to me and I was sure she had a pair of the stockings, too.

I put the stockings in my bag and suddenly I really wanted to get out of there. As if Julie and Jennifer read my mind, we all met at the makeup counter and said, "Ready?"

In an instant we were back outside.

"The coolest shorts!" Julie declared triumphantly.

"Socks, fishnets, some other stockings, and a belt!" Jennifer said. Then they looked at me.

"Stockings," I mumbled.

"Yay!" Julie said. "So what do you look so depressed about?"

"I don't know, I just feel nervous. I told you guys, I don't think I can do this anymore."

"But you just did!" Jennifer said.

"Why do you worry so much?" Julie said, sighing and not looking at me. She just kept walking and staring straight ahead. "Don't worry so much."

As we got to Sixth Avenue, Julie said, "I've got an idea. Let's go to Bigelow's. Anyone want a black-and-white ice-cream soda? They're so good there!"

Bigelow's was this old-fashioned pharmacy and ice-cream parlor on Ninth Street. I'd only been there once with my dad a long time ago, but I remembered it was pretty good.

I ordered a black-and-white ice-cream soda with chocolate-chip ice cream and chocolate syrup. I liked it with chocolate-chip ice cream instead of vanilla 'cause then you had all these chips at the bottom to eat at the end. That first sip was so incredible. Jennifer got one with strawberry ice cream and Julie got coffee ice cream with chocolate syrup, and we all tried each other's. I started to relax and felt the heaviness in my chest go away. Jennifer was telling us about her recent date with David Wine. (I had told Jennifer about my make-out with David last Christmas and she didn't care.)

"We went to see *Body Heat*," Jennifer said, cracking a slight smile.

"How'dja get in?" Julie asked. "Isn't that rated R?"

"Well, we were gonna ask someone on line to take us in, which would have been totally embarrassing, but then we didn't have to, 'cause they just gave us tickets. I guess it's good that David's tall," Jennifer said, relishing the word "David" in her mouth.

"So how was it?" I asked.

"Pretty groovy," Jennifer said, chewing her straw. "Sexy."

"Weren't you embarrassed to watch all that sex with David?" I asked.

"Nah," she said, waving her hand at me, like she'd done it a million times.

"Did you go to his house after?" Julie asked.

163

"Yes!" Jennifer squealed, and we all fell into a fit of giggles. The ice-cream guy behind the counter looked at us for a second and then went back to counting receipts or whatever he was doing. "But just for a little while. It took forever to get home from there. I took a taxi."

"You went all the way to Staten Island?" I said.

"Yeah! The ferry ride was, like, so romantic. . . ." Jennifer said dreamily, chewing her straw.

"The Staten Island Ferry? You're kidding!" Julie said.

"So? What happened?" I said.

"Well, nothing much, actually. We just made out a lot. Oh my God, he's such a good kisser!"

"I know!" I said, even though I didn't mean it, and we cracked up. I wondered if he did the rotating-tongue thing with Jennifer.

"But I have to tell you the funniest part." Jennifer paused, taking a long sip of her ice-cream soda like she was enjoying keeping us waiting. She swallowed and wiped her mouth with her napkin. "Oh my God. Are you ready for this? He has this huge . . . *poster* over his bed!"

We stared at her for a second. "What kind of poster?" Julie said.

Then she got all red in the face like she was gonna burst out laughing.

"*It's a poster of the Muppets!* He's, like, obsessed with the Muppets!" She was laughing so hard she could barely speak.

"You're kidding!" I said. "Kermit and Miss Piggy and Fozzie Bear, like, right over his bed?" We were all howling.

164

"Yes! *Framed!*" Jennifer said, trying to swallow her soda. This actually made me kind of like David more than I already did. I mean, just as a friend. But he really was one of the funniest people in our class.

"He told me he watches *The Muppet Show* every night," Jennifer continued. "Beaker and Dr. Bunsen Honeydew are his favorites!" More howling.

"Was he embarrassed at all?" Julie yelped, wiping the laughter tears from the corners of her eyes.

"No!" Jennifer said. "I couldn't believe it!" Then Jennifer started making the *beep-beep* sounds that Beaker the Muppet makes and we kept laughing for a while until I got stomach cramps.

"Have you guys told anyone about Bloomingdale's?" Jennifer said. The blonde lady cop popped into my mind. Shit, just when I was starting to relax. I hadn't even been back to the Lexington Avenue subway stop, let alone anywhere near Bloomingdale's. Would I really never go back there for the rest of my life? I imagined the scene of my return:

I would get just one foot into the revolving door to B-WAY. Instantly, deafening alarms would go off, a giant searchlight would shine in my face, blinding me, and I'd barely be able to make out a silhouette of the blonde lady cop, dressed in a police uniform this time, with a team of mean-looking policemen behind her. The blonde lady cop would point at me angrily and shout through a giant bullhorn: *"Julie Howe of One Fifteen Central Park West! You signed documents saying that you would never, ever return to Bloomingdale's for the rest of your life! You have violated that contract!"* Then I'd see my parents and Aunt Marty and some other relatives standing in the corner looking ashamed and disappointed in me. Maybe my mother would even be crying. And then all the cops would swarm around me, slap handcuffs on me, and lock me up forever in that little mug-shot fitting room in the basement.

"What about you, Julie?" Jennifer was saying to me, shaking me out of my fantasy. "Were you listening?"

"Oh, um. I don't know," I said. "What?"

"I asked if you guys told anyone about Bloomie's," she repeated.

"No, I haven't," I said, looking at my watch. Three o'clock. "Oh shit! I almost forgot! I have a rehearsal with my new scene partner, Demaris, at three thirty! I gotta go!" We slurped down the rest of our sodas and headed for the subway.

The next Sunday, Mom and I were both in the kitchen in the late afternoon. She was emptying my hamper into the washing machine and I was at the counter getting a snack. I could see her eyeing my shirts. Three new shirts I'd *gotten* from Macy's. They were all the same—long-sleeved with shoulder pads, in magenta, green, and black.

"New shirts?" she said.

"Uh-huh," I said, not looking at her. I took a bite of a pretzel.

"Where'd you get them?" *Oh God,* I thought, *she knows.* I never should have put them all in the laundry at once. My heart started to race and I inhaled silently.

"The flea market on Greene Street," I lied, acting like it was no big deal that she was questioning me. I pretended not to see the funny look on her face. Was lying a normal part of being a teenager, or was something wrong with me? When would I stop lying? And if I never did stop, what kind of person would I grow up to be?

I could only imagine she was thinking that these three shirts had "department store" written all over them. I wondered if she noticed the tiny rips where those white plastic things had been.

"You got these brand-new shirts at the flea market?" She paused. "Julie . . . is there something you're not telling me?"

For a few seconds, I just looked at her, stunned. I didn't know what to say.

"You look like the cat who ate the canary," she said.

"Um." I swallowed. "Can we go talk in my room?" I felt my voice get shaky. Mom put down the shirts and followed me. I didn't actually know if I was ready to confess. If I did, I hoped that would mean I'd really stop stealing once and for all. But of course, I couldn't be sure. The walk to my room was really quiet and serious like we were soldiers in line. Mom closed my door. I couldn't think of a time we had ever talked in my room with the door closed. I wondered if I should tell her about Bloomingdale's. No, that would just shock her. We sat down on my twin bed.

"I got those shirts at Macy's," I said. The tears started, and I didn't try to stop them. "But I didn't pay for them." We were sitting facing each other, but I could only look down at my lap.

I braced myself for the yelling to start, but then she said quietly, "You stole them?"

"Yeah."

"When?"

"Last weekend. I was with some other girls from school." I told her that everyone I knew at school did it. Even some boys. But I didn't mention Julie. That would have been a betrayal, I thought. I didn't tell Mom that I did it practically every weekend, that I thought I was a klepto. Or that I couldn't go back to Bloomingdale's for the rest of my life.

"Is this the first time you've done it?" she asked. I took another deep breath. Oh God. I wanted to lie again so badly. *Yes, Mom,* I wanted to say. *This was the first time. It was a dare. Some kids at school dared us. I swear I'll never do it again, I promise.*

"No. I've done it a bunch of times."

"Mm-hmm," she said. She didn't ask me how many times was "a bunch." Did she know that "a bunch" meant so many times I couldn't even count? Maybe thousands of dollars by now?

"Do you want to tell me more?" she said, like she didn't know what else to say.

I shrugged. "Are you gonna tell Dad?"

She thought for a second. "No. Not if you don't want me to." Why was she being so cool?

"Are you gonna punish me?" I said.

"I think you know what you've done is wrong. What if you had gotten caught, Julie? Do you realize what could happen?" Her face looked really worried, and she shifted a little on my bed.

168

"Yes." I blew my nose and continued to look down in my lap. *Oh boy, did I.* There was no way I was going to tell her about Bloomingdale's. Was not telling the same as lying? Mom took a deep breath.

Suddenly I thought about how when I was little and I had a bad dream, Mom preferred that I scream for her from my bed instead of coming to get her. The time I just showed up at the side of her bed in my feety pajamas, holding my teddy with no mouth, she nearly hit the ceiling. So she told me just scream *"Mom-my!"* as loud as I could when I had a bad dream. Then she'd come in my room half asleep in her white nightgown smelling powdery and like Mom-sleep-smell—a smell I loved—and she'd pull back my covers, get in bed with me, and say, "Tell me all about your dream. It's only a dream." She'd say, "I'm listening, I just have to keep my eyes closed." And I'd tell her about how I dreamed I was falling, or some shadowy gray man with no face was chasing me, or I was stuck in a fire, or whatever. When I woke up in the morning, I'd be alone in my bed but I wouldn't feel scared anymore.

"Do you talk to Joyce about this?" Mom was saying. "I know that's private, what you talk to Joyce about, but—"

"Yes, I do."

Then we were silent for a few moments.

"Please don't tell Ellie, either," I said. "She won't understand. She'll just make fun of me."

"It'll be our secret. Will you promise me you won't do it again?" she said.

"Okay," I said.

"Okay, what?"

"Okay, I promise."

"You can talk to me, you know. I know you think I'm some kind of ogre," she continued. "But if you need to, you can talk to me." She lifted my head so that I had to look at her. She smiled at me, but it was too hard to smile back. Then she got up and returned to the kitchen, closing my door behind her. *No, don't go, Mom,* I was thinking, but I couldn't say it out loud. *Stay here. Stay here with me on my bed. Let's get under the covers and I'll tell you about my bad dreams.*

Why didn't she yell at me and punish me? I was so ashamed; I deserved to be punished for all the awful things I had done. All the stealing. All the lying. All the pretending.

16

Only a Misdemeanor or Something

The next day at school I was totally dreading telling Julie about the talk I had with my mom. Like she'd think I was such a goody-goody for confessing. But I had to tell her this was it, once and for all—I wasn't going to steal anymore. Maybe I would tell her that I just decided to stop, but not 'cause I promised my mom. I had to wait to talk to Julie until homeroom, which I knew would be good timing 'cause homeroom was really noisy with everybody talking and being loud. Sometimes music students practiced there even though they were supposed to wait until music class. All morning I felt nervous, waiting for homeroom. Josh Heller smiled at me in the hallway, but I was so distracted I didn't even get excited. I got a ninety-seven on the quiz in Voice and Diction, and I had a pretty good acting class with Mrs. Zeig, but I still felt depressed.

"Hi!" Julie said, at the door to homeroom. She adjusted

her Chocolate Soup bag over her shoulder and seemed out of breath from running up the stairs. She noticed my face. "Are you okay?"

"Um. I told my mom," I said, just flat out like that.

"What?" Julie said like she was shocked, but knew exactly what I was talking about. She stuck her arm in mine and pulled me to the back of the classroom where there were two empty seats. In front of us, this kid Tyrone was loudly playing scales on his trumpet.

"She asked me about some shirts I got at Macy's," I said, sitting and noticing a heart that was carved in the desk. "And we ended up in my room having a talk. Julie, I never saw my mother so serious, oh my God!"

"Really," Julie said quietly, watching me closely.

"But the weird thing was she didn't even yell or punish me. I couldn't believe it. I kept waiting for her to start screaming, but instead she just, like, asked me questions and she had this really *concerned* look on her face." I shuddered, remembering it. "I wanted to lie and tell her some girls dared us, but I just couldn't."

"Us?" Julie asked.

"Don't worry, I never mentioned your name. She doesn't know who I was with."

Julie sighed and then was quiet for a second. "Wow, she didn't yell?" she said, letting her bag drop to the floor. "Here!" she shouted over the noise when Mr. Werner called her name for attendance.

"Nope," I said. "I couldn't believe it, either."

"Maybe your mom is cooler than you think," she said brightly.

"Well, I wouldn't exactly call it 'cool,'" I said. "I mean, she seemed really worried about me, and angry—and actually, it makes me kind of worried, too."

"C'mon, Jule, there's nothing to worry about—that's just moms for ya, they worry! It'll probably never come up again."

I swallowed hard. "Actually," I said. "I'm gonna stop."

Julie started laughing. "Seriously? 'Cause your mom found a couple of shirts?"

"Yeah, that, and 'cause we could get caught again," I said, lowering my voice even though everybody around us was chatting away.

Julie had a look of disbelief on her face. "Julie, I told you Bloomingdale's was totally abnormal! I bet the odds of that happening again are like . . . like the chance of getting hit by lightning twice!"

"What? Are you saying we'll never get caught again?" I tried to keep my voice down, but I felt it catching in my throat.

"Probably not, no!" Julie sounded defensive.

"How do you know that? I mean, like, I don't see how you can predict that!"

"'Cause we're good!" Julie said like, how could I forget?

"All right," I said, kind of sharply. "But I've really been giving this a lot of thought. Let's just say we *did* get caught again. I mean, I know we're only fifteen so the consequences wouldn't be so—"

"Exactly!" Julie interrupted. "Why are you getting so—"

"But what if they didn't let us graduate high school or something? What if we couldn't go to college?" I said.

Julie just looked at me, stunned. "Oh, Jesus. You have *way* too active an imagination!"

"It could happen," I said solemnly.

"No it couldn't! That's crazy! For stealing a pair of jeans or a couple of shirts? It's, like, only a misdemeanor or something; it's not even a felony—"

"Oh my God, listen to what you're saying!" I said. "You sound like a criminal! I don't even know what those words mean!"

"Have you ever heard of a fifteen-year-old going to jail?" Julie wanted to know, like she was some big authority on teenage crimes.

"No, but I have heard of reform school!" I said.

"That's only on, like, *Happy Days* and *Diff'rent Strokes*, or whatever. There's really no such thing as reform school—"

"Are you high?" I said, trying to whisper again. "*Of course* there's such a thing as—"

"All I'm saying," Julie said, "is that you're not gonna *not* be able to graduate or go to college! That's just impossible!"

I felt so frustrated, like someone was holding a pillow over my mouth, refusing to let me speak. It didn't seem to matter what I had to say. Julie would find a way to disagree. I looked away, trying to calm down.

"What?" Julie said, sounding pissed. "What are you getting so upset about?"

"What am I—? What about you? Why are you so pissed? You're acting like, like—"

"Like what?" Julie said.

"Like you're so offended, or something—"

"I'm not *offended*!" Julie interrupted. "You're just making a big deal out of nothing! I just don't understand why you're making such a big deal—"

"But it *is* a big deal! Why isn't it a big deal to you?"

"I don't know!" Julie almost shouted, and I felt a few kids looking at us. "Maybe I just don't *worry* like you do. Jesus Christ!"

"I'm just telling you I can't do it anymore! Is there anything wrong with that?"

"I can't believe you're gonna let one little talk with your mother change you—"

"Change me? How have I changed? I haven't changed!" I said, now hearing my voice get squeaky. I tried to ignore the kids around us who were acting like they weren't watching our fight.

"I don't know," Julie said softly. "You're being such a fucking *priss*!"

Then we sat there next to each other not saying anything. I could feel myself breathing heavily and I just kept thinking, *I can't believe this, I can't believe this. I can't believe she just called me a fucking priss.* I was sure Julie was wishing the bell would ring so she could get away from me. I wanted to scream, *"I am not a priss! You are a fucking kleptomaniac and you won't even admit it,"* but I could never shout that in front of the whole homeroom.

Then I remembered we had plans to go shopping after school on Friday. Julie must have been thinking about that, too, 'cause she broke the silence and said, "I guess we won't be hanging out on Friday, then."

"Well, we could do something else—" I started to say.

"Enjoy your new life," Julie said nastily, and got up from her seat just as the bell rang. "Natalie! Wait up!" she called to the front of the room, and I knew she did that for my benefit—Natalie would go shopping with her.

I just sat there in disbelief as everyone around me got up to go to their next class. The lump in my throat was enormous. I didn't even try to hide the warm tears running down my face. The room cleared out, but before Mr. Werner could notice me sitting there all alone, I got up and ran down the hall. I purposely pushed passed Julie and Natalie walking together so they could see me crying—I was hoping it would make Julie feel really bad for being so mean. I flew up the stairs to the third floor as fast as I could. I passed Reggie Ramirez and saw him do a double take, but I just pretended I didn't see him. I ran until I got to the girls' bathroom, closed myself in a stall, sat down and threw my head in my hands, sobbing, letting myself finally make sound. I didn't care if the dancers at the mirror doing their lipstick heard me crying. I didn't care if I was late to algebra. I was good at algebra and Ms. Gersh Bonime liked me. I knew Julie had gone off in her own direction; she had English.

How could this have happened to us?

17

Trying to Sound Normal

It was just a miracle that I made it through my study period, global history, and English without bawling my eyes out. I found Ms. Gersh-Bonime to hand in my homework and say I was sorry for not being in class but I wasn't feeling well, and I held it together through my rehearsal with Demaris in the basement. I couldn't decide if it was a good or bad thing that I didn't run into Julie. I was so scared this was the end of our friendship. Would this mean I'd be totally unpopular now?

When I got home, I barely said hello to Mom, who was sitting at her desk in the living room paying bills. Dad was probably in their bedroom reading or grading papers.

"Hi, pussy cat," Mom said, but I went right to my room and closed the door. I didn't even care what she was thinking; I just had to throw myself onto my bed and push my face into my pillow and cry. How would I ever get over this?

No one could possibly understand the way I felt. Talking to Joyce didn't seem to be helping me or curing me from stealing or anything. She asked questions, but she never gave me any answers or advice. How was I supposed to know what to do? Even Julie didn't understand my feelings, and she was supposed to be my best friend! If Mom came into my room to ask what was wrong, I'd make up some lie about I didn't know what. Then thinking about what a liar I was made me feel even worse. And Mom didn't come in, anyway.

I stared at my red phone praying it would ring and it would be Julie telling me how sorry she was, begging my forgiveness, saying I was the best friend anyone could ever have and she didn't mean to hurt me. But my phone just sat next to my bed like it was staring back at me, going, *Tough luck*.

Then, all of a sudden, it rang.

"Hello?" I said, trying to sound normal.

"Julie?" a guy's voice said.

"Yeah. . . ." My heart stopped.

"It's Josh. Heller. How are you?"

Oh my God! Josh Heller! Josh fucking Heller was calling me!

"Uh . . . good, I'm good," I said, sitting up.

"Whatcha doing?" he said. *Um. Crying like a baby?*

"Nothing much. I just got home." *I had a fight with my best friend about shoplifting, Josh Heller. How are you? Shoplifting is my obsession and I'm totally out of control.* Could he hear in my voice that I had been crying? I tried to sniff quietly. Oh my God, why was he calling me, what

178

could he want? Probably he forgot the French homework or something. I felt like I was having an out-of-body experience or something.

"Uh-huh," he said. His voice sounded deep and just . . . great.

Then there was this pause that seemed like an hour. I couldn't think of anything to say. I felt like such an idiot.

"I just felt like calling you," Josh said, just as I said, "What are you up to?"

"What?" I said. "Sorry." We laughed a little. Oh good, we were both nervous.

"No that's okay, I was just saying . . ." he started. "I just felt like calling 'cause it was fun that day. In French. You know, speaking French . . . or trying to speak French, right?"

Oh my God! Is this happening to *me*? Josh Heller thinks I'm fun to speak French with.

"Oh . . . yeah . . . me, too. . . . I mean . . . it was . . ." Suddenly I heard my parents fighting. I heard my Dad shout, *"Goddamnit, Helene!"* Then I couldn't really make out what my mom shouted back. I just heard her high-pitched voice like she was far away in the kitchen until I realized she was screaming at me.

"Julie! Time to set the table!" she hollered outside my door. *Fuck!* The one time I got a call from a guy and suddenly my parents were having a fight and I had to go out here and set the stupid table.

"Um, can you hold on for a second?" I said to Josh, feeling totally embarrassed. I hadn't heard the last few things he said, anyway.

179

"Sure," Josh said. I shoved the receiver under my pillow.

I opened my door and said into the living room, half shout-whispering, *"I'm on the phone. I will be there in a few minutes."*

"It's almost dinnertime—" I heard Mom say as I slammed my door.

"Hi again," I said, a little breathless. "Sorry about that." I decided to totally ignore my parents' fight. Josh Heller was calling me. This was too great, too rare an opportunity not to relish every second. Who knew when a boy might call me again, let alone Josh Heller? I tried to imagine his bedroom. I wondered if he was lying on his bed like I was lying on mine. Did he have brothers and sisters? Who did he live with? I didn't know anything about him.

I took a deep breath and said, "Um. I'm just curious. How did you get my number?"

"I got it from the phone book," he said. "You were the only J. Prodsky. I figured it had to be you. I'm at Tim Haas's house right now, by the way. Did you know his mom lives in the same building as Julie Braverman? So we were just out in the park and on our way back, and we ran into Julie's sister. Her name's Mandy, right? We talked to her for a little while and I remembered Julie's your friend so Tim and I were talking about you and he said why don't I call you now. I hope that's okay." Julie's my friend, yeah, right.

But wait, *They were talking about me?* Oh. My. God.

"Oh," I said. "Yeah, that's cool."

"Hey, T!" Josh suddenly screamed to Tim, who I guessed was in the room with him. "Turn that up! Can you hear that?" he said to me.

180

"Sort of. . . ." I said. "What is it?" The radio in the background got louder.

"It's one of my favorite songs. 'Africa' by Toto," Josh said.

"Oh yeah!" I said. "I love that song!" I felt so stupid for saying that—he probably thought I said it to copy him or sound cool or something.

"You do?" he said.

"Yeah," I said, hesitating. "I really like Toto. I wanna get their new album."

"Oh, I have it, it's *Toto IV*," Josh said. "I could make you a tape of it if you want."

"Really? That'd be great! Thanks!" I still couldn't believe I was actually talking to Josh on the phone.

"Only I might not be able to do it for a couple of days, 'cause the tape's in Long Island. That's where I live. In Merrick."

"Oh. Really? You come to school every day all the way from Long Island?" I asked.

"No, actually. I stay at friends' houses a lot. Especially Tim's, and Rick's in Brooklyn. My bubbe lives in Brooklyn, too."

"Your what?" I said.

"My bubbe. My grandmother. Aren't you Jewish?" he asked.

"Yeah, sort of. My dad is but my mom isn't. I mean, like, we get a Christmas tree and stuff."

"Oh. 'Cause 'bubbe' is what a lot of Jewish people call their grandmothers."

"Oh. Cool. Hey, wait a second," I said, changing the

subject. "Don't you have to live in one of the five boroughs to go to P.A.?"

Josh laughed a little. Oh man, he had such a cool, throaty, guylike laugh. "Yeah, you do. I lied so I could go. Long Island doesn't exactly have a school like P.A."

"Oh, right. Wow."

"They think I live with my bubbe in Brooklyn, but I really live with my mom in Merrick."

"Uh-huh. What about your dad?" I asked.

"He lives in New Jersey with my stepmom," he said matter-of-factly.

"Oh. Sorry, I hope that wasn't too nosy."

"No, it's okay. My parents got divorced a long time ago. When I was eight."

Then my mother started banging on my door. *"Julie!"* she shouted.

"I'm so sorry, I really have to go," I said to Josh. "We're about to have dinner." God, what a stupid thing to tell him. Now he'd think I was part of this dorky family that ate dinners together and stuff.

"That's cool . . . um . . ." he said, and his voice trailed off, kind of sounding like he was gonna say something else. Then it got a little weird. I didn't know how to get off the phone with Josh Heller! I really didn't want to.

"Um . . . have a fun time with Tim," I said.

"Thanks. . . ." he said, hesitating again. I waited a second or two.

Finally, I said, "Okay I'll see you in French."

"Okay," he said.

Should I say "Thanks for calling"?

"Okay, bye-bye," I said.

"Okay, see you in school. Bye," he said. And we hung up.

Oh my God! I had to call Julie! *Screw our stupid fight,* I thought, and I picked my phone back up and started to dial 8-6-4—when I heard my mother shriek, *"Julie Prodsky! I will not say it again!"* I hung up. Shit.

"Okay, okay, I'm coming!" I shouted. I'd have to wait until after dinner. Oh man, what agony. I opened my door and floated out to the living room.

I set the table in, like, thirty seconds, but it seemed to take Dad *forever* to bring out the stupid Shake 'n Bake pork chops and salad. Mom told me to go get Ellie.

"Ellie! Dinner!" I screamed.

"I could have done that," Mom said. "I said *go get* her!" She was nibbling on a handful of Cheez-Its. She didn't seem as angry as I expected. Maybe her fight with my dad was over. I started to feel relaxed. It was good that I didn't get a chance to call Julie—she could call me, after all. I didn't really want to be the one to make the first move.

I could feel myself beaming from talking to Josh Heller.

"What's the big smile about?" Mom said.

"Oh, nothing," I said.

"Who were you on the phone with?" Ellie said, pulling out her chair.

"No one," I said, unable to hide my smile. I took a swallow of milk, which I still liked to drink with dinner.

"Oh right, *'no one,'*" Ellie said, mimicking me. "Could it have maybe been . . . *a boy?*"

"Hmmm . . . very inte*rrr*esting," Dad said, rolling the "r" in "interesting." He was doling out the pork chops onto plates.

"Oh my God, you are all so nosy!" I said, feeling the red in my cheeks.

"Aren't we allowed to know? Or is it private?" Mom said.

"Okay, okay, it was Josh Heller!" I said, which made me smile and blush even more. I couldn't even take a bite of food.

"Ooooh!" Ellie said, and then she sang, "Julie's got a boyfriend!"

"I wish!" I said, kind of under my breath.

"Who's Josh Heller?" Mom said.

"He's just a guy in my French class; he's hardly my *boyfriend*," I said. And then Dad said, wasn't it funny, he had a student named *Josiah* Heller, not the same as *Josh* Heller really, but pretty close. Then he launched into this story about Josiah Heller and what an interesting background he had and blah blah blah, so I stopped listening.

I let my mind wander to gorgeous Josh Heller and what he was doing now at Tim Haas's house. Were they having dinner, too? I wondered what Josh's favorite foods were. . . Then when I zoned back in, Dad was explaining the complexities of the Carter administration. It was totally boring, but Ellie and Mom seemed interested. I couldn't really pay attention to anything 'cause all I could think about was: Josh Heller called me!

18

Can You Get into Flattery?

"Hello," Joyce said, adjusting her clipboard on her lap, her stubby legs in navy wool pants. She had on a blue-and-white sweater that I couldn't decide if I liked.

"Hi," I said.

We sat in silence for a second, and I suddenly realized there was so much to talk about, I didn't even know where to start. Mom finding out. Julie and me fighting. Josh calling me! I took a deep breath. I took another.

"What's up?" Joyce said.

"Not much," I said. "I mean, a lot, I guess. I don't know."

Joyce just waited.

"I mean, there's this guy . . ." I continued, and could already feel myself smiling. "His name's Josh Heller, and I have, like, the hugest crush on him in the history of the world and he called me last night for the first time!"

"Uh-huh," Joyce said, smiling like, *Go on*. She scribbled something.

"But then I didn't see him in school today, even though I spent, like, the whole day trying to bump into him, and I was thinking about him all day, hoping, praying we'd run into each other, but we never did." I took another deep breath.

"What would you have said to him if you had run into each other?"

"I don't know," I said. "I guess I'd say 'Hi.'" Then I thought for a second. "I guess it's good I didn't run into him! I'd probably look like such a fool!"

"Why would you look like a fool?"

"I don't know, I'd probably start babbling like an idiot or say something stupid. Sometimes I talk too much; I can be a total idiot! Especially if I'm nervous. Which I totally am in front of a gorgeous guy."

"What do you want him to say to you?" Joyce asked.

"I want him to ask me out," I said without hesitating. "On a date."

"Ah," she said. Then she waited again. I took a deep breath again.

"Are you feeling nervous now?" she said.

"Yeah," I said, exhaling. "All this talk about Josh Heller makes me feel kind of . . . I don't know . . . kind of . . . don't know if *nervous* is really the right word. . . ."

"What would be the right word?"

"I don't know!" I snapped. Sometimes Joyce really annoyed me.

"What's the matter?" Joyce said.

"I don't know, I don't really care what the right *word* is. I feel like this is so stupid."

"What's so stupid?"

"This! This conversation we're having! It's just a stupid crush! Nothing's ever gonna happen! I mean, it's not like Josh Heller could possibly be my boyfriend or anything. Or even ask me out!" Why wasn't I talking about my fight with Julie? Or stealing? Wasn't that what I was supposed to be talking about?

"Why couldn't Josh Heller be your boyfriend?" Joyce asked. "Is that what you want?"

Then I made this gasp-snort sound like, *Duh!* My mother hated when I did that. "It would be, like, a dream come true! But he probably just wants to be friends. Or he thinks I'm cute or funny or whatever, but not like a girl-friend. I'm too big a dork . . . I don't know. . . . I'm probably not cool enough."

"Well, what if you are?"

"Please."

We sat in silence for a few seconds. "So, what's bother-ing you?" Joyce said.

"I don't know," I said, rubbing my palms on my thighs. "I just can't stop thinking about Josh Heller ever since he called; I mean, haven't you ever liked anybody? Don't you know what it's like?"

"Yes," she said, in her calm voice, and she smiled. She recrossed her legs. "Of course I know what it's like."

"Well, okay then."

"But what I want to know is," Joyce said, "what's it like for *you*?"

"Like this!" I said, and my leg started bouncing away like it might break off and fly around the room. "I don't know, I guess I'm scared. Josh is so unbelievably cute and cool and—"

"What does it mean to be cool?" Joyce interrupted. "Who do you know who is cool?"

"Well, Julie, obviously."

"The other Julie," Joyce clarified.

"Duh, I mean, yeah," I said, thinking "duh" was probably obnoxious of me to say.

"How is she cool?"

"Well, 'cause she's beautiful and popular."

"So being cool is about looks?"

"No," I snapped. God, I sort of felt like I was talking to my mother. My mother never seemed to understand anything about teenagers. Like, she was always saying idiotic stuff like, "Why do you have to have *one* boyfriend? Why can't you have one for Friday night and one for Saturday night? And then have different ones the next weekend?" *"Because, Mom, it's not nineteen fifty-six!"* I always wanted to scream at her. *"This isn't* Happy Days!" I mean, how stupid can you get?

"Julie's also cool because she knows how to flirt and dress and say the right thing and stuff. . . ." I said.

"Uh-huh."

"And she's never insecure around guys," I said.

"Mm-hmm."

"So she's cool."

"Okay." Joyce paused. "And aren't you her best friend?"

"Yeah," I said, kind of hesitating. I thought I was.

"So wouldn't that make you cool, too—that a cool girl likes you enough to be her best friend?"

"Well, yeah." I thought for a second. "I guess. Except that it feels like a lie."

"What does?" Joyce asked.

"That I'm cool. I mean, maybe people think I am, but it's not true."

"How so?" she said.

"I don't know. Like, I know what I really am, deep down inside, but that's not what people see. Whatever they see isn't really me."

"Ah," Joyce said. "So who are you really?" she asked softly, leaning forward a little and looking me right in the eyes.

"Not good enough," was all I could think to say.

Friday in French, Josh Heller passed me a note that said, *What are you doing tonight?* Right away I felt a fluttering in my chest and I started smiling the biggest smile. My cheeks felt like they were up in my eyes, and I could not make the smile go down no matter how I tried. I turned to look at Josh, smiling like an idiot, and he smiled back at me. Then we both started laughing. We tried to laugh silently so Madame Craig wouldn't notice us. She was writing on the board, so I mouthed to Josh, "Nothing," and shrugged. Julie was trying to ignore me, but I saw her glance at us every now and then. Josh surreptitiously ripped out another little piece of paper from the back of his spiral notebook and wrote on it, *Want to see a movie?*

After school? Of course I wanted to scream *"Yes!"* immediately, but then I remembered my Friday job: putting away the groceries. I'd have to call my mom and beg her to let me out of it. Luckily the bell rang, so we didn't have to keep passing notes. Everyone's desks and chairs started moving as people packed up their bags and shut their books, and I was glad Josh and I could talk in the privacy of a noisy classroom. Out of the corner of my eye, I saw Julie look over at us, then she left for homeroom.

"Yeah . . . sure," I said to Josh. I slowly got my books together, wanting to make every second last.

"Great!" he said. "There's just one thing. I have to go back to Long Island after school. I promised my mom I'd pick the car up at the mechanic's. We can take the train there and see a movie, then I can drive you home."

"You have a car?" I said, trying not to sound too stupid.

"Well, it's my mom's car. It's a brown Chevy. Don't be too impressed," he said, swinging his bag over his shoulder. I was just impressed that he knew how to drive. I didn't know any New York City kids who had their licenses.

"Okay," I said, laughing. Total nervous laughter—I wondered if he could tell.

"So . . . should we just meet outside after school?" he said. He was so cute! I almost couldn't stand it.

"Yeah," I said. "All right."

"Okay then. You're sure you don't mind going to Long Island with me?"

"No, that's fine!" I said, though I really had no idea what I was saying and how I was going to get my mother to agree to this. But Josh Heller could have invited me to Africa, and I would have found a way to go.

"Cool," Josh said. "See you later!" And he headed down the hall.

As soon as I got to homeroom, I told Mr. Werner that I had to go to the bathroom. I raced down to the basement to call my mom from the pay phone. Thank God I caught her. She only worked a half-day on Fridays and had just gotten home.

"Mom!" I said, realizing I sounded breathless.

"Hi-ya!" she said, sounding in a pretty good mood. I imagined her in the kitchen glancing at the clock over the toaster oven 'cause she said, "Everything okay?"

"Yeah," I said, trying to catch my breath. "Everything's fine. I'm still at school. Mom, I have the hugest favor to ask you. . . ."

"Okay," she said. "What is it?"

"Um. I got asked out on a date tonight!"

"Honey, that's terrific!"

"Yeah, I know, but um, it starts right after school, so I can't come home first and put away the groceries, is that okay? Please please? I'll do something extra if you want; I don't know what, but I'm sure we can think—"

"Of course, pussy cat, don't worry about it. It's your first date!" Something about her saying that annoyed me, but she was being so cool, I couldn't complain.

"Thank you, Mom! Thank you so much!"

"You're welcome. So, who is he?" she asked.

"It's Josh Heller," I said, lowering my voice and looking out the glass door of the phone booth to make sure I didn't see anyone I knew. "He's in the drama department."

"You never told me about him," she said.

"Yes I did, Mom, I'm pretty sure I did," I argued. How annoying.

"Well, where are you going?" she asked.

"We're going to the movies, but I'm not sure which theater yet." It wasn't a complete lie. "But he said he'd bring me home. I swear I'll be home by eleven thirty, okay?"

"Will you have dinner?"

"Yes, we'll probably have dinner, too."

"Okay . . . I'd feel more comfortable if I knew where you were going."

"Well, we're gonna decide later, Mom. You just have to trust me. Josh is this totally smart guy and he's really responsible."

"All right," she said, still sounding unsure. "But you'll call if you're gonna be late or for any reason, right?"

"Right, Mom. Don't worry, I'll be fine!"

"Do you have mad money?" she wanted to know.

"What?"

"Do you have mad money?"

"I don't know. I don't even know what that *is*!"

"It's your own money to get home with in a cab or whatever, in case he makes you mad," she said.

"What? Why would he make me mad?" I said. Why was my mother so weird?

"You never know. . . ." My mother's voice trailed off.

"I have a little money. Mom, I gotta go. It's the middle of homeroom. I just wanted to call."

"I'm glad you did, sweetie pie. Have fun!"

So we were sitting next to each other in the Freeport, Long Island, Cinema, our shoulders touching, and all I could think about was how clean Josh Heller smelled. It was killing me, he had such good hygiene. He smelled like some kind of really nice soap. What kind of soap was it? I was racking my brain to remember. Zest? Dial? It was so strong, I couldn't *not* smell it; it was a good thing I liked it. We were seeing the movie *Diner* and I kept wondering, who was even in it? I thought maybe Mickey Rourke was, and some other cute guys, but I couldn't really be sure 'cause all I thought about the whole time was Josh Heller sitting next to me smelling so good. And our hands were so close to each other on the armrest between us, I was going crazy wondering if he was going to hold my hand or if something physical would happen.

During the movie at one point, he leaned toward me and whispered, "Look at that lady two rows in front of us. Doesn't her hair look *trapezoidal*?" That totally cracked me up. And trying to laugh quietly is practically impossible in a dark move theater, so Josh started cracking up, too.

"What, are you a geometry whiz or something?" I whispered. "Is 'trapezoidal' even a word?"

"Actually, I happen to be pretty good at geometry," he said. "I got a ninety-eight on the regents."

"Wow," I said.

Each time Josh leaned toward me I could smell him even more, but I kind of avoided looking him right in the eyes 'cause it was just too intense. When I looked at the screen, it was like the characters were speaking jibberish. I couldn't follow the story at all. Each time Josh sat back in his seat after whispering to me, I'd notice the profile of his teeth— I *loved* his teeth. There was a little gap between the front two.

"Can I tell you something?" I whispered. "And I hope you won't think this is weird to say, but—"

"You can say anything," whispered Josh. "I won't think you're weird."

"Okay." I inhaled. "I think you have great teeth." Then I started giggling again.

"Thanks," Josh said, laughing, too. "What's weird about that? That you think I have great teeth, or that I'd think you're weird for saying so? I mean, I don't think my teeth are so great, but it's not weird that you said that."

"Okay, good," I said, feeling really nervous. "I thought it might be weird to say it." *Try to calm down, Julie, just calm down.* But it was my first movie alone with a boy—how was I supposed to act?

"You have pretty great teeth yourself," Josh whispered. "They're so *white*!"

I thought about Joanie and Chachi on a movie date on *Happy Days*, and how once Chachi tried to touch Joanie's chest when reaching for the popcorn and she smacked his hand. I wouldn't know what to do if Josh tried anything like that. I mean, I wouldn't want him to think I was

a prude but, oh my God, there was his smell again. I hoped
I smelled good, too. Just before I left school to meet Josh
outside, I had run into Natalie in the girls' bathroom and
she let me have a spritz of her Jean Naté perfume. She was
so excited for me, she said, "Break a leg!" as I hurried off to
meet Josh.

After the movie, Josh suggested we go to this Chinese
restaurant nearby. It had started drizzling out, like light
mist, and neither of us had an umbrella, but I didn't care.
I was thinking maybe the rain would make the wispy hairs
around my face curly. I was hoping anyway. It was one of
my best looks, but it only happened when the weather was
just right.

"Is it okay if we walk?" Josh said. "It's only a couple of
blocks."

"Sure," I said. "I don't mind a little rain."

We walked across the parking lot to this little row of
shops: Merrick Hardware, Long Island Records, a station-
ery store, and Lam's Szechuan Garden in yellow lights at
the end.

A waiter led us to a red vinyl booth by the window where
we could see it was starting to rain harder. He threw two
enormous menus down on the glass table and went to get
us tea.

"You like Chinese food, right?" Josh said.

"I love it," I said. "Especially, like, spareribs and moo shu
chicken."

When the waiter came back, Josh ordered for us, which
was pretty cool. I didn't think anyone had ever ordered for
me, except maybe my dad and that didn't count.

"One order of spareribs, one moo shu chicken," Josh said to the waiter, and then he scanned the giant menu. "And one shrimp with lobster sauce. Is that okay?" he said to me.

"Great!" I said. The waiter took our menus and left.

"I think that was a pretty good movie," he said. "But to be honest, I couldn't really pay much attention to it."

I burst out laughing. "Me, neither!" I said, and he started laughing, too. Then we looked each other in the eyes, but I couldn't hold his gaze for too long. It just made my heart go crazy.

"Can you get into flattery?" Josh said.

"What? What do you mean?" I said. I had no idea what he was talking about, but I was pretty sure I started blushing.

"You have perfect eyebrows," he said. "They are just beautiful—the shape of them."

I was stunned. "Thanks," I said. "Wow."

Josh just smiled at me with his hands interlaced on the table. He was wearing this really soft worn-in rayon shirt—a button-down, kind of vintage. It looked really comfortable.

"And this might *actually* sound weird," he said, "but I really like your style. I like your taste in clothes." I wondered if I'd ever tell him most of them were stolen.

"Thanks," I said. "I like yours, too. I really like fifties stuff."

"Thanks," he said, looking so incredibly cute. This was all too much.

"This is a trip," I said. "I can't believe you just said all

196

that stuff." There were so many moments I couldn't wait to tell Julie. Then I remembered I couldn't tell her, so I tried to put Julie out of my mind.

Josh and I stared at each other for a moment, and I thought he might try to kiss me across the table. Even though I wanted him to, I suddenly got really nervous— it was hard to look into those intense sky-blue-marbly-crystally eyes. He reached across the table and took my hand. It felt so warm and guylike, just a little bit rougher and stronger-feeling than a girl's. I must have stiffened or looked down or something, 'cause Josh said, "Did I just make you uncomfortable?" But he kept holding my hand.

"What? No . . . I just . . . I don't know, I'm sorry." I laughed a little. I was kind of wanting to tell him this was my first date, but I didn't want him to think I was a total dork or desperate or something, so I didn't say anything. At that moment Josh released my hand anyway, 'cause the waiter came back with tea, the spareribs, and those crunchy yellow noodles and duck sauce.

"Don't worry, this'll be a good story," Josh said, putting his napkin on his lap, and I thought, *What good manners*. "One day we'll tell our grandkids that on our first date, I held their grandmother's hand and she kinda freaked out."

This cracked me up and I started to feel less self-conscious. Oh my God, our grandkids? I couldn't believe it. Josh Heller liked me.

By the time we left the restaurant it was pouring so hard you could barely see, so Josh grabbed my hand and we ran through the parking lot to his mother's brown Chevy and got totally soaked. Looking out the windshield, I felt like we were going through a car wash without the suds. Josh kept the wipers going at full speed and didn't seem bothered or nervous about the rain at all. I could tell he was a good driver and that he knew exactly how to get from Long Island to Manhattan. I trusted him, and I felt so grown-up sitting there next to him on the brown vinyl seat. Josh said there was a sweatshirt in the back that I could use to wipe my face or hair or whatever. The sweatshirt was gray and said YALE in navy lettering.

"Do you know someone who goes to Yale?" I asked.

"No, but I'm planning to go there. I'm applying early admission next year," he said.

"Wow," I said. "You must be really smart."

"I am," he said, smiling. "I mean, let's hope." Then I was having thoughts like, *Oh man, I'm on a date with a guy who wants to go to* Yale *and he's driving me home!* We listened to WPLJ and talked about our favorite songs and groups. Billy Joel's "The Stranger" came on and I was pretty impressed that Josh knew all the lyrics, and he could even do the whole whistling part, on key. I couldn't whistle, though I had tried to teach myself, like, a million times. Josh's singing voice sounded nice. We talked about the junior class rock musical, written by students from the drama department who auditioned to get in. It was directed by Mrs. Zeig, and everybody wanted to be in it. Auditions had been in February, and Josh didn't make it.

"Were you bummed out?" I asked.

"Yeah, I was. But Tim didn't make it, either. Rick did,

so now I don't see him too much after school."

"What did you have to do for your audition?" I asked.

"You had to sing a rock song. Acapella—do you know what that is?"

Of course I know what that is, I immediately thought. Then I realized, wait, maybe I didn't. But I didn't want to look stupid, so I just said, "I think so. Isn't that singing with no music playing?"

"Right," Josh said. "So I sang 'Beast of Burden' by the Stones." He looked straight ahead through the pouring rain.

"Cool choice," I said.

"I guess not really," Josh said, "since I didn't make it. Oh well, that's showbiz, right?"

"Right." I smiled at him. I liked him so much for being able to talk about getting rejected without seeming embarrassed. He was so honest.

"Can I ask you a personal question?" I said.

"You can ask me anything you want," he said. "I believe anyone has the right to ask anyone anything, and it's the other person's responsibility to say, 'No, I don't want to talk about that.' If it's something they don't want to talk about. You know what I mean?"

"Totally," I said.

"So what's your question?" Josh asked.

"Did you used to date Leah Reemer?" I couldn't help but think about Josh and Leah at Kahti Fearon's Christmas party, and I wondered what had happened between them. I knew it was none of my business, but I asked anyway.

Josh smiled and kept looking straight ahead through the sloshing windshield wipers. "Yeah, we dated our freshman year. But now we're just friends. Why do you ask?"

"I don't know. I feel kind of stupid for asking. But I saw you guys together a lot at Kahti's party and I just thought . . ."

"No, it's fine," Josh said. "That was around the time Leah's parents were getting a divorce. Her dad was moving out, so she was pretty upset."

"Oh," I said, feeling even stupider for having brought the whole thing up. Through the window I could just make out that we were on Broadway and 105th Street.

"Did you think I would ask you out if I was dating someone else?" Josh asked, shifting the car into park in front of my building and turning his body to look at me.

"Um . . . I don't know. I didn't really think you were dating her," I stammered, just as Josh leaned toward me, undid my seat belt, and kissed me. At first my lips quivered a little but Josh kept kissing me like he didn't care or no-tice.

Then he stopped for a second and whispered, "Besides, you're much cuter. . . ."

We kissed and kissed and he held my face, which felt so amazing I thought I might die right there in Josh's mother's brown Chevy. I suddenly understood what the big deal was about. This was nothing like kissing David Wine and our rhythmic tongue circles. When Josh kissed me, I felt this fizzy sensation in my chest go down to my stomach and then my crotch. And his breath smelled delicious. *He must have really good digestion,* I thought.

"Thanks for coming out to Long Island," Josh said.

"No biggie," I said. "Thanks for driving me home."

"Sure," he said. I didn't really know what was supposed to happen next. Did I just get out of the car? Say, "Let's do this again"? *Nah, better not to seem too desperate,* I thought, so I didn't say anything and just started fumbling with the door handle. Josh reached over my lap and opened it for me.

"I really liked hanging out with you," Josh said.

"Me, too," I said, and then we paused as the rain continued to beat down on the windshield. It was just pouring and pouring. What a night.

"Well, I better get upstairs," I said.

Josh leaned over and gave me one more kiss on the lips. More fizzes shot through my chest.

"Good night," he said, and I quickly got out of the car and ran through the rain to my lobby. As I waited for the elevator I could see my reflection in the tarnished gold elevator doors. My hair was still pretty soaked and my face was flushed. Did I look older and more experienced? I wondered. When you had a night like I just had, did it show?

"Hello, Yulie," Freddy the elevator man said in his thick accent.

"Hi, Freddy," I said, trying to fight my smile and wondering if he thought I looked different. But he didn't say anything else; we just rode up in silence. When he opened the elevator door on my floor, twelve, he said, "Watch yoo step!"

"Thanks," I said, searching for my keys. I was praying my parents would be asleep or at least in their room so I could walk through the living room without having to talk to them. Thank God, Ellie's door was shut and my parents were in their room, but I could see from the hallway their light was still on.

"Hello, pussy cat!" my mother said in a loud whisper. "Did you have a nice time? Did you get caught in the rain?" Fortunately, it didn't sound like she was getting out of bed.

"Um, no, not really," I whispered back. "I mean yes, I had a good time. I'm really tired, Mom. I'm gonna go to bed."

"Okay!" she said. She didn't ask me anything else.

I wanted to call Julie, who I knew would still be up, but I felt conflicted. I didn't care anymore about our stupid fight, and I knew Julie would really want to know about my first date with Josh Heller. Then again, she was so mean to me, saying, "Enjoy your new life!" I had never seen her so obnoxious, and she had been so cold to me since the day of our fight. I hugged my pillow, remembering how amazing it felt to kiss Josh Heller's lips, sitting in a car in the rain. How could I not tell Julie about it?

"Fuck it," I said out loud to myself, and dialed her number. My heart started beating in anticipation of her answering. I wasn't sure what I'd say much past "Hi." But her phone rang, like, eight times, and there was no answer. I hung up.

19

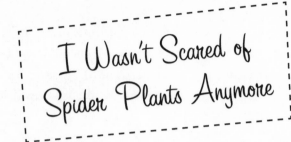

I Wasn't Scared of Spider Plants Anymore

The next morning, although it was a Saturday and I could have slept late, I lay in bed wide awake at seven thirty, staring at the ceiling. I could not stop thinking about Josh and our date. When I closed my eyes, I could remember what his hands on my face felt like. I bunched up a chunk of my hair and smelled it, and I could have sworn it smelled like Josh's soapy, great smell. I wondered so many things: Would Josh ask me out again? Would we kiss again? Or would we go further? I got nervous when I thought about fooling around or getting naked or whatever came after making out. I hoped he was patient, and yet I wanted him to be experienced, too—to know what to do so he could show me. I hoped he wouldn't mind how inexperienced I was.

I was still dying to call Julie so I could tell her about Josh, but I was scared, too. And anyway, Julie always slept late, so I'd have to wait. I wondered if Julie had asked Jennifer Smalls to go to Sak's with her after school. Would Jennifer Smalls be my replacement?

My mom was in the kitchen eating a piece of Branola toast from behind the newspaper. She folded her paper with a loud crunch and said, over her reading glasses, in a pretend loud whisper, "So, how was it?" She was smiling, so I started smiling.

"Good," I said. "We had a great time!" I added.

"Terrific! How was the movie? Whatdja see?" Mom said.

"Diner." I poured myself a bowl of granola. "But I don't really remember it."

I thought that might shock her, like she'd think Josh was up my shirt during the whole movie or something, but she just said, "Oh. Well it must not have been a very good movie, then."

I pulled the stool around to the counter and poured milk on my granola. *That's it?* I thought. Was that all she was going to ask? I was dying for her to ask me something else about Josh, but at the same time I wasn't sure if I wanted to tell her anything. I just kind of wanted a reason to talk about him since I couldn't get him out of my head. But she went back to her paper while I sat there eating and thinking, *C'mon Mom, ask me about Josh. Ask me where he wants to go to college or something. Anything.* Then my mind wandered to Josh saying, "Anyone has the right to ask anyone anything, and it's the other person's responsibility to say, 'No, I don't want to talk about that.'"

"Do you think I have good eyebrows?" I asked my mom.

"What?" she said, creasing part of the paper with her fingernail to mark her place.

"Josh thinks my eyebrows are *perfect*," I said, and I couldn't stop smiling again. "Can you believe that?"

"Of course I can," she said, "but I can't say I've given a lot of thought to your eyebrows." Then the weather report came on WQXR on the radio over the toaster oven, and Mom said, "Oh, shh, I want to hear this."

Later that same day, I went biking through Central Park. It was the second weekend in March, and it was suddenly sixty degrees! I had grown just enough to reach the pedals on Dad's bike if I lowered the seat—the tires on my bike were totally flat. Feeling the sun on my face, I thought it was the most beautiful day ever. I felt like life couldn't possibly get better: I had finally had a date with Josh Heller, I got to experience what really good kissing felt like, and spring had arrived! Of course, the whole Julie thing was nagging at the back of my mind, but I wasn't going to let that ruin my day. I thought of trying to call her again, but then thought, *Forget it.*

Outside it was like New York City had come out from under a rock. So many people were out in their gym shorts and terry-cloth sweatbands jogging, skateboarding, roller-skating, and blasting music on their boom boxes. Little kids and dogs were running around, and I felt like I could have biked the park's whole outer loop twice, even up Heartbreak Hill.

I got home from biking totally sweaty, and my inner thighs were a little sore. I was putting down the kickstand, leaning the bike against the big living-room bookshelf where Dad kept it, when I noticed Mom was looking at me like the cat who ate the canary.

"I have something to tell you," she said. Uh-oh. I couldn't even imagine what she was gonna say. She was getting up from the couch surrounded by a pile of manuscripts that she'd brought home from *Ladies' Home Journal*.

"What?" I said, undoing my small army bag from the bike.

"I did a bad thing. I answered your phone," she said in a small voice.

I breathed a sigh of relief. "Mom—" I started.

"I know you want your privacy!" she said. "I know it's none of my business, but I was putting some clothes on your bed and it rang, and I don't know what came over me; I just answered it."

I stared at her for a second. I wasn't mad exactly, I just wasn't sure what to say. I was kind of surprised Mom was acting like *I* was gonna yell at *her*. I tried to think of how I could use her guilt to my advantage.

"But . . ." Mom said, her voice getting brighter. "I think you're gonna be glad I did answer your phone."

"Mom—who was it?" I didn't know whether to hope it was Julie or Josh. My life was so complicated.

She pulled out the small piece of paper that she had been holding behind her back and taunted me with it, enjoying herself.

"It's a boy. . . ." she teased.

"Was it Josh? Mom, come on, was it Josh?" I demanded as she smiled at me. "Just tell me!"

"It was Josh Heller!" she said handing me the paper. The note was written in Mom's neat script: *Call Josh Heller, 516-555-4703. 3:15pm*. Mom always wrote down the time someone called. She must have learned that a million years ago when she was a secretary at Doubleday.

Usually if my phone rang and I wasn't home, my parents ignored it. My dad had just gotten a telephone-answering machine for their phone. He hooked it up to the phone in their bedroom, the one that sat on Mom's vanity. It was the coolest thing—it was a tape recorder set to tape someone's voice so you could know who called when you were out. Whenever we played back the phone messages, though, we always heard the click of someone hanging up the phone like they didn't want to leave a message.

Call Josh Heller, 516-555-4703. 3:15pm. I almost couldn't believe my eyes. He called me. I mean, I sort of expected him to, but the fact that he actually did kind of surprised me. Did that mean that he had a good time last night? That he was gonna ask me out again? When should I call him back?

I closed my door and kicked off my sneakers. I took off my red hooded Performing Arts sweatshirt and sat on my bed. I stared at the hanging plants over my double windows. Dad had insisted on keeping them in my room because I got the best sunlight in the apartment, he said. I didn't really care, 'cause he took care of them. I didn't have to water them or anything. Ellie told Dad she didn't want any hanging plants in her room 'cause they were "too seventies."

When I was a little girl, spider plants scared me. In the dark of my room, trying to fall asleep, I'd imagine the spider plant would become a giant spider and eat me whole. But at fifteen, I wasn't scared of spider plants anymore. I stared at the spider plant, noticing the yellow in some of the leaves. I sat cross-legged on my bed, holding Josh's message, unable to move.

The next Thursday after school, Daisy, Jennifer Smalls, and I went to Serendipity, the delicious ice-cream place that was kind of near Fiorucci, where Jennifer insisted we look for a new outfit for me for my second date with Josh Heller. It felt kind of weird that Julie wasn't with us. Jennifer said Julie had a doctor's appointment, but I thought, *Yeah, right*. She was probably avoiding me.

"He's taking you to *Avery Fisher Hall*?" Jennifer said as she took a big gloppy bite of her frozen hot chocolate. Serendipity was famous for their frozen hot chocolates— amazing gigantic chocolate slushies with tons of whipped cream and chocolate shavings on the top. Frozen hot chocolates came in these huge glass goblets, and some of Jennifer's spilled out over the edge, which gave me a pang at all those delicious slurps wasted. But that day I was having a sundae with coffee ice cream, cookies-and-cream ice cream, and hot fudge.

"Wow," Daisy said. "That's pretty fancy."

"I know!" I said. "At first I was really impressed, but then he told me his mom works for some music company and got tickets for free. He says she gets tickets all the time."

"Is he taking you out to dinner first?" Jennifer said.

"Yeah, he said we should go to the Saloon 'cause it's right across the street from Lincoln Center. Did you know the waitresses there are on roller skates? It's pretty cool."

"Groovy!" Jennifer squealed. I was psyched that she was being so excited for me. Suddenly she gasped. "Oh my God! I just realized something!"

"What?" I said, holding my heart. She totally scared me.

"Maybe he'll ask you to the Spring Dance!" Jennifer got all squealy and giggly.

"Shhh!" I said. "We haven't even had a second date yet! Are you crazy? Are you trying to jinx me?"

"I'm sorry, I'm sorry," Jennifer said, still giggling with her hands over her mouth. "You're right. Let's just focus on the second date. When is it, anyway?"

"Saturday night!" I said. I was both scared and excited.

"What are you gonna wear?" Daisy asked.

"Oh my God, I have no idea!" I said. "I hope we find something at Fiorucci. Maybe just a new top, if it's not too expensive—something that goes with my skirt with the buttons. . . ."

"Oh yeah, that skirt!" Jennifer remembered. "Well, who cares if it's expensive—you know what to do. . . ."

"I know," I said. "But I'm not really doing that any-more. . . ."

"Oh, right," Jennifer said, seeming disappointed. I thought I saw her roll her eyes, but I wasn't sure. I didn't know what Julie had told them about our fight. They knew we weren't speaking and hadn't in a couple of weeks, but Jennifer and Daisy hadn't taken sides.

Daisy whispered, "You want me to get something *for* you?"

"No," I said. "That would be, like, the same thing."

In Fiorucci, Daisy went right down to the jeans department and Jennifer and I stayed on the first floor in the back where the blouses were. The only thing I liked was this tight purple cotton top with black dots all over it. It was thirty-two dollars, which was more than I had. But I tried it on anyway. Jennifer and I were in the dressing room together, and she said it looked good on me.

"Really?" I said. "Even though I don't have a big chest?"

"You've got plenty," Jennifer said, circling me as I stood in front of the mirror. I knew she was searching for a plastic tag. "You want me to pull off the price tag?" she whispered. "There's no plastic; that's a good sign. . . ."

"No," I whispered back. Then in my regular voice, I said, "Are you sure I can wear something this tight?"

"Definitely," Jennifer said. "Guys love tight stuff." Then whispering again, she said, "C'mon Jule, this is an easy one. It'll roll right up in your bag—and thirty-two dollars is a lot for a little piece of cotton. I don't think it's worth it."

She had a point. Oh man, it was so tempting. I could hear myself saying, as I had said to myself so many times, *Okay, maybe this time will be the last time.* I took off the shirt and held up a bunch of other shirts that I didn't really like 'cause they seemed itchy and hung them back on the hook. Jennifer rolled up the purple shirt and started root ing around my Chocolate Soup bag to hide it. I felt that familiar feeling of my heart beating in my throat.

We went to the earring counter, where Daisy was shifting her weight from foot to foot, but I couldn't tell if she had a pair of jeans on underneath her pants.

"You guys ready?" she said.

"Almost," Jennifer said. She had a couple of sweaters over her arm. "Let me just try these on. I'll be quick."

Jennifer came out of the dressing room all smiles. "Ready!" she said. We went to get our free Fiorucci posters, which I didn't really want 'cause they were kind of ugly— this weird cartoon of some European rock band I didn't know, and it was mostly in this puke green color. I felt like the purple shirt in my bag was burning a hole in my side.

We got outside and Daisy said, "Where to next?"

"How 'bout Bloomingdale's?" Jennifer said. "Just kidding!" I wasn't really listening to them as we walked a few steps away from Fiorucci.

"Hold on a sec," I said, and suddenly, without even thinking, I ran back into Fiorucci. I headed straight to the back of the store where the dressing rooms were. Now there was a salesgirl who wasn't there before.

"I think I left something in there," I lied, pointing to the curtain where we had been.

"Sure, have a look!" she said, and waved me past her. I exhaled a small sigh when I realized she wasn't going to follow me in. Inside the dressing room, I pulled out my balled-up shirt and hung it on the hook without a hanger. Then I fished around my bag for my orange Reminiscence heart-shaped sunglasses.

"Found them!" I said to the girl, coming out from the curtain, holding up my glasses.

"Oh, good," she said, smiling, but she was busy sorting items on a rack. I could feel my heart slowing down to normal and the blood coming back to my cheeks. Jennifer and Daisy were still waiting for me outside.

"Sorry," I said under my breath. "I had to do something."

They just looked at me for a second, and I knew they knew. Then someone said, "C'mon, let's get the bus."

20

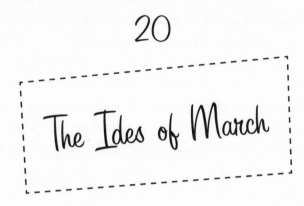

The Ides of March

That night I decided, *Enough of this stupid fight*, and I tried calling Julie about three times, but her phone just rang and rang, and I couldn't imagine where she was. Maybe she was out with Oliver. I tried calling Mimi's phone, too, but there was no answer there, either. I had this horrible feeling in the center of my chest like a pain and an ache, and I just couldn't believe that Julie could stay mad for *three weeks* because I didn't want to steal anymore.

The next day I got to homeroom just as the second bell was ringing. Julie and Natalie were in a whispery conversation. I slid into a chair next to them. Julie kind of had her back to me.

"Hi," I said.

"Hi," Natalie said, and Julie said hi, too, but barely looked in my direction.

"All right, all right, quiet down! Quiet down!" Mr.

Werner said. Everyone was quiet for about a second as he started attendance, then they went back to their conversations.

"Here!" Julie said when Mr. Werner called her name and she barely turned her body to the front while continuing to talk to Natalie. I suddenly felt like it was the first day of school all over again and I didn't know anyone.

When the bell rang at the end of homeroom, Julie walked so quickly to the door I could barely catch her, but I got her arm and said, "Julie."

She turned around as kids pushed passed us.

"What's going on?" I said, holding back the tears. was not going to cry. If she was still mad at me for a dumb reason, I was not going to let her see me cry about it.

"What?" she said.

"This stupid fight. Why are we doing this? Why are you, like, ignoring me?"

"I'm not ignoring you. What do you mean?"

"You've been avoiding me for weeks and being cold and just now you, like, clearly didn't even want to say hi to me." I forced my voice not to get high-pitched and caught in my throat.

"What—Mr. Werner told us to quiet down," she said, which was, like, the worst excuse I ever heard. "I gotta go now," she said. "I have dance."

I just stood there for a second like, *What the hell?* swallowed hard. Then I dragged myself downstairs to class.

* * *

I got home that day feeling totally depressed. As I was dumping out my book bag on my bed, I looked at my loose-leaf notebook, the one Julie and I had decorated together with stuff from cool lipstick ads and lettering from pictures we had cut out of *Seventeen* and *Glamour* magazines. My phone rang. *That's gotta be her,* I thought, *calling to say she's sorry.* She would probably tell me I'm still her best friend and she'd ask me if I wanted to hang out tonight.

"Hello?" I said.

"Hi!" Josh's voice said, sounding upbeat.

"Oh, hi!" I said, feeling a weird mix of disappointment and relief.

"I can't really talk right now 'cause I'm going to have dinner with my dad and stepmom, but I just wanted to see if we're still on for tomorrow."

"Yes, sure," I said. "Six o'clock, right?"

"Right. Do you want me to pick you up, or should we meet at Lincoln Center?"

"We can meet at Lincoln Center," I said. "That's fine." I wasn't ready to introduce Josh to my parents or Ellie.

"Okay . . . um . . . let's just meet at the fountain, then. You know the big fountain, right?"

"Yes, the fountain. Six o'clock," I repeated.

"Um . . . " Josh paused for a second. "Are you okay? You sound funny."

"I do?" I said, noticing my voice getting high. He totally caught me off guard. Man, was he observant! "No, I'm fine," I stammered. "I'm just, it's nothing." I couldn't decide if I should tell him about my fight with Julie.

"All right. Well, whatever it is, will you tell me when I

see you?" Josh said. "I mean, you don't have to, but—"

"No, it's okay," I said. "It's just a whole big thing. Sure, I'll tell you later."

"If you feel like it," he said.

"Okay," I said. "I'll see you at six."

"Great," Josh said, and we hung up.

Saturday night, March fifteenth at six o'clock on the dot, I was at the Lincoln Center fountain. *The Ides of March,* I was thinking, since we had just finished reading *Julius Caesar* in English. Ellie let me borrow one of her antique dresses, the yellow one with the tiny pink flowers that almost looked like apples. I was wearing it with my pink plastic belt. For some reason, I felt kind of relieved to not wear anything stolen. I wore white tights, my pink flats from Capezio, and a light pink scarf in my hair. I only had on a little bit of makeup: liquid eyeliner, Iridescent Baby Pink lipstick, and some blush. Standing there waiting for Josh, I started to doubt my outfit—I looked like an Easter egg. Thank God I had my jean jacket on, 'cause it was a little chilly out, and I hugged it around me with my hands in the pockets. I felt this weird kind of nervousness, like when I was about to perform in acting class, but I kind of liked it.

"Hi," Josh said, appearing out of nowhere. I could see his breath. "You haven't been waiting long, have you?"

"Like, two minutes," I said. He leaned forward to kiss me but I got confused and turned my head a little, so we sort of kissed half-lip-half-cheek. I laughed stupidly, bu

216

Josh just smiled. God, sometimes I was such a dork.

"I have something for you," he said, pulling a brown paper lunch bag out of his pocket.

"You made me a sandwich?" I said, which made Josh laugh. Without skipping a beat, he said, "Yes. Pastrami on white with mayonnaise. That's your favorite, right?"

"Eww! No! Who do you think I am, Annie Hall?" I said.

"I can't believe you got that," Josh said, looking surprised and pleased. "*Annie Hall* is one of my all-time favorite movies. Sometimes you remind me a little of her."

"Really?" I said. "Thanks. I think." I wondered how I was like Annie Hall. Did Josh think I was ditzy?

"The way you dress, sometimes," he clarified, like he was reading my mind. "Anyway, so now you deserve this even more." He handed me the paper bag.

"Wow, thanks. . . ." I said. "Should I open it now?"

"Sure."

I stuck my hand in the paper bag and could immediately feel it was a cassette tape. I pulled it out.

"Cool, *Toto IV*!" I said, reading Josh's small block-lettered handwriting. Side A had a list of all the songs, including "Africa," the song we said we loved on the phone that time. "Thank you," I said, feeling like I didn't know what else to say. *Should I kiss him?* I thought.

"You're welcome," he said, putting his hands back in the pockets of his red baseball jacket. "I wasn't sure what to put on Side B, so I just put Billy Joel's *Turnstiles*. It's one of my favorite records."

"Great," I said. *I'll listen to it till I've memorized every word,* I thought.

Then he took my hand and said, "C'mon, the Saloon i right across the street. Are you hungry?" Oh man, holding his warm hand was, like, the coolest thing.

As soon as we walked into the restaurant, a tall girl ir long ponytails and a tight yellow T-shirt rolled up to us or her rollerskates and stopped short.

"Two?" she said, holding white plastic menus that said "Saloon" in script on them.

"Yes," Josh said, motioning for me to go first. I felt so unbelievably short following the roller-skating hostess to our table near the window. We could watch all the people passing by. That was one of my favorite things to do— watch people. New York City was especially good for that Mrs. Zeig said becoming a keen observer of "human being being human" was one of the secrets of good acting. "Watch like doctors!" she would shout at us when we observed each other in a scene or a monologue or whatever.

Josh asked me if I liked white wine. I liked wine coolers like Bartles & Jaymes, and my parents had let me try a sip of their wine now and then, but I wasn't really sure if could say I liked it. I didn't want to look stupid, and bee always tasted like metal to me, so I said yes.

"Two glasses of Chardonnay," Josh told the waitress sounding so grown-up, and I held my breath for a second to see if she would card us, but she didn't. Then I had thi moment of total euphoria, looking out the window a Broadway. I felt like, I can't believe this, I'm on a second date with Josh Heller.

The concert at Avery Fisher Hall—it was some orch estra from Vienna or something—was pretty boring, bu

Josh did funny things like pretend he was playing the flute when the flute part played or the cello or whatever, and he kept passing me tropical fruit Life Savers.

We got out at about ten thirty, so I still had a whole hour to be with Josh before I had to get home. We walked with the crowd of people, and it was still pretty nice out. Josh took my hand and said, "Let's go sit by the fountain."

The dark gray marble felt cold on the backs of my thighs, through my tights, and I started feeling nervous again. I wondered if I'd ever get good at being on a date.

"That concert was pretty boring, wasn't it?" Josh said.

"Um, yeah," I said, and we both started laughing. "But I didn't mind."

"Do you play any instruments?" Josh asked.

"Well, I played the piano when I was younger but I hated practicing, so I stopped."

"I play piano a little," Josh said.

"Really?"

"Yeah, I taught myself mostly."

"Cool. Where do you practice? Does your mom have a piano?"

"No, but there's one at my dad's in New Jersey. And I sometimes play the ones at school."

"I'd love to hear you play sometime," I said, hoping that didn't sound stupid.

The Lincoln Center fountain was surrounded by three famous white buildings: the Metropolitan Opera House, with these huge archlike windows; the New York State Theater, with a balcony around its middle; and Avery Fisher Hall. A few other people were sitting around the fountain or strolling across the plaza, but I noticed it had gotten less noisy.

"Are you cold?" Josh said.

"A little bit. But I'm fine. Are you?" I said.

"A little bit. Let's walk. How 'bout if I walk you home?"

"All the way to One Hundred Sixth Street?" It was like forty blocks. I was thinking we should get on the subway.

"Well, let's see how far we get," Josh said.

We held hands again and started going up Broadway. We got to a block in the Seventies and stopped to look in this bookstore, Shakespeare & Company. We stood there for a second with our noses almost pressed up against the window. Josh's part of the window kept fogging up whenever he exhaled. I was wondering if his breath smelled as good as it did the last time, but I wasn't close enough to tell. Then all of a sudden we were kissing again. Right outside the window of Shakespeare & Company. Josh's lips were smooth, and he tasted like Chardonnay and pineapple Life Savers. I liked it. Even his stubble felt kind of cool. I noticed the difference from our first kiss—I felt just a tiny bit more relaxed. We stopped for a minute, and Josh rested his arm on my shoulders, playing with the ends of my hair.

"I just had the urge to do that again. Did I surprise you?" he said.

"Yeah," I said, slightly catching my breath. "It's okay though."

"I have to ask you a question," he said. Oh my God. This was only our second date; could he be about to ask me to the Spring Dance? *Don't jinx it by thinking about it Julie.*

"What are you doing Saturday night, April twenty-fourth?" Josh smiled. *Oh. Shit, I jinxed it.* The Spring Dance was in June.

"Um, I don't know. That's, like, a month away. Nothing, I guess."

"Do you want to come to a party at my dad's house in Montclair? It's Dad and my stepmother Marlene's anniversary. They have a big party every year. It's pretty cool, actually, and I can invite whoever I want."

"In New Jersey?" I said.

"Yeah," Josh said, still smiling, still playing with my hair. I was loving that.

"Um. How would I get there?" I said.

"The bus. It's not a long ride. I can pick you up at the bus station."

"It's at night?" I asked.

"Uh-huh." Josh smiled.

"So . . . how would I get home?" I said.

"Are you really wondering, *when* would you get home?"

"Kind of. I mean, my curfew's at eleven thirty, and I don't know how I'd get home by then, coming all the way from New Jersey."

"Well, the party usually goes pretty late. But you could sleep over. If you want. In the guest room, of course." Josh smiled his big smile at me.

"Sure," I said, now unable to stop smiling back at him. Did Josh actually just ask me to sleep over at his house? I couldn't believe it!

"That . . . sounds . . . cool!" I said. I had no idea how I'd get my mom to agree to that but I'd figure it out later.

*　　*　　*

I got home at eleven forty-five, but luckily I saw my mom's
light go off and she didn't say anything. I knew she had
been waiting to hear my key in the door before she could
sleep. I changed into my nightshirt, brushed my teeth and
washed my face, got in bed, and tried calling Julie again. "I
don't care if you're mad at me," I was going to say, "I just
have to tell you that Josh invited me for a sleepover!" I
mean, how could I go on with life without Julie knowing
that?

Julie's phone rang and rang again with no answer. I
had this quick little fantasy in my mind that maybe she
and Mimi and Mandy had moved. No, that was impossible.
My clock radio said 12:05. It was March sixteenth, almost
three weeks since I told Julie I wasn't going to steal any
more.

21

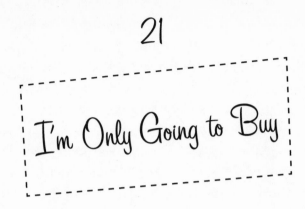

I'm Only Going to Buy

At first I really wanted to lie to my parents about staying over at Josh's dad's house in New Jersey. I wanted to tell them I was having a sleepover at Julie's instead.

But Julie and I still weren't speaking. We pretty much ignored each other in class, in the girls' bathroom, or after school on the subway platform. It felt so stupid, but I wasn't going to be the one to break the silence. After all, she was mad at *me*, so it was her turn to call. I wasn't going to call her anymore.

Josh and I had been on two more dates, one to see the movie *Casablanca* at the Regency, and the other hanging out at Rick DiBiassi's house drinking wine coolers and watching TV with a bunch of other kids. But Josh and I sat next to each other the whole time and kind of played with each other's hands. So I counted it as a date.

The Sunday morning a week before Josh's parents'

party, Mom was in bed reading the paper—a time when she was usually in a good mood.

"Mom? I have to ask you something," I said.

"Okay. . . ." she said, folding down a corner of her paper and looking at me. I was sitting on the end of her bed near her feet, which were under the covers.

"This guy Josh—um . . . remember him? Well, Josh invited me to sleep over at his dad's house in New Jersey. Next Saturday night, April twenty-fourth. It's his dad and stepmom's anniversary party." As soon as I said the word "Josh," I started smiling. So my mother started smiling.

"Uh-huh," she said, crunching the paper in her lap. "How are you going to get to New Jersey?"

"I'm gonna take the bus and Josh will pick me up. And then I'll come home the next day," I said slowly.

"Mm-hmm . . ."

"And Mom, his parents will be home the whole time. You can even call his dad."

"Leave me the phone number on my table." She pointed to her vanity.

By Wednesday, Mom hadn't called Josh's dad and it was driving me crazy. Every time I heard her on the phone in the kitchen or her bedroom, I strained my ears to see if I could figure out who she was talking to. But it was always my grandmother or Aunt Marty or somebody else. Not Mr. Heller. So after dinner and *Masterpiece Theatre* were finally over I said, totally nonchalantly, "So can I stay at Josh's on

Saturday, Mom? Did you ever call Mr. Heller?" I said it like I had just thought of it that minute.

"What? Who's Mr. Heller?"

"Josh's dad. *Mom*," I said, trying not to sound annoyed. "Remember? I asked you about going to Josh's in New Jersey?"

"Oh yes, yes, I'm sorry. It's hard for me to think at this time of night, Julie." God. It was only nine o'clock.

"So did you call Josh's dad?"

"Did you give me the number?"

"*Yes!*"

"Oh, okay, pussy cat, you can go, I just wanted the number so I'd know where you are."

Sometimes, I just didn't understand my mother at all.

The night before Josh's party, I knocked on Ellie's door. I wasn't really sure why, but I thought maybe I could try talking to her. I felt scared about my sleepover with Josh, and I needed somebody to tell me which nightgown I should pack.

"Yeah?" Ellie said. She was working on some college application stuff on the typewriter.

"Can I come in?" I said, peering around the door.

"Sure," she said.

I stepped in and she looked up. I didn't say anything.

"Yes?" she said.

"I just wanted to hang out in here. Is that okay?"

"Okay." She shrugged and went back to the typewriter.

"Are you gonna watch *Donny and Marie?*" I said. When Ellie was in the eighth grade, she saved up $120 and bought a small black-and-white TV that was covered in denim fabric with orange stitching. Dad had taken her to some warehouse in Queens to buy it.

"Um. I guess so. I hadn't really thought about it." She slowly plunked at the keys.

"Can I watch with you?" I said, sitting on her bed.

"I guess so," she said, keeping her eyes on her paper. "But it's not on for a little while, right?"

"Yeah," I said. Then we didn't say anything again for a minute. Finally Ellie looked up from the typewriter.

"What's wrong, Julie? You're acting weird." I inched myself farther onto the bed and leaned against the wall.

"I guess I feel kind of nervous," I said.

"How come?" Ellie said.

"Well, you know I'm going to Josh's house tomorrow night in New Jersey?"

"No, I didn't know that. How was I supposed to know that?" she said, sounding a little huffy.

"Sorry I didn't tell you. I thought you heard me telling Mom, and I only just found out that Mom and Dad would even let me go."

"Okay, so?"

"So, I'm nervous. Like, I can't stop thinking about what nightshirt I should bring."

She sighed like I was the biggest pain in the ass. "Well, what does it matter?" she said. Maybe this was a mistake. I had no idea she would be so obnoxious.

"It totally matters!" I said. "Josh is gonna see me in it!

226

Wouldn't you care what you were wearing if a boy you liked was gonna see it? God! I thought maybe you'd be understanding, but I guess you're just not capable of that emotion!" I got off her bed and headed for the door.

"Julie, wait. I'm sorry."

I stopped at her door with my hand on the knob. I was fighting back the tears.

"Are you crying?" she asked.

"No!" I said, totally crying. Then Ellie started laughing, and she came over to me and turned me around.

"Stop laughing at me!" I shrieked, sounding like a baby.

"I'm sorry, I'm sorry, I'm not laughing at you, but it is a little funny. I'm sorry, Jule." She stood there facing me with her hands on my shoulders, but I kept my head down. "You want me to help you pick out a nightshirt?" she asked.

Even though Ellie got nice after that and said she swore my long white Fiorucci nightshirt with the two angels on it was perfect for my sleepover with Josh, I decided to go shopping on Saturday morning. I had almost a whole day before I had to get the bus to New Jersey, so I went to Macy's. I hadn't been there since a few months before with Julie, back when we were friends and I was stealing. We had gone one day after school and each got a pair of Calvin Klein jeans. Julie also got a magenta velour V-neck top and just as we were leaving, we pocketed some earrings that were on those little plastic squares 'cause there wasn't a salesperson anywhere. As usual, we made it out of the store, no biggie.

This time I walked through the first floor to the escalators feeling a little nervous, but I kept telling myself, *I'm only going to buy, I'm only going to buy*. I went to the junior floor and it was kind of crowded. Looking through the nightgowns and nightshirts, I found some flannel ones on sale but they were too warm and too long. There were some pink gingham short nightshirts with matching bloomers, but they seemed too girly. Then I saw some plain yellow, blue, and green nightshirts. They were $9.99. I had just about enough with tax. I took two smalls and two mediums in different colors and went to the dressing room. There was a lady with enormous boobs counting some shorts. I noticed her huge chest because the glasses she wore on a chain around her neck rested there like they were sitting on a shelf. As soon as the lady saw me, she yanked my four hangers out of my hand and said, *"Four!"* loudly and headed down the dirty green carpeting trail to the dressing rooms. *"This way!"* she said, and her boobs led us to an open door. I was wondering if she was hard of hearing or something 'cause then even louder she said, *"Bring everything out when you're done, all right?"* She wasn't mean or anything, just loud.

"All right!" I shouted back. It just came out that way.

Inside the dressing room I felt relieved that she had counted my nightshirts so I'd have to be a total idiot to try to steal one, and yet part of me was trying to figure out how to do it. As I tried on the green size small, I actually thought about waiting until the lady was distracted. I wondered whether or not I could quietly tiptoe past her with a rolled-up nightshirt in my bag. But I couldn't be sure she was really deaf. Then I remembered to keep telling myself, *I am only going to buy, I am only going to buy,* and I tried on the blue one in a medium. It fit better than the small, but I liked the green color. So I chose the green medium.

I handed the loud lady the three I didn't want. *"Thank you, darlin'!"* she said, and I went to find the cash register. My heart was pounding in my chest as I actually took out my wallet and paid for the shirt. I went out the Sixth Avenue exit wondering if I was cured forever.

"Yeah, it's okay," Ellie said when I got home and showed it to her. "But I still think you should wear the Fiorucci one."

My heart sank. A part of me was wishing I could call Julie and say, "Can I come over and show you my new nightshirt and you can tell me which one to wear to Josh's?" But I decided to trust Ellie, and I packed the Fiorucci nightshirt in my LeSportsac overnight bag. As I packed, I kept imagining kissing Josh and feeling his hands in my hair.

22

Alone in the Tennis Bed

"So nice to meet you," Marlene, Josh's stepmom, said in a deep, gravelly voice as she met us on the white-carpeted landing a few steps up from the front door. Marlene was a roundish woman in a white terry-cloth robe with her hair all up in a towel like a turban. A few pieces of frosted blonde hair peeked out onto her forehead.

"Excuse the towel, I just showered," she said, as she wrapped both her warm hands around mine. One of her long pink nails lightly scratched my wrist. "Oh, pardon me!" she said and started cough-laughing like a smoker. Her voice was so husky she almost sounded like a man. I counted nearly ten gold chain bracelets on her wrist and a gigantic diamond ring. She had several gold necklaces on, too, hanging off her tanned, somewhat wrinkly neck. I wondered if she showered with all that jewelry on.

"That's okay," I said. "Um. Nice to meet you, too." We heard a timer go off in the kitchen.

"Ooh! That's the pigs 'n blankets. You kids are my tasters, all right? I'm trying out some new hors d'oeuvres, all right? Whaddaya say?" And she scampered off to the kitchen, where I heard her open the stove. Josh rolled his eyes and smiled.

"Don't mind her—she's pretty cool actually," he said. "Nothing like the evil stepmother you hear about."

"Josh!" Marlene shouted from the kitchen. "Why don't you show your friend the tennis room? Take her bag downstairs."

"Yup!" Josh shouted back, taking my overnight bag from my arm. "I was just going to do that." He touched my hand. "Follow me." We went down a bunch of small white-carpeted steps to the basement.

"It's the guest room," Josh explained. "We call it the tennis room."

The tennis room had white carpeting and kelly green wallpaper with white tennis rackets dancing all over it. There was a double bed neatly made with a matching green-and-tennis-racket bedspread and throw pillows. On each side of the bed stood white night tables with lamps that were made of that fuzzy yellow tennis-ball stuff. There was a white bureau with brass pulls on the drawers, and on top was a piece of kelly green material that matched the walls and the bedspread. It was sewn like someone had made a place mat out of extra material.

"I guess you could say Dad and Marlene are kind of obsessed with tennis," Josh said, trying not to laugh, which of course made us both start cracking up. Josh was about to show me his room when we heard Marlene scream his name.

"Yeah?" he said as we went back to the kitchen.

"Would you and your friend like an RC Cola? Or I have Fresca, I have orange soda, and I have Dr. Pepper!" Josh looked at me.

"Dr. Pepper's fine," I said.

"Two Dr. Peppers and her name's Julie," Josh said, rolling his eyes again at Marlene.

"*Julie*, of course. Forgive me, sweetheart, if I didn't have my head screwed on. . . ." Her husky voice trailed off as she dumped the tray of pigs 'n blankets onto a paper towel on the counter. "Blow on them first," she said, as she licked some flakes of dough out of her nails.

The doorbell rang. Marlene squealed a little as she tightened her robe around her chest and pulled the terry-cloth belt. "That's my liquor man!" she said. "Just a minute!" she called to the door. "Josh, take some mustard out of the fridge—you kids want mustard?" And she ran out of the kitchen to get the door.

"She has all the liquor delivered whenever she has a party," Josh explained. "It's a lot of bottles."

"Gotcha. She is really funny," I said.

"Yeah," Josh said with a mouth full of hot dog. "Oh! Hot!" He fanned his mouth and opened the jar of mustard.

"Let's get out of here," Josh said after we had eaten more pigs 'n blankets.

"But what about the party?" I said.

"We'll come back when it gets going," he said. "There's

a cool park around here I want to show you."

I ran back down to the tennis room to get my jean jacket. Just as we hit the front door, we ran into Josh's dad.

"Well, hello!" he said. Mr. Heller was roly-poly like Santa but had brown hair and a brown beard and moustache. He was wearing a white alligator tennis shirt and white shorts that were too tight, and he was a little sweaty.

"You must be Julie!" he said. He wore a gold chain and a pinky ring. "I'd kiss you, but I'm all shvitzy." I'd never heard that word before, but I got the gist. Even though Josh was eager to leave, his dad didn't seem to notice, and he launched into all these questions, like was I planning to be an actor professionally when I graduated or was I going to college first, and did I have a backup plan if acting didn't work out.

"Oh shit!" we heard Marlene's deep voice shout from upstairs.

"What's the matter?" Mr. Heller yelled up to her. Josh looked up the stairs, waiting for Marlene's response.

"I forgot ice!" Marlene screamed. "Josh! Would you and your friend mind going out to get some ice? Just run down to Luigi's and get a few bags. You have money?"

Josh's dad pulled a twenty out of his money clip and pressed it into Josh's palm.

"No problem!" Josh shouted up the stairs.

"You're a doll and I love you!" she called back.

The party was pretty cool for a while 'cause the weather was nice enough to be out in the backyard. But a lot of people stayed inside in the nearly all-white living room singing along with the hired piano player at the baby grand. He was kind of a Liberace guy with totally sprayed silver hair and lots of rings, and he played Barry Manilow and Captain & Tennille songs.

Marlene was drunk and acting pretty funny. She was singing at the top of her lungs in her husky manlike voice and kept introducing me to people as "Josh's friend." Josh must have sensed when I had had enough of being surrounded by all these grown-ups I didn't know. He took me by the hand and led me to his parents' bedroom. The first thing you saw when you walked in was the king-sized water bed across from a huge TV. *Pretty cool,* I thought, but then I noticed there wasn't really any other place to sit. Josh kicked off his shoes and slid back into the rolling bed, then he patted the area next to him like I should do the same. We sat on top of the down comforter and Josh put his arm around me. We watched some old episode of *The Twilight Zone*, and I couldn't help but laugh every time the water bed made us bob up and down. Luckily Josh laughed, too.

We started making out, which I kind of knew would happen. I hoped I tasted as good as he did. We were kissing for what felt like a long time and I was playing with Josh's black hair when we heard the *Gilligan's Island* theme coming out of the TV.

"That's not exactly the right music, is it?" Josh said as he got up to turn it off. Just his getting off the bed left me riding a pretty big wave. As he walked back to me going up and down on the bed, I couldn't help but look at his

234

crotch. Oh my God, I could see through his jeans that he was hard, and I felt both scared and excited. He saw me look there—I guess I hadn't really tried to hide it—so he looked down quickly, looked back at me, smiled, and shrugged. He turned on the clock radio and "Do You Really Want to Hurt Me?" by the Culture Club was playing.

"It's okay?" Josh said, referring to the music, and I nodded.

"Wait," I said, "aren't you worried someone might come in?"

"Nah." Josh smiled mischievously. "The door's locked." He got back on the bed and we hugged lying down as the bed rocked us to the music. "So you're trapped," he whispered.

Then he kissed me and I giggled, making our teeth touch. Boy George was singing and Josh's hand snuck behind me and pulled the bottom part of my shirt out of my jeans to the beat of the music, which made me laugh again. I was wearing this white cotton top that was kind of like a pirate shirt—it had three buttons going diagonally from my collar bone down my chest. Josh unbuttoned them all pretty smoothly but I could tell he was stopping himself from reaching inside. He touched me over my shirt, and it felt so warm and nice. I stuck one of my legs between his and our legs hugged. Then Josh took my hand and moved it a little over his hard-on. Julie had warned me that guys did that sometimes, and it made me kind of nervous.

"Um . . . wait a sec," I said, interrupting our kissing. "Is it okay if we go slow?"

"Okay," Josh said, and I moved my hand away. As we lay there rocking in the waves, I realized I had had to pee since back when *The Twilight Zone* started, but everything felt so nice I just didn't want to get up. We started to hear sounds of people leaving the party and I was wondering when Josh's parents might knock on the door.

"What?" Josh whispered, and I thought, *Oh my God he's so aware*. How did he know my mind was wandering?

"Uh," I stammered. "I'm sorry, but I really have to pee."

"Oh!" Josh said, and laughed. "Down the hall, the first door on your right." Then I heard him sigh, and I couldn't tell if it bugged him that I interrupted us. Or that I asked to go slow?

The bathroom had a seashells theme—the shower curtain had a bunch of different kinds of shells on it in various shades of tan and brown, and the towels all matched perfectly in beige with white seashells along the edges. I finished peeing and was washing my hands when I noticed there was no more music playing from the living room downstairs.

Then I thought I heard Josh's dad's low voice outside the bathroom door saying something like, "Just be in separate bedrooms in the morning, all right?" I turned the water off to hear Josh's response but I only heard some steps creaking a little on the carpet. I peeked back into Josh's parents' bedroom and no one was there, so I went down to the tennis room to change into my nightshirt. I had just finished brushing my teeth in my own private tennis bathroom, and there was a soft knock on my door.

"Come in," I whispered. Josh padded in wearing his socks, gray Yale sweatshirt, and sweatpants. He smelled like toothpaste and looked so incredibly cute. I wondered what was gonna happen with us in the tennis bed.

"Hi," he said.

"Hi," I said.

"Do you mind if I stay down here with you for a little bit?" he said.

"No," I said, and I took a deep breath.

Josh was kneeling on the bed. He reached over my shoulder and turned off the tennis lamp on the bedside table, so the room got pretty dark, but we could still see each other. He pulled me gently toward him, and we kissed again for a little while kneeling like that, and as we started to lie down, Josh said, "I'm really . . . into you, Julie." He sounded out of breath. Then he very quietly whispered, "I want you," and all I could think was that it sounded like a line on a soap opera or something—like this totally *adult* thing to say. And even though I was flattered, I had this feeling like Josh had said that line before. He was starting to really grind his crotch into mine—I could really feel how hard he was since all that was between us now were his sweatpants and my thin nightshirt and underwear. I couldn't tell if he was wearing underwear under his sweatpants.

"I'm into you, too," I whispered back, and pulled away a little. "But I feel like I should tell you something."

"Uh-oh," Josh said, propping himself up on his side.

"No, it's nothing bad. I mean, I'm sure you probably already figured it out. I haven't gone all the way with any-

237

one yet." I felt kind of embarrassed, but at the same time I wanted to just say it. I giggled a little and put my hand over my eyes.

"Oh," Josh said. "Well, okay. So?"

"I wasn't sure if I should tell you. I just thought you should know. I guess I've kind of been holding out. I mean, not like I'm waiting to be married or something like that, I just want to be sure I really like the person it happens with the first time." Josh looked slightly perplexed.

"Okay," he said again, but something told me it wasn't. Then I started having a kind of yawning fit. Like when you're so tired you feel like you've been up for twenty-four hours straight or something. I mean, I've never been up for twenty-four hours straight, but it just suddenly hit me how tired I was. I wasn't sure what time it was, but I knew it was late.

Neither of us said anything for a minute. I wondered if Josh was sorry he had asked me to sleep over. But then he broke the tension and said, "By the way, cool nightshirt," as he ran his hand over my shoulder and upper arm. I shivered a little. "Are you cold? You want a sweatshirt?"

"Sure," I said, and he took off his Yale sweatshirt. I put it on. It smelled like him and was all warm.

"I hope you can go slow," I said, as we lay back down. "I mean . . . you know what I mean. Right?"

"Yeah," he said, snuggling with me. "I do. I think I can. And if I can't, well, that's just something I'll have to find a way to deal with." He grinned at me. I had no idea what he meant by that, but I don't remember what I said next 'cause I think we kissed some more, and then I woke up and the clock said 9:10 in the morning and I was alone in the tennis bed.

For almost the first two weeks of May, I tried not to go to clothing stores. I used the multicolored pen I got in my stocking at Christmas to put a big purple check on each day of my calendar that I didn't go. I made it eleven days in a row. I stopped going to Reminiscence and even Postermat, where they didn't even sell clothes, 'cause I thought if I was too close to a clothing store I might get tempted. I also decided to see how many days I could go without wearing any stolen clothes. This part wasn't so easy. I actually did not own a pair of jeans that wasn't stolen. Well, not any good jeans. I had this old pair of Lee's that still fit me but I hated them 'cause they weren't as cool as my Girbauds or Fioruccis. I couldn't even count how many times Julie and I had been to Fiorucci and left with jeans. I had so many pairs.

For every day I didn't wear stolen clothes (I decided that jeans were exempt from this rule), I put a green star on my calendar. While I was at it, I started to write on my calendar whenever Josh and I were together, like an after-school time when we hung out with other people, or a Saturday-night date, or whatever. On those days I put an orange "J+J." Since our first date that rainy night, we had seen each other nine times. I wondered how many dates we would have before I could call him my boyfriend. And did I have to be Josh's girlfriend for him to ask me to the Spring Dance? It was about a month away. Although I wasn't writing it

239

down, I couldn't help but figure out that it had been forty-seven days since Julie and I had spoken.

About a week later, Jennifer Smalls and I were outside together at lunchtime—it was another really sunny, warm day. We were trying to decide where to get lunch.

"I can't believe how soon the last day of school is," Jennifer said, as we walked down 46th Street toward a deli on Broadway.

"I know," I said. "Doesn't it seem like this year went so fast?"

"Yeah," Jennifer said. "The juniors will be seniors next year—won't that be weird?"

"Totally," I said, but I was thinking about the summer fast approaching and whether I'd see Josh.

"I'll probably cry at graduation," Jennifer said, cracking her gum. "And I'm not even friends with any seniors!"

"Wow, we'll be sophomores," I said.

"Yeah. We'll no longer be the youngest! *Wheee!*" Jennifer screamed, and started skipping ahead a little and spinning. She practically ran over two people turning the corner from Broadway.

"Oops! I'm so sorry!" Jennifer said, and her gum flew out of her mouth and landed on her big chest.

"Jen, your gum!" I said. We both started laughing hysterically. I stopped walking and was doubled over laughing. Then I looked up and suddenly realized who Jennifer had bumped into—Josh and Leah Reemer. My heart kind of did a backflip into my stomach. Leah and

Josh stood frozen, staring at us. Josh let out a little laugh.

"What the . . . ?" Jennifer said quietly.

"Oh, shit," Josh said. "Hi," he said to me, sort of looking down.

"Hi," I said, feeling my face get hot and a burning start behind my eyes. It was obvious Josh and Leah were just now arriving at school. The bell for lunch had rung like a minute ago and they couldn't have been on their way back already. Oh my God, all I could think was that they were coming from Leah's house, since Josh stayed at his friends' houses in the city all the time. They had probably had a sleepover. I was positive he was wearing the same shirt he'd worn to school the day before. Sometimes it was a curse to have such a good memory, but I was positive. My eye fell to Leah Reemer's chest. She was wearing a gray Yale sweatshirt. Oh my God. Josh slept with Leah Reemer. He slept with her because he thought I wouldn't.

23

Boys Will Come and Go

"What a total and complete asshole!" Jennifer Smalls said, angrily dropping the brown plastic tray on the table in front of me. The fries spilled out of the paper sleeve, and I watched all the individual grains of salt bounce onto the tray. We were at McDonald's across the street from school. Jennifer must have dragged me or carried me or something, 'cause it felt like *poof* we were there. I had no memory of crossing the street. I had started crying as soon as we were far enough away from Josh and Leah Reemer, and now felt like I'd never stop. I was slumped over in my orange chair where Jennifer had left me with the last tissue she found at the bottom of her book bag. She pushed the fries toward me and began squeezing ketchup onto the paper place mat.

"Ugh! I can't believe it!" she said to no one in particular

lar. "That asshole thought he'd never get caught and *bam*! We run smack into him! I mean, what are the chances? What a complete and total asshole!" she said again. I just sat there sobbing.

"Julie, have a fry. Do you want a fry?"

I shook my head and wiped my eyes with the tissue. It was soaked and shredded.

"Here. Have a napkin," Jennifer said.

I took a napkin to blow my nose and left the shredded tissue on the table.

"I just can't believe it," Jennifer said, almost under her breath, shaking her head. She came and sat in the chair next to me, even though it was connected to another table. I just kept crying and watched my tears leave big dots on the thighs of my Fiorucci jeans. Jennifer put her hand on my shoulder. "What a fuckhead!" she said. "And Leah Reemer, that slut! I never liked her!" Jennifer watched me cry for a few seconds. "I'd totally be crying, too. It's so fucked up. I just can't believe it."

"I thought he really liked me," I managed to say through my tears.

"He totally likes you!" Jennifer insisted. "I mean, come on, you had so many dates! Maybe he's just a big idiot."

No shit he's an idiot, I thought, he just totally fucking cheated on me. I looked at Jennifer for the first time since her gum had fallen out on her chest. Why did she wear such tight shirts? It annoyed me. Why did she want to show everyone her big chest like that? I was suddenly hating Jennifer for not being Julie. I knew she was trying, but I didn't want to hear that Josh was an idiot. If Julie were there, she would

243

have said the right thing. I didn't know what it was, but it would have been the right thing.

"So, he probably had sex with her, right?" I said, not really expecting an answer, and it made me cry even more to say that out loud.

"Oh . . . " Jennifer said, her voice sympathetic, and she handed me more napkins. "I don't know. . . . They used to date, right? I mean, yes, probably, Jule, they probably had sex. He probably doesn't *like her* like her, though, you know? But it doesn't matter anyway, you don't need him! You deserve better! I mean, what a complete and total asshole." Nothing she could say could make me stop crying. It felt like there were just oceans and oceans inside of me and the tears would never stop pouring out.

"What do I do?" I sobbed. Jennifer kept trying to comfort me while I cried more.

"I don't know. . . ." Jennifer's voice trailed off like she was thinking about something else. She chewed on her straw and stared off into space for a minute. "I guess he'll take Leah to the dance now, huh?" she said.

It felt like someone kicked me in the chest. I hadn't even thought about the dance! Jennifer kept looking at me so sympathetically with her eyebrows all scrunched up in her forehead, but I couldn't stop thinking it should have been Julie with me running into Josh and Leah Reemer. Julie would never have said anything about the dance. Julie probably would have yelled at Josh or told him off or something. Where the hell was Julie? Why wouldn't she call me? How long was this stupid fight going to last?

*　*　*

Once I got to Joyce Kazlick's office, I started crying again, so everything was totally blurry. I got ahold of myself and launched into the whole Josh and Leah Reemer story. After about twenty minutes, I suddenly noticed that Joyce had gotten a perm. Now her Dorothy Hamill haircut was kind of like a tight little soft afro. The curls below her temples looked a little too long, almost like sideburns. I thought of this picture of me, Ellie, and my mom and dad taken on the beach at Cape Cod in, like, 1976 or something when my dad had huge sideburns. I was nine and Ellie was twelve. It was a black-and-white picture, and both my sister and I were squinting 'cause the sun was in our eyes. I wondered who took that picture since my dad was in it and he was usually the one taking the pictures. It was the only photo I could remember with all four of us. Then I thought of the conversation I had with Dad the other night when I just flat-out asked him if he and Mom were going to get a divorce. He laughed, like what a crazy thing for me to say. "Your mother and I have our differences," he said, "but no. No plans for a divorce." Then he changed the subject like we had been talking about the weather or something meaningless.

"How long has it been since you talked to Julie?" Joyce asked, shifting her weight in the vinyl chair. This was totally weird, I thought, since I hadn't even been talking about Julie.

"I don't know, about two months, I think," I said. I sat

there slumped in my chair, playing with the bottom edge of my bowling shirt. The whole run-in with Josh and Leah had happened only two days before, and I was still totally depressed about it.

"Do you want to call her?" Joyce said.

"I've tried, but she's never home. I'm pretty sure she knows what happened with Josh 'cause Jennifer Small probably told her." I still couldn't believe it wasn't me who told Julie everything that happened.

The day we ran into Josh and Leah Reemer, I got home from school and put Billy Joel's *Glass Houses* on my record player. I sat on my light blue carpet and cried and cried. I played the song "All for Leyna" over and over like eight hundred times. Billy Joel sang about how everything he did was all for Leyna, a lady who killed herself by standing on some train tracks or something, and that he wanted to throw himself into the sea and drown 'cause he couldn't live without her. He sang about how he was failing in school, he couldn't sleep, he was losing his mind, he just wanted Leyna one more time. I felt so pathetic, I could totally relate to this song. Then I played *Toto IV*, the tape Josh made me because I must have been a masochist. How would I ever get over Josh Heller?

"What do you want to happen now?" Joyce asked me and I realized I was having trouble focusing. It was like my mind was in a million places. I thought about her question for a second.

"I want my friend Julie back," I said surprising myself. I sat there for a second, hugging Joyce's box of Kleenex. "I really miss her."

I started to wonder if maybe I was more upset about the Julie stuff than the Josh stuff. Julie was my best friend, after all. I remembered one of our sleepovers when I lay in the trundle bed next to Julie's bed, all tucked in, and we talked into the darkness until we fell asleep.

"Remember," Julie said, "boys will come and go, but true friends are here to stay."

At the time I thought I had heard someone say the same thing on some TV show like *Eight Is Enough* or something and I thought to myself, *What boys will come and go? When will I meet just one boy who will come and go?* I hadn't even had one. Was Josh my first heartbreak experience, or was Julie?

"We have to stop," Joyce said. "But let's continue with this next time."

"Continue with what?" I said, under my breath. God, I sounded like a typical angry teenager. I let the box of Kleenex fall into my chair and closed the door behind me.

I got home after six and Ellie said Mom and Dad were at some concert and did I want fish sticks or chicken pot pie?

"Fish sticks," I said, throwing my book bag on the couch. "Do we have tartar sauce?"

"Yeah. I'll make them. You can clean up, okay?"

"Okay," I said. I didn't have the energy to argue.

"Hey, Julie . . ." Ellie called from the kitchen as I went to turn on the TV.

"Yeah?"

"What happened to your friend Julie?" she asked. My

heart started racing. Had something happened to Julie and Ellie knew about it but I didn't?

"What do you mean?" I said, turning down the volume.

"You don't seem to hang out at her house anymore. Are you guys still friends?"

I breathed out. Oh, Ellie was just being nosy.

"Well, sort of," I said. "I don't really know." I didn't know how to tell Ellie about Julie and me without bringing up the whole stealing subject.

"Did you guys have a fight?" she asked.

"Not really," I said, knowing these non-answers were going to annoy her.

"What do you mean 'not really'?" she called, still in the kitchen. I could hear her scraping the cucumber for salad. exhaled loudly.

"How come you're so interested?" I shouted back.

"Just curious. *God*. Excuse me for living."

I stood at the TV, changing channels. News. News. Doublemint gum commercial. *M*A*S*H*. Some part of me wanted to tell Ellie everything. To start with learning how to steal at Fiorucci and end with Josh cheating on me and maybe even ask her what I should do. Instead I went into the kitchen and sat on the stool at the counter and watched Ellie make salad.

"What's going on with your college applications?" asked.

Ellie sighed. "Oh, nothing. I'm just waiting to hear at this point."

"RISD's your first choice, right?" I said.

"Yes. I hope and pray I get in."

"I bet you will," I said.

Ellie looked up from the salad bowl. "Why do you say that?"

"'Cause you're a good artist," I said, stealing a tomato out of the bowl.

"Oh. Thanks. I didn't think you noticed my stuff," she said quietly into the bowl.

"Well, I do. Jesus, Mom and Dad sure fight enough about where you're going to college."

"They just fight about money," Ellie said. "If I get into RISD and don't get a scholarship, Dad'll want me to go to a state school like SUNY Albany or someplace."

"Would you go there?" I asked.

"Not on your life!" Ellie said. "If I get into RISD, I'll beg, borrow, or *steal* to go—I don't know, but somehow, I'll find a way."

I couldn't help but cringe a little when she said "steal."

Just before dinner the next Sunday night, I thought about calling Josh at his mother's house on Long Island. I knew he usually spent Sunday nights there, and we had been ignoring each other in French ever since the run-in. I hadn't answered my phone in a few days 'cause I didn't know what to say to him if he called. Josh had called my parents and left, like, three messages, but I kept tossing the little notes into the garbage. I dialed the Long Island number I'd memorized months ago, and wondered if this would be the last time I'd call it.

"Hello?" Mrs. Heller answered. Josh's mother still went

by Mrs. Heller, even though she and Josh's dad had been divorced for eleven years or something.

"Hi, Mrs. Heller," I said, feeling a little nervous. "Is Josh home?"

"Yes he is. Who's calling, please?" She sounded like a secretary or something. Great. How many girls were calling him, that she didn't know my voice?

"This is Julie."

"Oh, hello there, sweetheart!" she said in her heavy Long Island accent. "How are you? When will I get to meet you face-to-face?" Before his mother could say anything else, I heard Josh grab the phone and shout, "I got it!"

"Hello?" Josh said, sounding a little relieved, or maybe I was just hoping I heard that in his voice.

"Um. Hi," I said.

"Hi. Hold on a sec. Let me take this in the other room." I heard his mother's kitchen radio and various other sounds, like pots clanking. Then Josh screamed, "Mom! Hang up!" The kitchen receiver clicked and Josh said hello again.

"Hi," I said again.

"I've been trying to call you," he said. "Did you get my messages?"

"Yeah," I stammered. "I just wasn't sure—"

"I know," Josh said, interrupting. "Listen, Julie, it's not what you thought. I don't *like* Leah Reemer; we're just friends. . . ."

"How many of your friends are you sleeping with?" I asked, shocking myself with my bluntness. It took Josh a while to say something. I was dying to break the silence 'cause it felt so uncomfortable. It took every ounce of strength I had to wait for him to talk.

"I'm not going to lie to you," he said quietly.

"Good," I said.

"Something did happen with Leah," he said, sounding really solemn and serious. "But I don't want to go out with her. I want to go out with *you*." Then there was another long silence. "I want to date you, too, Josh," I wanted to say, "but now I don't know what to do." I wanted to call him an asshole but I just couldn't.

"And I was going to ask you something," Josh broke the silence.

"Uh-huh?" I said.

"Well. Um. I'll understand if you say no, if you just, like, hate me now. But I was wondering if . . . if you'd go to the Spring Dance with me."

"Oh my God," I whispered into the phone, and let out a big sigh. "I don't know, Josh, I don't know what I'm supposed to say to that. . . ."

"Don't say anything then. Just think about it. We have a few weeks still to get tickets."

When I hung up the phone, I went right to the kitchen. My mother was hunched over the counter reading a yellowed page from *The New York Times Cookbook*. There were several open cans of clams on the counter, parsley on the cutting board, and an empty box of Ronzoni linguini.

"Mom, I know you're gonna kill me, but I'm not going to be home for dinner tonight," I said. She looked up at me over her reading glasses, keeping her finger on a spot in the cookbook. The other hand went right to her hip.

"Why not? Where are you going?" she asked.

"I'm going over to Julie's. I just have to talk to her right now, it's really important."

"Oh, honest to Pete, Julie. . . ." Her voice was on its way to shrieky. "I already have a pound of spaghetti in the water!"

"So, we'll have leftovers, Mom; I'll take it to school tomorrow," I said. I was trying really hard not to whine.

"I just hate to waste food like that," she said, like she hadn't heard me at all.

"It's not a waste! I'll eat it, I promise. I just have to go to Julie's now, Mom, please? Please, c'mon, it doesn't have to be such a big deal."

"Well, if it's not such a big deal, why do you have to go to Julie's right now?"

"'Cause I just do, Mom. I need to talk to her. I meant, it wasn't a big deal—"

"All right!" she said, cutting me off. She was angry but I decided to ignore it.

"Thanks, Mom!"

I was out the kitchen door, racing to get my sneakers as I heard her complain loudly, "I just don't get any help—I might as well be the maid!"

24

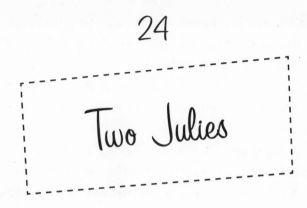

Two Julies

I practically ran to Julie's building on 99th Street and Riverside Drive. It was as if Julie were headed for the airport and I had to catch her. The truth was, I didn't even know if she was home. I didn't feel like calling first. I wasn't even sure what I was going to say. "Julie, we have to talk," I rehearsed under my breath as I hurried across West End Avenue toward the DON'T WALK sign. "Hi, Julie," I said to myself, "we need to talk. . . . I'm sorry I didn't call first, but it's important. . . . Are you busy? Can we talk for a minute? It's important." I couldn't even imagine what her response would be. Would she be mad at me for just showing up? Would she refuse to talk to me? What if Mimi or Mandy answered the door—then what would I say? I started to think about what to do if Julie wasn't home, and I was so deep in thought and walking breathlessly that I almost smacked right into Julie on the street. She was wearing a

bright magenta T-shirt that said PARACHUTE on it, so you'd
think I would have seen her.

"Hi," I said, totally stunned.

"Hi," Julie said, looking pretty surprised to see me, too.
"Where are you going in such a rush?"

"Um . . ." Suddenly this struck me as funny and I
started laughing. "Your house," I said. Julie cracked a smile
too, but looked a little confused. Before she could say any
thing else, I said, "I really need to talk to you." I tried to catch
my breath.

"Okay," she said. "Do you want to come upstairs?" We
were at the top of the hill on 99th and West End Avenue,
standing in front of the building on the corner. It was a nice
May night, kind of warm out.

"Nah, let's just sit on these steps for a little bit—is that
okay?"

"Okay," Julie said.

So we sat and I took a deep breath. It was kind of a shock
to just stop running so abruptly like that. She didn't seem
mad. She seemed nice, like the Julie I knew. But maybe I
had just caught her off guard and she didn't have time to
get mad. Suddenly I had no idea how to begin. Tell her
about Josh cheating on me, even though Jennifer Smalls
probably already did? Tell her about Josh asking me to the
dance and should I say yes even though he cheated on me?
Ask her what happened to our friendship? Remind her
that she said true friends would always stick around even
though boys would come and go, and wasn't she a true
friend? Before I even said anything, Julie said, "Actually

this is kind of weird. I just tried calling you from my dad's. But I guess you had already left."

"You tried calling me?" I said.

"Yeah." Julie looked down at her red-painted thumb-nail.

"How come?"

"'Cause I wanted to talk to you, too." Oh my God! This was definitely a sign of our connectedness. We both knew we needed to talk at the same time! What were the odds?

"You did?" I asked. "What did you want to talk about?"

"I don't know. . . ." she said. "You can go first." I could hear her voice start to go up like she was trying not to cry, and she kept looking down so I wouldn't see it, and that made me feel the tears behind my eyes. I thought, *The two of us, we're a mess. How did this happen?*

"I thought . . ." she said through tears, without holding them back now. "I knew I would cry." She cried for a little bit and I didn't know what to say. All I could think was, Julie was maybe the only person I could cry in front of and not feel self-conscious.

Finally I said, "Um . . . I think you should probably go first. Did something happen?" It was so weird that *I* was saying that to *her*. I was the one things were happening to!

She shook her head and sniffled. "No. Well, yes. But the something that happened was a couple of months ago. The night of your first date with Josh, actually." She paused for a second, took a deep breath, started crying again, and quickly blurted out, "Julie, I'm sorry I've been so horrible. I mean, I never meant to stop being your friend. I never meant for all that stuff to happen. I just didn't know how to tell you—"

"Tell me what?"

"I'm just so sorry," she said, still crying. Then her nose was really running and neither of us had any Kleenex. "I feel terrible . . . especially that day in homeroom when you asked me why—"

"Tell me what, Julie? What happened?" I said.

Then, through her sobs and runny nose, she tried to catch her breath. "Remember that Friday we were gonna go shopping together? *I got arrested that day.* At Sak's," she said quietly.

"Oh my God," I said, and I took one of her hands. "Tell me."

"I was in the women's department. You know, the fancy expensive section?"

I nodded.

"Well, I was trying to get this silk vest, but it had a plastic tag and I had my little scissors—"

"How much?" I just had to interrupt.

"Um. I think it was, like, a hundred seventy-five dollars or something."

I gasped. Now Julie's crying had subsided a little.

"And Jule, there were two-way mirrors there! And a hidden movie camera! They showed me a videotape of me cutting the vest and taking the plastic thing off!"

"Oh my God" was all I could keep saying.

"So this lady security guard comes out of nowhere the second I step out of the dressing room and she grabs my arm and pushes me toward this totally scary, like, French guy in a suit with a big black moustache and he takes me

256

by the wrist and twists my arm behind my back and he pushes me into this dark room behind the dressing rooms. He was so mean. He was such an asshole!"

I just sat there with my mouth open.

"Wait," Julie said. "It gets worse. They actually *hand-cuffed* me. . . ." And her voice got squeaky as if the memory upset her all over again. Down came more waterworks. "Of course, I was hysterical." She took her hand out of mine to wipe her nose with it, and then she rubbed it on her jeans. "Gross. Sorry," she said, and we both started laughing. She took my hand back. I just continued to watch her.

"And there were other security guards in the back room, thank God. I mean, I was so scared of what that French guy was gonna do—"

"How did you know he was French?" I asked.

"His accent. *Vhat do you sink you are doing, Mees, eh? I am going to call zee police!*" she said, doing kind of a bad imitation of a French accent. "I can't do a French accent. Anyway Jule, I just couldn't believe it. I was, like, totally bugging out. I was screaming that I was fifteen, they couldn't arrest me, and the French guy kept saying he could and they were gonna put me in a home for girl criminals and I was crying so hard I could barely see anything and they kept saying they were gonna call the police!"

"Oh my God," I said softly.

"And I wanted to tell them it was my first time and it was a dare and all that stuff, but I knew they wouldn't believe me cause they had the videotape and I had scissors, which they took from me, by the way—"

"No—"

"*Yes*. They grabbed my bag, you know the Esprit one with the turquoise netting?" I nodded. "They grabbed it and dumped it out on this dirty carpet to make sure I didn't have any other stolen clothes—thank God I didn't—and they went through my makeup bag and took my scissors!"

"Jesus," I said. Julie kept crying.

"Jule," she sniffled, her nose still running. "I've cried so much about this, I didn't know I could cry any more." She was breathing short, shallow breaths.

"I wish I could have been there for you," I said. "Take a deep breath." We both inhaled a big breath together. Julie laughed a little and let out a huge hiccup, which totally made us laugh more.

"It's so good to talk to you," she said, taking another deep breath. "I'm so sorry," she said in her squeaky voice, and started crying again.

"It's okay," I said. "But tell me the rest of what happened, 'cause I have a lot to tell you, too."

"Okay," she exhaled again, curling her bottom lip so her bangs flew up. "Somehow I convinced them to let me call my mother, who was actually home—total miracle! She was pissed 'cause she was getting ready for a date with this new guy—oh God, there's so much to tell you. There's this new guy she's dating—Nathan. Nate. He's a carpenter. Anyway, so she comes all the way to Sak's to get me and by then this policeman is there and I'm still crying and all she cares about is that she's totally late for her date with Nate—" Then we both burst into hysterics. "*She's late for her date with Nate!*" we said together in rhythm, laughing.

"I didn't mean to say that," Julie said, still giggling. "It just came out! Anyway, Mom was like, 'So what's the big deal?' to the French guy. 'My kid tried to steal a silk vest?' Like, what's everybody freaking out about? And even though she assured the policeman I'd never steal again, he wrote me a ticket! So I have this court date in a few months but Mom called Harvey, who she broke up with, but he's a lawyer, and he'll help us. And everyone at Sak's thought Mom was totally crazy, of course, like I needed another reason to feel embarrassed, and somehow we got out of there and Mom says, 'Julie, please, you should know better,' or something, like no biggie really, and she hugs me and puts me in a cab to go home so she could go meet Nate."

"You're kidding," I said.

"No," Julie said. "And I cried the whole cab ride home."

"Did you tell anyone?" I asked.

"I told Mandy and that was it."

"Really? Not even Jennifer Smalls? Or Natalie?"

"Nope." Julie shook her head.

"Why didn't you tell me?" I asked, trying not to sound hurt.

"I don't know, I guess . . . I just . . ." she said. "Well, you had just said you were gonna stop. . . ."

"Uh-huh," I said. "Have you been mad at me this whole time for that? I kept telling myself that couldn't be true."

"Yeah, well, I guess I was," Julie said, looking me in the eyes. "You got kind of weird about the whole thing."

"What do you mean?" I said. Now my voice was getting squeaky. I was scared we were gonna fight again and then not talk for God knows how long.

259

"I don't know, you were just bugging out and acting kind of uptight about stopping. I felt like you judged me or something. Like that time we went to Patricia Field with Jennifer Smalls."

"I just couldn't do it anymore," I said, barely whispering. "Even though I did get something that day."

Julie just stared at me.

"There was this other time I went to Fiorucci with Daze and Jennifer. I actually took a shirt and made it out of the store, and then I went and put it back. I just couldn't go through with it," I said.

"I heard about that," Julie said.

"Oh." We paused and sat there a second. I felt like Julie was still mad at me, but I didn't think I should apologize.

"Anyway, I was also pretty ashamed," Julie said, crying again. "I felt so stupid—that's why I didn't tell you."

"Uh-huh," I said. "I didn't know what to think. I wasn't sure. I just couldn't figure out how you could stop talking to me over stealing." Then I started crying again, too. "It was so weird."

"I know, I'm sorry—" Her voice dissolved into sobs.

"I know," I said. "You don't have to say sorry anymore. But are you still mad at me 'cause I stopped?"

Julie just cried silently and shook her head.

"Have you stolen anything since this Sak's thing?" I asked, lowering my voice.

Julie nodded. "Yes," she said.

"Julie!" I said. "I know you're gonna think I'm being uptight or whatever, but come on!"

"I know," she said. "I don't think you're uptight. You're

right." I could feel my forehead was all scrunched up.

"So what happens at the court date?" I said.

"It's July seventh, so at least school will be out. Harvey says I just have to go down there with him and look like I'm a really unhappy fucked-up kid, and he says the worst is probably I'll have to pay a fine." I must have had a horrified look on my face and Julie knew exactly what I was thinking.

"No! There's no chance I'm going to jail!" she said.

I exhaled and Julie sighed, too. "God, it's so good to talk to you," she said. I suddenly felt this wave of calm.

The world had completely stopped while Julie and I sat on that stoop and talked, until we realized we were both starving, so we walked to the Blimpie on Broadway. I thought, *Julie Braverman and I actually talked again. It's all going to be okay. She's going to help me figure out the Josh stuff and we're going to be best friends again.* I thought about Joyce Kazlick and that she'd be proud of me, if therapists felt proud of their patients. I wasn't sure. I liked going to Joyce, I realized. Even though I wasn't planning to steal again, I wanted to keep talking to her.

Whoever thought up the Blimpie was a genius. I mean, putting oil and vinegar on a ham and cheese hero with the lettuce, tomato, and mayo—I loved the tangyness of it. We bought Blimpies, sodas, chips, and brownies and brought them back to Julie's house, where no one else was home. I had told Julie all the Josh Heller stuff while we waited on line for our sandwiches. She said he was a total asshole for going off with Leah Reemer, and as I had imagined, she said if she had been there instead of Jennifer Smalls, she would have told him off. Julie said it was a good sign that he tried to call me so much right after the run-in, that he apologized, and that he said he didn't want to date Leah Reemer. But the whole Spring Dance question was a toughie.

"Well, let's put it this way," Julie said with her mouth full of Blimpie. We were at her round kitchen table, using the paper wrappers from our sandwiches as plates. "Do you actually *want* to go to the dance?"

"I don't know. . . ." I tried to imagine what it would be like. The dance was going to be at the St. Moritz Hotel on Central Park South.

I imagined the Spring Dance would be in some big ballroom with chandeliers and gold wallpaper. When I told my Mom that Josh asked me to the Spring Dance and that it was at the St. Moritz Hotel, she said, "Ooh! Fancy schmancy!" I imagined myself really dressed up in a taffeta 1950s dress I'd find at Unique Antique Boutique. My dress would be red with black velvet spaghetti straps and tiny black velvet flowers woven all through it. I'd wear red lipstick. I saw Julie in purple—a deep purple antique dress under which she'd wear a big poofy petticoat. She'd have a little purple clutch purse and we'd both have beautiful wrist corsages. And nothing we wore would be stolen. We'd have receipts for everything. But Julie hadn't been asked to the Spring Dance.

"If you were gonna be there, I think I'd want to go more," I said, realizing Julie would probably want to go with Oliver, but he didn't go to P.A. "Are you still going out with Oliver?" I asked.

"No," Julie said, like, *Don't remind me*. "He went back to England, that schmuck."

"You're kidding!" I said. I was shocked.

"Nope. He broke the news to me, like, a week before he had to leave. His visa was up or something, I don't know. And of course he waited to tell me till the morning after I spent the night and had sex with him again. I really wanted to tell you that, too. . . ." She looked sad again.

"I wish you had," I said.

"Me, too." Then we both looked at each other and smiled.

"Don't say it!" I started laughing.

"I'm sorry!" she shouted, and kind of laughed, too.

"No! You are not allowed to say sorry any more! I forbid it!"

I shoved the last bite of my ham-and-cheese Blimpie in my mouth.

"I've got an idea: How about you ask Rick DiBiassi to go to the dance?" I suggested. Julie thought for a second. She certainly had the guts for something like that.

"Nah, that'd be weird, he's gotta ask."

"Yeah."

"And anyway, as much as I still think Rick is totally gorgeous, I don't really care about the Spring Dance. It's for juniors. It's not like it's our Spring Dance or the *prom,* you know?"

"I know," I said, watching Julie toss her empty bag of chips into the garbage. "But what if I don't have a boyfriend our junior year? When will I get a chance to go to a cool dance with a boy again?"

"Well, that's not a reason to go, just 'cause you got asked. It's sounds to me like if you're wanting to go only if I go, then you don't really want to go." I thought about this for a second. She was right.

"Besides, Jule," Julie said, looking me square in the eye. "Wouldn't you rather get asked by a really *good* boyfriend? One who won't pressure you about sex and then cheat on you? Let's wait for really good ones."

"Was Oliver a good boyfriend?" I asked.

"I guess not," Julie sighed.

"What if neither of us has a date for our Spring Dance?" I asked.

"Then we'll go together," Julie said, brushing crumbs off the table into her hand. "Let's make a pact on it!" she said, looking up like she had a lightbulb over her head.

She held out her pinky to me. I curled my pinky around hers and we pulled. It was official: if neither of us had boyfriends in June 1984—our junior year—we'd go to the dance together.

I managed to avoid Josh for a whole week before I worked up the guts to talk to him. I was kind of nervous about actually confronting him, but Julie told me, "You can do it," and in my heart, I knew I could. But whenever I imagined talking to Josh, my heart started racing like I was stealing clothes or something. One Friday after school, a week before the dance, I found Josh alone by the front steps to P.A. Tons of kids were outside listening to their boom boxes and talking and stuff, but he didn't seem to be with anybody.

"Hi," I said, taking a deep breath.

"Hi," he said, and I couldn't tell if he was glad to see me or not.

"Listen . . ." I plunged right in. "I can't, I don't think I can go to the dance with you." Josh thought for a second and kind of squinted at me 'cause the sun was in his face. I stood there adjusting my book bag, feeling totally self-conscious.

He nodded a little before he spoke. "Okay . . . how come?"

"Um . . ." I didn't expect him to ask how come. I thought he'd just say, "Oh well, have a nice life, bye," or something.

"I just don't . . ." I started. I wasn't sure how to put it. "I just don't . . . feel right about it," I said.

"'Cause of the whole Leah thing?" Josh said, sounding kind of pissed off.

"I don't know, I guess that's partly—"

"I told you, I don't want to date her!" Josh said, interrupting.

"What are you getting pissed off for?" I said. Then I sort of said under my breath, "I mean, *you* cheated on *me*!"

"Excuse me? I didn't exactly cheat on you! It's not like we were girlfriend and boyfriend!" he said. Ouch.

"What?" I said. I felt a combination of wanting to kill him and my heart breaking.

Later, I would think of all the great things I should have said, like, "ANYWAY, I'D RATHER BE WITH

SOMEONE TALLER!" or "I LIED ABOUT YOUR TEETH—GET BRACES, ASSHOLE!" or even just a simple "FUCK YOU!" and "EAT SHIT AND DIE!" But nothing even remotely like that came to mind.

"Well, anyway," I said, as if it wasn't clear, "I don't think we should go out anymore. So obviously I'm not going to the Spring Dance with you." And then I actually added, "Have a nice time!" I looked him in the eyes one last time and turned away to walk to the subway, resisting every impulse to look behind me to see if he was watching me walk away. I felt like an idiot for wishing him a nice time, I mean, *why* in God's name did I say that? But it didn't really matter 'cause I did it. I broke up with him.

"Julie Prodsky, you are just *too chill*!" Julie said when I told her everything later on the phone. I was a little depressed about Josh, but I also felt kind of relieved. I just couldn't believe he turned into such an asshole after he seemed so nice. Maybe this whole ordeal would make me feel older somehow. I could chalk it up to one of life's bittersweet experiences. You had to roll with the punches, or you weren't really living a real life, right? Didn't somebody important say that in a song or something?

"What are you doing tomorrow?" Julie asked. Tomorrow was Saturday.

"Nothing . . ." I started to say.

"Good! 'Cause we're going shopping!"

"What? No, Jule—" I got scared that she meant we were going *getting*.

"C'mon, c'mon, you can't refuse. We need to celebrate! Let's go down to the Village!"

"All right," I said, feeling unsure.

"Am I your best friend?" Julie wanted to know.

"Yeah. . . ." I said.

"And do you trust me?" she asked. I'd never heard such determination in her voice.

"Yeah. . . ."

"Okay, then, meet me at the subway at eleven in the morning."

Saturday morning I showered, scrunched my hair with mousse, got dressed, and took a twenty-dollar bill I kept in my undies-and-sock drawer that I had been saving for a special occasion. Today seemed like the perfect day to buy myself a present. I went into my parents' bedroom to tell them I was going out. My dad had gone to the roof of our building to sit in the sun, and Mom was sitting at her vanity, putting foundation on her face.

"Hi," I said.

"Hi, pussy cat," Mom said. "You look nice; where are you off to?"

"Julie and I are going down to the Village to go shopping."

"Have fun," she said, looking in her mirror at her eyelids; then she turned and looked at me. "Shopping, hmm? You're not—"

"No, I don't do that anymore Mom," I said, lowering my voice, sitting on the end of the bed. "I promise."

267

Mom squinted at me like she was trying to decide if I was telling the truth.

"Really?" she said.

"Yes," I said, looking her in the eyes. "I swear." I crossed my heart.

"All right," she said skeptically. I changed the subject.

"I do have to tell you something," I said, taking a deep breath. "Josh and I broke up."

"Oh, I'm sorry, sweetie," she said, frowning. "What happened?"

"He just turned out to be a total jerk, so I'm not going to the dance with him."

"Well that's all right, there'll be other dances," Mom said.

"That's what Julie said," I said.

"Julie's right. Now you know what you have to do, right?" Mom said.

"What?" I said.

"You just have to open the front door and shout 'Next!'" We both kind of laughed.

"Oh, *Mom*," I said, getting up and walking out the doorway, "you're so weird. If only your advice was, like, for people on this *planet*!"

Sometimes, like maybe once a year or something, my mom wasn't all bad.

Sitting in the red vinyl booth at the Greene Street Diner, Julie and I ate our grilled-cheese sandwiches, and I had such mixed feelings. I was happy to be hanging out with her again and to be in the Village, my favorite place in New York City, but I was also kind of nervous about what she was gonna do once we got in a clothing store. A part of me wished we could go back to last fall, before she taught me how to steal, to before I knew how she got all those jeans. But that was impossible and anyway, I'd never want to go back to knowing Julie less than I did now. In a way, our whole stupid fight had made us closer.

Our waiter came over to the table. He was a short older man with smiling eyes and a big belly.

"How are you pretty girls?" he said with a Greek accent.

"Fine," Julie said, and looked at me.

"Yeah, can we have the check please?" I said. The waiter took out his pad and flipped through a few pages till he found our order.

"You girls sisters?" he said, not looking up. Julie and I laughed, like, *He's kidding, right?*

"No," I said, and then not knowing why, I just blurted out, "I'm Julie." The waiter looked at me and smiled.

"And I'm Julie, also," Julie said.

"Ah!" the waiter said. "Oh! Two Julies!" He laughed a hearty, throaty laugh as he put our check on the table.

It felt like ages since I'd been to Reminiscence. I had always wanted a pair of the purple painters pants with the dark blue stripes, the same pair Julie had.

"Try them on anyway," Julie said, even though I said I couldn't afford them. "Don't you want to see how they look on you?"

"Okay." I shrugged. We went to the dressing rooms in the back with a few shirts and pairs of pants each, and I was thinking how this totally felt like old times. But some other part of me just knew I wasn't going to steal anything. What Julie was gonna do, I wasn't so sure about.

Julie stepped out of her dressing room wearing a canvasy kind of lavender jacket with big white buttons and looked in the full-length mirror. I came out as she was pushing up the sleeves. I put my hands in the pockets of the painters pants.

"Those look great on you!" Julie said. "Look at how great your butt looks!" I turned my butt toward the mirror to see my profile—not bad.

"Very nice," this girl who worked there said, from the ladder she was sitting on above us. She was refolding this enormous pile of different colored balloon pants.

"Dontcha think?" Julie looked up to the girl.

"Oh, yeah," the girl said. "And I swear, if something doesn't look good, I don't say anything at all."

"I don't think this jacket is really me," Julie was saying back to the mirror.

"I like it," I said. "Cool buttons."

"It's more you; you try it on," Julie said, and she was totally right. I loved the jacket; it *was* so me. It had no collar and these big plastic buttons, kind of like an old-fashioned railroad worker's jacket.

"That's on sale," the salesgirl called down. "I think it's only ten dollars."

Ten dollars was still kind of a lot. But I couldn't take the jacket off. The sleeves looked so good pushed up, I kept turning in front of the mirror to see the different sides. I went back in my dressing room to change, unable to decide whether to buy the jacket. Julie, I realized, was in some other part of the store. I peeked into the dressing room she had been in to see if she had left anything in there, and it was empty. I started to feel nervous. I handed my painters pants up to the lady on the ladder.

"Thanks," she said with a pen in her mouth, and went back to refolding. Julie was at the front of the store, looking through the Hawaiian shirts. She had a few articles of clothing flung over her arm.

"What are you doing, Jule?" I said under my breath.

"You don't need to talk like that," she said, though she was whispering back. "You trust me, remember?" I sighed.

"I think I'm ready to go," I said.

"Okay, just give me a few more minutes." She looked at the jacket still over my arm. "You should buy that," she said. I held it out in front of myself one more time. I really did love it. *Don't think too much,* I told myself, and I went right up to the front counter to pay.

The girl at the front wrote "painters jacket" on the receipt. She put my jacket in a plastic Reminiscence shopping bag with pink-and-black leopard spots and handed me my change. It felt cool in my hand. As I put my money back in my wallet and took the bag, I couldn't stop smiling. For some reason I thought about Ellie and that I was excited to show her my new jacket. Ellie had gotten into the Rhode Island School of Design, and she had gotten a half-scholarship, which was enough for Dad to relax.

I looked around for Julie and suddenly she was right

behind me with the painters pants I had tried on over her arm and her wallet out. She was smiling. I looked at her, a little confused.

"Jule, you're buying those?" I said. "You already have that exact same pair."

"Duh!" she said. "They're for you, silly!"

"What? You're kidding!" I didn't know what to say.

"Cash or charge?" the salesgirl said.

"Cash," she said proudly to the salesgirl, who wrote and cranked out her receipt like she did mine.

"You didn't *get* anything?" I whispered as we walked out of the store. Julie shook her head and held her arms up.

"You can search me!" she said. She handed me the Reminiscence bag with the pants in it. I noticed how different new pants looked with the tags still on.

"Julie, it's too much," I said, but I held the pants to my chest.

"Oh shush, it's no biggie," she said. "Hey, you're sleeping over tonight, right?"

"Of course," I said. We had a huge hug. "Thank you so much. I can't believe you got, I mean, *bought* me those painters pants!"

"You're welcome. Ooh! Let's go into Capezio—I gotta show you this new lipstick!" Julie said. "It's called Dewberry Pink. Ruby has it and I tried it on at her house—it's amazing!" Capezio was right next door to Reminiscence.

As I watched Julie skip up the three white steps to Capezio, the image of seeing her on the top step of P.A. the first day of school flashed in my mind. It seemed so long ago now, like that was a different Julie. I was a different

Julie now, too—I wasn't the Julie who was so scared of not finding a friend. And I was no longer Julie Also. I remembered our first after-school subway ride, the first time I saw Julie's closet, sitting at her kitchen table laughing so hard we had tears running down our cheeks. Now we even had battle scars—we'd had our first fight and survived. Somewhere deep inside of me I had this really strong feeling: I will know Julie Braverman forever.

Acknowledgments

Klepto began in 1998 as a one-woman show called *Goodnight, Diary*. It was based on the diary I kept during my teenage years. After many staged readings and workshop productions, the consistent feedback I got was, "This might make a good teen book." But I didn't know how to turn theater into young-adult fiction. I am indebted to so many people who helped me with that conversion process: Daniel Judah Sklar, Elizabeth Law, Victoria Labalme, Nadette Staša, Kevin Mandel, and Victor Warren were the most influential in those early days. I am grateful to Annette Cunningham for "funding" our Friday artist workshops in the summer of 2000, during which both of us banged away on our keyboards, let the creative juices flow, and tried very hard not to answer the phone.

Throughout my high school years and countless sleepovers and hours spent at my best friend's house, I was awed and fascinated by her myriad family members and their boyfriends, girlfriends, and spouses. I remember thinking, *Someday I'm going to write about this.* For those years and all the juice, spice, and wisdom given to me by the Kravats, Buschmans, and Zinkers, I am profoundly grateful—especially to Annie, my second mom, and to Jenny, of course. Everyone should have a best friend like Jenny.

To Joan, Dan, and Susan Pollack, thank you for providing so much good material and for loving me and being proud of me. Thank you to the Kners, Nina Rowe, Regina Sheer, and Huck Hirsch, all of whom changed the course of my childhood. I am grateful to the Performing Arts' Drama Department Class of 1985 students and teachers— you know who you are even though I have changed your names in this book.

To Jennifer Belle for her excellent feedback and support and her fantastic workshop, including Colleen Cruz, Scott Jones, Elin Lake Ewald, Leslie Ross, David Zaring, Brenna Tinkel, Robin Swid, and Sarah Bennett, thank you.

Thank you to my husband, Rob Handelman, for his willingness to read anything I write, talk endlessly about my process, give me the guy's-eye view, and take Charlie away when necessary.

Many thanks to my agent, Merrilee Heifetz, for reading my book in one day and cheering me on immediately.

Finally, I am not only grateful to Joy Peskin, a first-time novelist's dream of an editor, but I am also moved by her endless enthusiasm for this book. From our writing sessions in Prospect Park to pretzels and Pirate's Booty on her living-room floor, I will always treasure her keen editorial eye, her sense of humor, and that simply, she "got" me.

Jenny Pollack grew up in New York City and graduated from the High School of Performing Arts and Barnard College. Back in the eighties, she *got* from Fiorucci, Macy's, Sak's, Bloomingdale's, Betsey Johnson, Patricia Fields, Reminiscence, Aca Joe, Parachute, and who knows where else. She hasn't *gotten* anything since then. She is still best friends with her best friend. Jenny lives in Brooklyn with her husband, Rob, and son, Charlie, and their two cats, Mike and Harry. *Klepto* is her first novel.